HARK

Sam Lipsyte

GRANTA

Granta Publications, 12 Addison Avenue, London W11 4QR

First published in Great Britain by Granta Books in 2019
This paperback edition published by Granta Books in 2020
First published in the United States in 2019 by Simon and Schuster, New York

A CIP catalogue record for this book is available from the British Library.

1 3 5 7 9 10 8 6 4 2

ISBN 978 1 78378 323 6
eISBN 978 1 78378 322 9

Offset by Avon DataSet Limited, Bidford on Avon, Warwickshire, B50 4JH

Printed and bound by CPI Group (UK) Ltd, Croydon, CR0 4YY

www.granta.com

MIX
Paper from
responsible sources
FSC® C020471

For Sylvia

"My glory was fresh in me, and my bow was renewed in my hand."

—JOB 29:20

PART ONE

One

Listen, before Hark, was it ever harder to be human? Was it ever harder to believe in our world?

The weather made us wonder. The markets had, the wars.

The rich had stopped pretending they were just the best of us, and not some utterly other form of life. The rest, the most, could glimpse their end on Earth, in the parched basins and roiling seas, but could not march against their masters. They slaughtered each other instead, retracted into glowing holes.

Hark glowed, too.

He came to us and was golden-y.

It wasn't that Hark had the answer.

It was more that he didn't.

All he possessed, he claimed, were a few tricks, or tips, to help people focus. At work. At home. Out for coffee with a client, or a friend.

(Listen, before Hark, was it ever harder to find focus?)

Hark gathered his tips together, called it mental archery. Pretty silly, he liked to say.

But some knew better. Some were certain he had a secret, a mystery, a miracle. For what was mental archery but the essence of Hark, and what was the essence of Hark but love?

In this hurt world, how could that hurt?

The hunters of meaning had found no meaning. The wanters of dreams were dreamless. Many now drifted toward Hark Morner.

This is, like, the backstory.

The front story is about a bunch of people and a movement they launched under the banner of Hark, a movement that maybe meant nothing at all. Or maybe it did mean something. It's tough to tell. The past is tricky, often half hidden, like a pale, flabby young man flung naked into a crowded square. The past doesn't stand there, grant ganders. The past clasps its crotch, scurries for the cover of stanchions, benches.

History hides. That's its job. It hides behind other history.

Fraz Penzig, one of the front-story people, knows all about it. He used to teach some history, though he hasn't taught it in a while, not since the middle school cut staff by a third. His wife, Tovah, told him that life is not a zero-sum game, but Fraz senses that if it were, he would be the zero sum.

Lucky for him that Tovah is still employed.

He's grateful for the medical, though he happens to have his health at the moment. Not that it's something you can ever truly own, or bequeath, like a house, or a houseboat, or a parcel of land in the hills, but Fraz does have his health.

Oh, maybe he feels frail on occasion, a tad pulped, bones shot, frequently fevered, on the verge of the verge of death, but make no mistake, he's hardy. His twinges, his spasms, his stabby aches, they're chronic, like all the other minor hurts, the gym injuries, the sprains achieved mysteriously on the can.

He's terminal, but not quite near the terminus.

Like when he had that raisin on his head, went to the raisin doctor.

"It's nothing," the doctor said.

"Nothing?"

"I mean it's something. It's just what people get. On the way down. You want I light-saber that bad boy off?"

Also, forty-six years on this hard turd of a world and Fraz's mind is still, by his lights, pure silk. He knows younger types already fried, or brined, not just with drugs or booze, but merely from rising in the morning, moving about in their private biospheres of panic and decay, the hours at work, the hours of work at home, the hours of work with spouses, fathers, mothers, children, the stresses laced into the simplest tasks, the fight-or-flight responses to kitchen appliances, not to mention the mighty common domes, with which the individual bubbles Venn: the fouled sky, the polluted food, the pharma-fed rivers full of sad-eyed Oxytrout, the jeans on outlet shelves in their modalities of size—skinny fit, classic fit, fat shepherd fit, all dyed a deep cancer blue. And the wave rot, of course, the pixel-assisted suicide, the screens, the screens, the screens.

Yes, Fraz is lucky, privileged, if you please, not just to be alive but to still live here, his locus, his home grove, the city that never sleeps, but paces its garret in a nervous rage, the city of his kin.

Once he had some vague ambitions, semi-valuable skills. Now he tutors schoolkids part-time, does favors for an old friend of his late father.

He's also lucky Tovah's affections don't hinge on his ability to generate revenue. Or maybe her affections hinge on nothing now.

But fie on such wallow-world musings. Fie on these flurries of own-negs. Today he will shrug off the cape of self-hate. Fraz has upsides. He's a doting father. He's one of Hark's apostles. He spreads the word. Also, he's rich in nutrients, solid from the gym, with, despite a certain overspreading doughiness, some noteworthy detail on his tris and delts. Truth is, he'd rather be a male waif, but he got Jewed (he can say it) on the genetics. His narrow band of endomorphic choice will always come down to this: lard barn or semi-cut chunk.

Today he's headed downtown for a meeting with the mental archery brain trust: Kate Rumpler, the young heiress who funds their institute; Teal Baker-Cassini, the discipline's leading intellectual light; and Hark Morner himself, their radiant, inscrutable guru. They will take their booth at the Chakra Khan, sip kale-and-peppermint toddies. They have much to discuss. Demonstration videos. Scheduled appearances. The True Arrow, a new feed on Hark Hub.

Fraz wishes they could meet at a coffee bar, or a full-service bar, or a full-service meat cart. He likes the street meat, the tangy skewers. He doesn't mind the toddies. But the candles, the garden scents, menace his dainty machismo.

Listen, such are the sacrifices one makes for the cause, for mental archery, for love.

Two

Today, Hark and Fraz ride north toward some bluffs above the Hudson.

Pickering, New York, once the largest manufacturer of frozen waffles in the country, has invited Hark to speak on the rudiments of mental archery. Near the town an ancient billboard juts from a cliff. Boys in earth-tone plastic helmets clutch honey-brown, frost-stippled discs. The tagline reads: GENTLEMEN, START YOUR TOASTERS. Fraz recalls this ad campaign from his childhood, though he remembers it as "Gentlemen, Start Your Waffles." Could the company have survived longer with his version? Fraz berates himself for foolish speculation, then berates his inner berater for stifling winsome or playful thoughts, for from such lazy perambulations through the noggin's grottoes profundity can effloresce—ideation's lush, dark bloom.

But now he's thinking too much. Clumps of overthought thoughts accrue, cloud him.

Fraz switches to a vacant setting, watches the roadside world slide by: fields, houses, malls, rivers, malls.

In mental archery, this is called unstringing your bow.

Hark unstrings his bow a lot. Falls into silence, self. Fraz turns from the window to study Hark, the soft electrics of those gold-flecked green eyes, the ninja sinews in his neck, the spiky, creamy meringue of his hair. Sometimes Hark appears born of a fabled tribe from a fold in space. Today he's a young man on a bus. He hunches, scribbles in a battered, yellow journal.

When Hark does speak, his voice is an enchanted river with roars and hushes and thick, crystal swerves. It carves a course for Fraz to follow, to flow toward, out from his fetid backwaters, his brack stink.

Fraz met Hark by chance in a bookstore. He'd ducked in out of the summer heat to kill time before a tutoring gig. The streets were a hot, greasy griddle, and Fraz was bent on the assassination of a tiny segment of time.

Also, he wanted a book. He was depressed about the political situation and he wanted a book that was either about the political situation or not about the political situation at all. This book would either explain with unerring exactitude the intractable shittiness of the political situation, or it would transport him to another place, a magical forest of shittinesslessness, for example, or perhaps transport him to another time, a time that did not flinch in the face of Fraz's determination to kill it, that did not almost literally (but not, obviously, literally) fall to its knees (if time can be said to have knees, which surely it can't) and beg for its feckless life.

Yes, he was depressed. Or was he just sensitive? Maybe his was the reasonable response to the situations, the political situation, the economic situation, the situations at home with Tovah and the kids. Or, to bring it into Harkian focus a bit more, the Tovah situation. What was actually, probably, literally known to Tovah as the Fraz situation.

One had to seize perspective on these things.

He could sense Tovah's displeasure, her weariness. The qualities in Fraz she once claimed to adore were maybe not such adorable qualities anymore.

He wanted a book to tell him what to do about all these situations. He knew there were books like this, though he'd never read them. But he didn't see any books in the bookstore. He saw a man instead, and a dozen other people in metal chairs. A hand-lettered sign on the table read: MENTAL ARCHERY WITH HARK MORNER.

A pile of stapled pamphlets lay beside it.

Fraz took a seat as Hark spoke in his freshwater voice, riverine and delicious, about the force of an imaginary arrow.

And Fraz, a fellow who really hadn't been able to focus on anything for too long, not for years—not since preparing history quizzes for his pupils (Who led the Swedish intervention in the Thirty Years' War? When considering the Triangle Shirtwaist Factory Fire, how would one define a shirtwaist?)—began to focus. The situations, the perspectives, they retreated from what he was often hesitant to call his mind.

If this was not the answer, perhaps it was the path to one. He would follow in this young man's footsteps, like the boy in the snow behind that good Bohemian king, as long as the king wasn't the other kind of Bohemian. Fraz's artsy days were done.

What had Hark said that made all the difference?

Hark said "Boy." Hark said "Space." Hark said "Apple."

Hark said "Time."

Someday soon you, too, will understand.

"I'm Meg Kenny," the woman at the Pickering station says. "We're so happy you decided to come."

Why do people greet Hark this way? Yes, they have decided to come, for the money, of course, for the opportunity to share Hark's techniques and maybe to rescue the audience from the happiness hustler or protein priest who might arrive in their stead.

Meg steers Hark to her car. Fraz follows with the gear, the bow in its canvas sleeve, a shiny cloth quiver with a few arrows, some pamphlets, a ripe Fuji apple for the William Tell portion. Mental archery requires no actual archery, but the bow proves a vital prop, as well as an effective transitional object for beginners. The arrows are for show, or maybe—and Fraz hopes the day never comes—for a feeble try at self-defense. You can't pierce much with flat tips. Stun a pigeon, perhaps.

Meg drives along worn streets lined with vintage waffle boom houses. They cruise past a structure of wood and glass whose canted roof, with its rows of pegs, suggests, not subtly, the hatches of a Belgian iron. The garage of another home curves into the shape of a syrup jug. They zag into a main square, park near a bronze statue, a bewigged fellow in colonial dress.

"Who's that?" Fraz says.

"Who?"

"The statue guy."

"Who cares?" Meg says.

She seems less hostile than depleted.

"I do. A little."

"I'm sure there's a plaque."

They stare at the statue.

"I'm sorry. That was damaged of me," Meg says.

"Pardon?"

"The statue is Hector Pickering. Born and raised here. Fought in the Continental Army. Hanged as a spy by the British, though there is no evidence he was a spy. His last words, in fact, were 'There is no evidence I am a spy.'"

"The town is named for him?" Fraz says.

"No, for his father. A landowner named Priam Pickering."

"You're really up on the history."

"I'm the town historian. I'm also chief clerk and cultural coordinator. When we had a decent budget, we used to bring exciting people here."

"Thanks," Hark says.

"He speaks!" Meg says to Fraz. "Sorry. It's been a tough spring. Todd left me for that cunt at the flower shop."

"You should try to forget Todd," Hark says. "The lean dog, the hungry dog, will soon claim him."

"The hungry dog? What is that? Are you some kind of soothsayer? You do tarot, too? I hope this isn't what your talk is about."

"Not at all," Fraz says. "Hark has a very serious message."

"I'm trying to help people focus."

"Focus on what?"

"He doesn't do *what*. *What* drives hearts apart."

Hark jerks in his seat, flicks his fingernail a few times against the dashboard.

"He's antsy," Fraz says. "Let's get going."

"Fine," Meg says. "I could use some focus anyway. Meanwhile, I've got paperwork for you. Then we can set you up in the space. Did you bring books to sell?"

"Pamphlets," Hark says.

"Priam Pickering wrote pamphlets. Mostly about how to detect biscuit theft among servants. They're on display."

"These are probably a little different," Fraz says.

An hour later Hark stands in the shade of a band shell. Was there ever a band? Not in many years, Fraz guesses. The audience looks old, slumped in varying stages of rheumatoid torment on the wooden slats of their chairs. Retirees. The last generation permitted to retire. They've come to listen to a fervid man from the metropolis, his canary-yellow chambray shirt dark with a zealot's sweat.

". . . And so to reiterate: The targets, which are your work goals, your life goals, your spiritual goals, may always shift. But once a master archer, a true disciple of, say, the bow wielder Ashur, chief god of the Assyrians, or of Apollo and Diana—mythical figures your Priam and Hector Pickering would have read about in their Greek primers—you will always remember to anticipate. One aims at the future, but not a static future. One shoots where the stag, the target, one's chance for fulfillment, are about to appear. You lead your prey. You don't dress for the job you want. You dress for the job your child will someday be denied. A glass tureen of sour-cherry soup slides off the table and you catch it, centimeters from the floor. How did you do that? The body anticipates. The body remembers. The body is drenched in sour-cherry soup. Because all time is now. But you must let yourself feel it. If you stop shouting, if you grow silent, easeful, the body will launch the spirit's shaft true. To save his son, William Tell did not shoot an arrow at an apple, which probably, in an age before genetically modified crops, was a pretty scrawny piece of fruit. All Tell did was reach out and gently tap the apple from the top of his son's head. Can you understand this? Focus does not mean to simply gawk at something. It is to transform it. Tell knew this. And it has nothing to do with your tools. The English used the long bow and revolutionized war. The Mongols used a short bow and also revolutionized war. Size matters, but only the size of your patience. Your attention. The size of your ability to refuse mere perception, to refuse the given, to refuse the boon, as the poet said. It has nothing to do with archery, really. Archery is a metaphor. We could easily be talking about volleyball, or handcrafted butterscotch. But better we talk about the bow. It is primal. And so are the fears we must vanquish to live the lives we deserve."

Hark swivels from the lectern, raises his bow to the sun.

"I have pamphlets for sale."

The applause is florid, bone weak. Hark takes questions, signs autographs for the throng. Fraz hovers about, throng management.

"I'm not sure I grokked it all," a withered woman tells Hark, "but it's wonderful. You are wonderful. We need this. My family needs this. My grandson is on all these drugs for his ADHD and he still can't focus. And my daughter, with all her hot and cold yoga and big talk about mindfulness, she just stands around in the kitchen texting and posting on her phone all day. You should see her face when she does it. Her jaw all slack like a junkie."

"Very philosophical," calls a man with a cane. "And none of that Continental balderdash!"

"He's so strikingly handsome," a woman in line says to Fraz. "I feel better from listening to him. More focused!"

"I'm glad to hear it," Fraz says.

"I'm a senior citizen, so I have no trepidation telling you that you yourself are not handsome."

"I admire your lack of trepidation," Fraz says.

A man about seventy, with a long white filament of hair that sprouts from the meat of his nose, seizes Hark's wrist, remarks upon the plenitude of carp in nearby streams. He mentions the make and model of his bow, offers to guide Hark if he ever returns to town.

Fraz watches, frightened of his urge to tug at the strand of hair.

"I've never hunted," Hark says. "Thanks for the invitation, but like I said, my archery is a metaphor."

"Can't eat a metaphor," the man says. "Can't freeze it in the basement for winter."

"My father once told me something similar."

"Smart man. What kind of bow did he use?"

"He used a police service revolver. He hunted people."

Most balk at this, Hark's stock reply about his detective father, but the man gives a grave nod, as though now that the subject of stalking human game has been broached, they may speak as honest men.

Fraz's phone vibrates, a private number.

"You can hack that," the man says to Fraz. "See who's calling."

"Oh, no, thank you."

"Ignorance is bliss, huh?"

"Information has buried us."

"I'll tell you," the man says. "Looking back, over the years, there were times I could have used a lot more information."

He pinches the silky white strand from his nose, winces, drapes it on Fraz's shoulder.

"Noticed you eyeing it."

Meg taps Fraz's arm.

"We need to get you guys to the station."

The train is late. They buy iced chais, sit on nifty trapezoidal benches.

"Your talk," Meg says. "It was terrific. It really addressed some of my personal struggles."

"Okay," Hark says.

"The audience loved it. Mrs. Lawrence said she already felt the power of focus, as you called it."

"I didn't call it that."

"She said she felt better about recently discovering her late husband had cheated on her. I told her not so fast. I told her about Todd. I know I told you about Todd."

"The flower shop."

"I guess it wasn't cheating at first. We have an open thing. But the rule is: No feelings. You married?"

"No," Hark says.

"No? A catch like you? Ever get lonely?"

"It's no matter. I'm devoted to helping people through mental archery now."

"I'm married," Fraz says.

"Good for you," Meg says.

"But who knows?"

"Who knows what?"

"It's rocky. Marriages are difficult. Sometimes. Or maybe not really."

"Whoever she is," Meg says, "hold on to her. It would be a disaster for you out there."

"Out where?" Fraz says.

"Anyway, Hark. You really are something. I'm just honored to be sitting here with you."

"Thanks."

"God," Meg says. "I think my blood sugar is dropping. I should get a bar or something. This happens to me. I'm usually laden with snacks. Energy bars. Trail mix. But today when I left the house I was . . . unladen."

"Go ahead and get something," Fraz says. "We're fine."

"No, I can wait," Meg says. "I don't want to leave Hark by himself."

"He's not by himself," Fraz says.

"Next time we drive," Hark says.

They sit in silence and it reminds Fraz of that faraway time, earlier in the day, when they stared at the statue.

"Priam Pickering," Fraz says. "You don't meet people with first names like that anymore."

"No, now they're named Todd. Todd's father was a manager at the factory. Mine worked the batter vats."

"Gentlemen, start your waffles."

"I really need that bar now. I feel faint."

"Go ahead," Fraz says.

"No," Meg says. "Hark, tell me more about William Tell."

———

Back in the city, Hark and Fraz hike down Broadway to Kate's. The doorman deals them his usual smug nod. They're the strange dudes with the odd hours. Though Hark is the official houseguest, Fraz floats back his best freeloader scumbag grin, an ancient reflex.

Up in the plushness, Hark unpacks his gear.

Fraz would love to lounge with Hark on one of Kate's austere midcentury armchairs with a glass of Scotch and some Mahler or Debussy, or maybe a little West Coast jazz, on the stereo. A soothing and sophisticated close to the evening. But Hark dislikes classical, and jazz, both coasts. Inland, too. Hark disdains most music, really. Choral is okay.

Fraz turns on the TV. A blindfolded man waist-deep in a river grapples with a giant catfish. Numerals tick on the screen.

"Heck," the voice-over says, "I was pretty sure that catfish was going to gobble my freaking arm. And you can't see it, but the slimy bastard crapped on me."

"I hear America singing," Fraz says.

"You do?" Hark says.

"No, I just mean . . . forget it."

"You know I'm bad with the sardonic. Or was it sarcastic?"

"I wonder where Kate is," Fraz says.

"She's out tonight. You can leave now. I'm fine here. Go home to your wife and kids."

"I can stay."

"Please, just go. I'm tired. And turn this horrible show off."

Fraz holds out the remote, taps the screen dead.

"Okay, then," he says. "I'm tutoring for a few days this week, but I'll call tomorrow."

"Good."

"Well, that was fun today."

"We did the work," Hark says.

"That Meg woman really liked you."

"How so? She doesn't know me."

"You're right. Maybe I mean she liked your message."

That's not what Fraz means, but it's hard to talk about ordinary feelings or observations with Hark. To suggest that someone might be attracted to Hark in a carnal fashion seems near apostasy, though there is no ostensible reason for it, nothing in the pamphlets. It's just Hark's natural stiffness, a trait that maybe gets mistaken for purity, earns him the trust of his disciples. Or perhaps it is, in fact, a sign of something noble, ascetic. Maybe Fraz is too impure to know the difference.

"There is no message," Hark says now. "As you know. But perhaps she will help us in our endeavor to share my techniques with others."

"Perhaps so."

"I am comfortable with uncertainty. You might learn to be as well."

Home, in bed with Tovah, Fraz dreams of Meg. The town guide chews on her arm to get her blood sugar up, scales the statue of Priam Pickering, peers up at the sky.

"Hark!" she says. "Where are you, my love? Why have you forsaken me?"

It's one of those dreams where Fraz retains partial creative control.

"That's great, Meg!" he calls from a canvas director's chair perched high above, beyond, or beside the dream. Keep rolling, keep streaming. Welcome to the new night logic. Cue Mahler, and the major West Coast catfish noodlers. Cue that cunt Todd from the flower shop.

Let fall your quiver, my children, quiet your mind, unstring your bow, fly forth, forever unfletched.

Three

Tovah's on the train with the twins. She sits between them, keeps them yoked in relatively loose, pro-wrestler choke holds. They are temporarily immobilized and thus unable to assault each other or fellow riders, both of which are distinct possibilities with these maniacs, especially this morning. Meanwhile, she texts emendations to her supervisor's proposal to the provisional head of development at the Blended Learning Enhancement Project. Her supervisor, Cal Kronstadt, possesses what Tovah knows the business community deems leadership qualities, meaning he's equal parts fool and lout, a human facsimile on a ceaseless quest to collect his salary and cover his butt.

Apropos of which, the reason she's here on the subway restraining her kids in semilegal grappler grips, instead of already at her desk, is because one or both of her children have, as she put it as concisely as she could on the phone to the doctor, "concerns of the ass." More specifically, ass worms. Tovah may have ass worms, too. What happened was that all of their assholes started to itch and Tovah looked this symptom up, discovered a detailed photograph of a hairy, nearly microscopic worm. Somebody had earned enough trust from this creature to achieve a lively, candid shot as the critter regarded the camera with unamused scorn, mostly expressed through what Tovah supposed were eyes but on further inspection might have been anal orifices themselves. Tovah tried to call Fraz but hasn't been able to reach him. He could be tutoring, or doing a favor for Mr. Dersh, or, most likely, cleaning and jerking, perhaps at the gym, more likely at home.

The twins' noses nearly touch in Tovah's double clinch.

"Jesus, Mom, stop, let me go!" David says.

"Seriously," says Lisa.

"Hush it, guys!"

The names of her children sometimes embarrass Tovah. They were Fraz's idea. He had declared himself the creative one, which is how people (men) describe themselves when they aren't the competent ones. Tovah has a degree in poetry and two chapbooks, even if that was a thousand lives ago, but somehow he bulldozed her on the kids' names.

Fraz fretted, as he explained at the time, that what you called your children made your aesthetic too visible. You had to be clever. You could give them names culled from your particular ethnic tradition, or the names of major martyrs, or storied boroughs, neighborhoods. Tremont and Sunnyside were possibilities. You could also bestow family monikers. Tovah wanted to call the boy Jonah, after her uncle, and the girl Sarah. But Fraz insisted there was another familial tradition to uphold. His father, Frank Penzig, had named his son after an incident in which he misheard a page at the airport. He could have sworn the woman was saying "Fraz Penzig, please come to gate number five." Fraz's father had been bold and imaginative enough, Fraz told Tovah, to remember that moment in the Pan Am departure lounge and celebrate its uncanniness by naming his only child "Fraz." But what was uncanny about it? Tovah had studied the uncanny, written an undergraduate paper on the manifestations of *das Unheimliche* in sitcoms of the late 1980s. Frank had just misheard an airport announcement. What was uncanny about being a half-deaf doof?

Meanwhile, Fraz decided to honor his father by rebuke, bless his twins with top picks from Fraz's birth year, 1969, the kinds of names he would most likely have received if sired by a less inspired or perhaps less hearing-impaired man. *David and Lisa* was also the title of a tragic, popular 1962 film about mental illness. Penzig men: always hovering just outside of an inside joke they have played on themselves.

Tovah loosens her choke grips. The twins flop back in their seats, rub their necks, groan. They peer about the car for pitying looks, or perhaps an undercover agent from the Bureau of Alcohol, Tobacco and Bitchfuck Moms to bust their mother for abuse. But the other riders, ingrates, ignore them. Grown-ups are sick, thinks Lisa, and maybe David does, too, since their eight-year-old twin minds beam thoughts and emotions back and forth, or at least that's what it feels like, or what people tell them it's supposed to feel like.

Tovah asks her children if their assholes still itch.

"Not as much," David says.

"Not as much," Lisa says, mimics the high, sweet tone of her brother's voice, reaches out for a nasty flick of his earlobe.

"Mom! She's bullying me. Like a predator! Stop predating me!"

"Live with it," Lisa says. "I came out first."

"Both of you, stop at once!"

Tovah's itch is faint at best. Could it be that new cheap detergent Fraz bought, so proud of his thrift? She never did see a worm, except in the photograph. But it looked so real and wanting to nestle in the rectums of her family. Did she overreact? How can an overworked working mother overreact? The intestinal canals of your precious spawn teem with maggots, your husband slacks off on a job that barely keeps him in breath mints and your dolt of a supervisor gets promoted based on your due diligence. Overreaction is an impossibility. Mothers don't even empty machine pistols into middle school playgrounds. Those jobs are controlled by the Young (Disturbed) Boy Network.

Maybe the doctor will have some cold, soothing cream. A nice, cooling ointment or salve in her butt could absolve this galling day, so long as Fraz doesn't figure it for a goddamn invitation.

Four

Kate Rumpler settles into her business class seat, cradles the cooler on her knees.

"Excuse me," the flight steward says.

He wears a minuscule arrow-shaped stud in his nose.

"Yes?"

"Would you like me to help you store that in the overhead bin?"

"Bin?"

"The case. On your lap."

"It's a cooler," Kate says.

"Funny, it really does look like a cooler."

"That's what it is. And it can't go in the bin. Can't leave my person."

"What do you have in there?"

Kate nods at the stickers on the lid.

"Oh, wow. Do you have harvested organs in there?"

"People love that word."

"What word? 'Organs'?"

" 'Harvest.' 'Harvested.'"

"You got a liver in there? The way I hit the pisco sours last night, I'm definitely going to need one soon."

"No livers today. Just bone marrow."

"Does it pay well?"

"It's volunteer."

"That's wonderful."

"I like your nose stud."

"Well, archery is just a metaphor."

Kate nods.

"Could be butterscotch," she says.

The steward winks, passes Kate a few extra packets of party mix.

"On me. Enjoy. Relax. Unstring."

After the steward leaves, Kate spreads a napkin on the top of the cooler and pours out the party mix, sorts the debris, crumbled cheese twists, pretzel splinters, tortilla shards. She neatens her heaps until it all resembles a tiny industrial dump site. But edible. Though she'd never eat it.

Kate has many names for the marrow. Maybe today it's the marinade, the gravy, the gruel, the bloody goddess, the hema goblin, the caviar, the soul paste, the crude. Or perhaps it's the Ronko, the root juice, the marbled Juan, the one percent, the Roman senator, the traveling salesman, red river, red rider, hip spooge.

She never knows the lives she saves. All the information is protected. Kate only ever knows the cities and, if she desires, and Nestor, the coordinator, is in a weak ethical state, the results. Usually she delivers life, unless she misses a connection, in which case she delivers nonlife. Kate takes comfort in the starkness of that. Her troubles, she has come to believe, stem from being too enamored of the non-stark.

Kate began to carry the coolers after a court acquitted her of manslaughter. A kind of penance, though she never felt much guilt. The man slaughtered, Uncle Conrad, had been her father's business partner and mother's paramour toward the end of America's long boom. Years later, in Ann Arbor, the night before her cousin's wedding, he'd knocked on Kate's hotel room door, tottered forth in a seethe of gin, muttered something about the "moist splendor" of Kate's mother's "sex, circa 1985." He licked Kate's face with his salmon-brown tongue, pinched her breasts.

"I watched these melons grow," he said. "Like a fucking farmer, I watched."

"Conrad!" Kate said. "Stop!"

The old man was too big to bat away. Kate broke free, retreated. He cornered her with a mating call of gargled phlegm. Kate lowered her shoulders, rocketed out of her squat, cracked him in the chest with the heels of her palms. Uncle Conrad flopped back onto the carpet and his fine-veined, feather-fluff skull stove upon the brass knob doorstop that jutted from the floor. The old gropist had expired, according to the coroner's report, "slightly before instantly." The long boom was a sudden bust.

In the quaint jargon of her lawyer, Kate missed prison by a "twat follicle." Her mother's hostile testimony, with claims that her hussy of a daughter had harbored designs on her former flame, might have proven disturbingly suasive to some American juries, but this dozen had surmised there was not quite a person inside Mrs. Rumpler's stunning floral print wraps. Kate's father proved a heatless sort who, when queried about his personal values, quoted Rilke on marriage—all that guardian-of-solitude gark—and ancient Chinese naval tracts on life in general.

The trial confirmed Kate's early suspicions: Her mother had never loved her and she'd never been a daddy's girl.

Soon after the trial, the Rumplers crashed their Piper Aztec in the White Mountains of New Hampshire. It seemed preordained, or maybe just ordained, or perhaps merely evocative, as Kate had spent years scrunched up in Rumpler hobby planes. Now she was twenty-nine and had inherited from her inheritor progenitors enough money to live however she wanted.

The courier program seemed like a virtuous hobby while she figured out what this particular however entailed. But lately she's decided to stop the steady runs. Since she stumbled onto some crude early videos of Hark, Kate's life has commenced a slow, enormous pivot. She might possess most everything, but Hark seems to have seized on something crucial, elusive.

Yes, mental archery might smack of gimmick, and even Hark, once in a while, pokes fun at the dour mien of his acolytes, but that's just his playful surface nature, for he's dead serious underneath, and the only truth that matters is that out on her mat, stringing or unstringing her bow, or holding a pose like Rainforest Hunt or Arc of Totality, her body stretched and coiled at once, her skin slippery with a light coat of cleansing sweat, her mind at peaceful communion with a chorus of cosmic vectors, Kate achieves a serene and exalted state that neither her mother's delusional jealousy nor her father's pill-distant disdain could ever wither or shame. Her focus shatters the hurt.

There is no question about putting her wealth at Hark's disposal. Too much is at stake. You have the state of the world, for starters. Forget about the falcon not hearing the falconer. These days the falconer just totally ignores the falcon, checks celebrity news on his phone. The poor falcon soars around forsaken, bereft, eats spoiled bratwurst discarded on a rooftop, pukes. Or that's how Fraz framed the situation at a recent meeting.

"It's from a famous poem."

"I don't remember the sausages," Teal said.

"Tovah liked to recite it to our twins when they were little."

"Sounds snuggly."

Kate laughed, as she does at about half of what Teal says. The other half she maybe resents, for even in her old college friend's compliments lie buried accusations about Kate's privilege. Still, they are buddies for life, vowed it on graduation day, always an odd, semi-feigned drama with them, a treasure, a curse.

"Falcons," Hark said. "That's good. I like falcons. As long as it's all about focus. As long as we don't lose focus on focus."

Hark is always focused on focus. Others speak of what mental archery might mean for politics, for communities, for resistance against the forces of distraction and atomization, forces which Teal, former Fulbright scholar and ex-con, says reside at the core of oppression and imminent environmental collapse. Kate's more drawn to fragile and private spheres, a caseworker approach. She wants to heal the world one broken person at a time. They argue tactics, but never with severity. Hark stands apart from such discussions, refuses to claim any grand purpose for mental archery.

It's better that way. They can stay on task, as Teal likes to put it, produce the videos, maintain the Website and mailing lists, travel with Hark to his talks and sessions, protect him from spiritual mash-ers, push for small-market radio, craft the book pitch. Marketing, Kate supposes you'd call it, and if that word sounds cynical for some-thing as holy as mental archery, only the process is tainted.

The message, which does not officially exist, is pure.

Now the plane banks into what the pilot describes over the inter-com as their initial descent into Chicago. The napkin with her party-mix heaps slides across the cooler top. Soon, the pilot says, they will commence their final descent. When does the initial descent blur into the final? Somewhere in your mid-forties, Kate figures. She has less than a decade. Not much time.

Strawberry jam, strawberry sturgeon, the shortcake, the hot shot, the cream of bone, the inside scoop.

O'Hare is murder when you've got the marrow.

Five

Today's tutee's cleft hand is a lump with a pointer finger, nubs cousinish to thumbs, but he can hold a pencil, which he uses now to circle sentences in the textbook spread before him. He hunches with Fraz at an antique oak desk in an ornate study on Park Avenue.

"This clause is trippy," the tutee says. "I don't get it at all."

"Let me see."

Rich kids with deformities fascinate Fraz. Their blights are an extra injustice, a cosmic prank. Will this lad with the congenital mishap ever get to rev a custom-built Ducati, or grip the till of a teak-decked daysailer? Will he be welcomed by handsome and ravishing peers, invited to caress fellow trust fund vaginas and penises with his raw, scaly permafist? It's all so splendid and poignant.

Fraz hates rich people because he believes in his heart they are better. Most people won't acknowledge this fact, think they're equal to the rich, just unlucky for now. If the majority ever susses out the truth—that the wealthiest have evolved, by dint of breeding advantages and technology, into a smarter, sleeker, more disease-resistant caste—there will be a bloodbath. Fraz hopes it's a bubble bloodbath. He's got a towel picked out.

Right now, though, Fraz must buckle down, guide his young charge through pedagogical thickets. He's distracted by the boy's shirt, which bears this rebus: a decal of a truck, followed by a human ear set in parentheses, a sketch of a clothes iron and the letter y. Fraz, a T-shirt connoisseur, does not approve.

"Truck ear irony?" Fraz says.

"The ear means 'sounds like,'" the boy says.

"Truck fear irony?"

"As in 'sounds like truck,'" the boy says. "As in 'fuck irony.' Is it that difficult?"

"For me," Fraz says. "Do you know what irony is?"

"It's bad," says the boy. "It means you don't care."

"Who told you that?"

"My wellness teacher."

"Your wellness teacher is wrong. Your wellness teacher sounds like a font of illness. Irony, kid, means you care too much."

"Liar!" the boy says.

"But it's true."

"It's not."

"On the other hand, look at your hand."

"My what?" the boy says.

"No Ducati, buddy."

"Excuse me?"

"Like, you can afford it. But can you rev it?"

"I don't know what you are saying, but I do know you can't talk to me this way."

"What do you mean? I'm trying to assuage."

"What does 'assuage' mean?"

"It's on the vocab sheet."

"Mother!"

"I think we can stop for today," Fraz says. "You're really on top of the material. You don't even need a tutor."

"Don't come back."

"I understand completely."

Fraz the Castoff wanders the avenues, crosses to a commercial street, a bistro with a bar.

"I'm Tommy," the bartender says. "I'll be your bartender."

It seems obvious that Tommy will be his bartender. Fraz resigns himself to industry etiquette, the catalogue of inanities which includes the dread question "Are you still working on that?" and this courtesy of utmost insincerity: "Take your time."

Fraz orders a sexy new stout from Vermont, peers up at the TV. Ball game graphics zoom, burst. The home team ace hasn't allowed a hit in six innings.

"Fella's got a no-no going," Fraz says.

"You just fucking jinxed it," Tommy the bartender says, a bitter curl to his lip.

"Hardly," Fraz says, or maybe lectures, overspill from his tutoring session. "I think that's just the teammates and the announcers who have to keep quiet when there's a no-hitter going. Surely we here in this remote location may sing of impending glory."

"If you say so."

A sharp crack sounds from the TV. The visiting team's designated hitter, a pasty behemoth, has smacked one over the high blue wall. The bartender regards Fraz's nearly full pint glass.

"Still working on that?"

"I'm still drinking it, if that's what you mean."

The bartender snatches the glass away, pours the stout down a sink, plops a bar rag down near Fraz's folded hands.

"I need to know," Fraz says. "Do you really believe I had something to do with that home run?"

"It's not about what I believe."

"But it is."

"You're not welcome here."

"I would never return anyway," Fraz says. "It's random I'm here in the first place."

"You say that now," the bartender says, runs the flat of his hand through his brush cut. "But a day will come. It always does. You'll be shit out of luck. You'll be in Shitsville. Or Fuckberg. Or Anal Fissure Township. Or Anal Fissure Heights. One of those municipalities. Just looking for respite. For a soft place to lay your ugly head. But there will be no respite. There will be no room at the inn."

"Excuse me?"

"And the stable will not be available, either."

The bartender reaches below the bar, comes up brandishing a tiny, wooden Bat Day baseball bat.

"Leave, or I'll jab this in your eye, you jinx, you stout-ordering douche."

"What's wrong with stout?"

"Nothing, until *you* ordered it. Now leave."

———

Fraz finds a bench at the rim of a park. Sick pigeons peck near his shoes. A shame it's too late to shoot back home for some Fraz time. The kids at school, Tovah at work, he could watch porn, eat spelt pretzels, read a bracing report about white poverty in a general interest magazine, watch more porn.

Fraz is on a weird preggo jag. You have to rummage through loads of clips for a scene that doesn't reek of heartbreak, or morose surrender. What you want are dignified professionals in warm, loving open relationships who happen to be knocked up and extremely horny. He's found a few out there in the nether-ether.

He's not certain of the craving's source. Maybe he hungers for life's abundance, joneses for a taste of that hormonal fantasmagoria again. He recalls those months with Tovah, how he lusted for her heat, her bloat. Those had been beautiful days.

They'd met at a café poetry reading, Fraz at the bar on his semi-regular stool, annoyed to discover his quiet cappuccino was about to be interrupted by a local women's writing collective.

"I just wanted a coffee, not to listen to some pretentious losers air their fucking twaddle," he complained to the woman next to him.

"I'm with you," she said. "Last thing I care about is a bunch of pathetic bitches who don't even have the balls to put their heads in the oven get up there and spout some convoluted babble about their dumb feelings. Keep it to yourselves, you coddled wenches. Nobody cares."

"Totally!" Fraz squealed, delighted. "Coddled wenches!"

He should have known she was one of the poets. His gut fluttered in shame a few minutes later when she drained a cognac, punched him in the shoulder and strode up to the lectern to read.

It wasn't that he hated poetry. He hated bad poetry. Or so he'd always told himself. But he hadn't really known anything about it, he realized, until he heard her. Her poems were short, with a high, clean music. Funny right up to the moment they tore your throat out. You could see versions of her in these terse songs, a roving bird, an ancient seer, a bored girl, a tender troubadour, a comedian, a brute. He fell in love right there in the café.

Somehow her words made his better. He heard himself sound like a human with Tovah, witty, kind, alert to the suffering of others. For hours at a time he wasn't Frank Penzig's preternaturally nervous and bitter son. They spent days together after the reading. She welcomed him in stages, as though she'd decided to stare through that dolt on the stool to something worth her gaze. He was shocked and grateful, but also afraid, perhaps, that he could never sustain the heart she summoned in him. But for a long time he could squash that fear. Also, she wasn't perfect. She was quick to cruel judgment and frequently misplaced jar lids. She tended to let the garbage bag slip down into the pail and demanded he be the one to reach into the muck and tug the edges out. He grew enamored of her flaws, though, because they balanced out his, and because by dint of this equilibrium they could cultivate what he called a level loving field. She said she appreciated the idea a fuck load more than the phrase.

They moved in together after a few months, cooked simple meals, or no meals. They watched premium cable, read each other's favorite novels, screwed and cuddled on a scratchy plaid sofa they reveled in despising.

They never discussed a life without children. Never seemed to consider the choice. He pretended it was mostly her idea, her programming, her biological mandate, but he felt fatherhood encoded in him, too. It was not quite biological. It was Jewish or something.

They never discussed a life with children, either. Not in any pragmatic sense. What they imagined parenthood to be was more like a film montage with a baby in it. They were maybe pitching each other a movie that would star the two of them and an as-yet-uncast infant and in this film they would love each other and the child and even learn to love the sofa in a sober fashion. Riding this wave of undeniable creative momentum, excited as Hollywood executives about the so-called project, they dove into development, which mostly required them to screw and cuddle at very particular times of the month. Eventually, the project got greenlighted.

Fraz watched Tovah's body swell, thrilled to it. Her belly was the antidote to death.

Tovah still made poems. But now she'd made a baby. Two of them, in fact. Twins ran in her family.

After a while she got a job in educational technology. Now she makes money for both of them. She never makes poems anymore. Fraz thought a raise he was about to receive would give her more time to write, but they cut his job instead. The zero sum. He wanted to join her in making things but felt so paralyzed, so lazy, sad. Tovah is often sad, too, but never lazy.

Fraz announced new plans after his layoff, major endeavors: bookshelves, bathtub mead. He'd work on the family go-bag, to which he'd been adding supplies over the years. The huge vinyl duffel was long past its existence as an object anyone could carry in a crisis. It took up the entire floor of their hall closet, a shrine to the futility of planning.

In lieu of end-of-days days that never seemed to arrive, here were Tovah and Fraz locked in low-key, quotidian apocalypse. A desalinization straw would not save the marriage. What would?

Point is, he still pines for her. But does she want him anymore?

There are signs of hope. She doesn't rebuff him when he makes his move, not exactly.

When she's in the mood, she'll say, "If you want to have sex, I won't consider it marital rape."

It's not like the days when she'd cross a room to kiss him, but it's a start.

Can Hark, or the teachings of Hark, make him worthy of her attentions, the brush of her fingers, her lips, again? Can he become the better man he glimpsed his future self to be when they met? Can their hearts trace the path of the true arrow?

Tune in next week. Fraz always does.

But sometimes he still dwells on that swollen era, when Tovah resembled one of those ancient clay figures from biblical lands. Not to mix religious signifiers, but he could flog the bishop to a Hittite fertility goddess all day.

Too bad they never made an actual home movie of themselves.

Fraz could have shot a pretty decent one. He'd studied film as an undergrad, made a short documentary.

One day the professor told the class that only a few of them would succeed and those who did wouldn't be the most talented ones.

"The rest of you will experience a failure of nerve."

Fraz knew he was not talented and also likely to experience a failure of nerve. He figured there would be time to recover from that failure. But there doesn't seem to be much time for anything. Mr. Dersh expects him in an hour. Bizarre, the way Tovah calls him a layabout since he lost his job, when his day teems with to-dos.

———————

Old Man Dersh's main concerns are tech and crap. His firm invests in start-ups and he also owns factories that manufacture a portion of the world's geegaws and doodads, the finger fans and fly swatters and water pistols and much else plastic and on hooks in the 89- and 99-cent stores. He owns stakes in the Thai prawn industry, though he assures his friends he finds slavery abhorrent.

"They'll grow out of it," he says of the man brokers on the docks of Bangkok.

Mr. Dersh swore Fraz to an oath of secrecy on the subject of his business ventures. They were beyond nondisclosure agreements. Mr. Dersh and Fraz's father went back, had been born on the same Brooklyn block. The vow was a sacred act to Fraz, who knows himself to be a jaded sentimentalist with a love for authority, no matter how much he yearns for outlaw cool. He still cries at war and sports movies, or any other depiction of homosocial sacrifice. It's a genuine disability. He should qualify for benefits.

Now Fraz waits in Mr. Dersh's penthouse office suite overlooking the park. A silver-pink cloud nudges the windowpane, an immense, fluffy beast. It was Mr. Dersh who set up the tutoring gig Fraz has just fled, and he hopes word of his possibly inappropriate behavior hasn't already reached the old man.

"He'll see you now," says Vera, the assistant, Mr. Dersh's grandniece. Fraz is not the only beneficiary of nepotism here.

The inner office, vaulted, walnut, is familiar, but a different Dersh, a younger version, stands at the standing desk.

"Fraz, buddy!"

"Nat. Is that you?"

"It's me, pal!"

Nat the Gnat, Fraz and the other kids used to call Mr. Dersh's son, with a silent but somehow still audible G.

Window light soaks the rich knit of Dersh's necktie, dances off his shaved head.

"How are you, Fraz?"

"I'm okay, Nat. Where's your dad?"

"Here's the thing, Fraz. You're not going to believe it. He had a stroke. Just the other day."

"You're kidding me."

"A few strokes, really. Maybe dozens. Most of them micro. But a few of them macro. It was terrible."

"How is he now?"

"How is he now, Fraz?"

"Yes."

"He's dead. Gone. The only reason I sound so calm about it is the shock. And that I didn't love him that much. But, see, the only reason I just said that is the shock."

"I'm so sorry. I wish I'd known . . ."

"No worries."

"But, my family . . . yours. We go back."

"It's okay, Fraz."

"I didn't see it in the news."

"It wasn't. We are in the middle of a deal. We'll announce his death soon."

"Oh."

"He lived a good, longish life. I know my dad helped you out from time to time. And I intend to follow that tradition."

"That's very kind of you."

"Nat the Silent G Nat is your buddy."

"Look, we never meant to hurt your feelings or—"

"Just messin' with you. Hey, the old man's going where he belongs."

Dersh pokes his finger toward the ceiling.

"Of course he is," Fraz says.

"Not heaven, man. The moon! We're all going. The Dershes, I mean. Booked to launch next year with an Azerbaijani outfit. We're going to have another service for my father there."

"Scatter his ashes?"

"Scatter? Fuck no. We're going to bury them on the moon! Near the Sea of Tranquility. Deep, so his shit doesn't float off."

"Smart," Fraz says—dumbly, he guesses.

"Well, that's it for now. As soon as we announce my father's death I'll be grieving for a while."

"You must be grieving right now."

"Sure, man. But remember, the shock. It's funny seeing you at this moment, right? I mean, our fathers grew up together in Brooklyn. My pop always said, 'That Frank Penzig, he's not made for this world. Too sweet. Too kind. That's why he's a poor schmuck teaching community college and I'm rich.' But I never really agreed with him. Your dad was a dick, you know? Guy once threw a football straight at my nuts. Do you remember this? We had that barbecue. You all showed up in your shitty station wagon. That detail sticks in my head for some reason. Even as a kid I asked God to make sure I'd never end up driving a shitwagon like your dad's. Anyway, we're playing touch and your old man is automatic QB and I'm waving from the flat for a screen pass. He gets this glint in his eye and bammo! My balls burned for a week. What a duckfucker, right?"

"Sure," Fraz says.

"Great. How is that wife of yours?"

"Of mine? Oh. I mean, we're not that patriarchal. I don't own her."

"Who said you did?"

"No, you're right."

"She's still your wife? You're still her husband?"

"Yes."

"That's a shame."

"What?"

"Just joking. You know how lucky you are to have such a gorgeous, intelligent woman, don't you?"

"Gorgeous?"

"Oh, my God, you blind slug. She's a knockout. You don't think your wife is hot?"

"Of course I do."

"She's a poet, too, right? She's got soul. Deserves so much more than a baloney pony like you. And I mean that. Just kidding. But it's true. But don't sweat it. But be careful. Other men would mangle for such a wise, witty, joyful piece of pussy."

"Hey, maybe that's enough, Nat."

"I know, I'm standing here babbling. I've got meetings. And we're not exactly generating revenue just squawking. I'll call you when I need you. Be well."

In the anteroom, a stern fellow in a padded military sweater watches Fraz from behind some ficus leaves. Fraz knows better than to wave to Major Van Brunt, retired mercenary and Dersh security chief since Fraz's boyhood. Fraz still remembers the day Van Brunt barged into the Dersh bathroom where little Fraz sat at stool.

Van Brunt, an Adonis with a pencil mustache, fresh from the bush but in a dapper goon's blazer, perched on the lip of the whirlpool.

"What are you doing?" Fraz asked.

"I'm here to make sure you don't steal anything."

Fraz looked about at the gleaming gold fixtures, the plush blue bath mat, the pearl-studded tissue box, the regal mirrors and sconces of rare ore.

"Okay," Fraz said.

"And when you leave, don't flush."

"Why?"

"That's need-to-know. How old are you?"

"Twelve."

"You don't need to know."

Now Fraz scurries past this gaunt relic of a young, strapping creep, rides the elevator down to the clumped squalor of the streets, the city proper, his world beneath the clouds.

Six

It's Tuesday, but the twins have no school. (Teacher development? Can't they develop on their own time?)

Tovah works from home. She'd rather work from work.

At home, there is noise, the screeched incoherence of sub-tween hearts, dishes in the sink, smudges on the walls, Popsicle sticks in the sheets, guinea pig scat on the rug. At work, except for the infrequent twinkling of devices, and the occasional Cal Kronstadt implosion, a voluptuous silence reigns. Her colleagues are kids, but not the smelly kind. There are massage kiosks and nap chambers, screens in the walls to guide you through the beige maze of corridors. Vending machines dispense organic snacks, tech accessories and health-monitoring gear, at no cost.

At work, the free cafeteria is a sun-flooded garden stocked with exquisitely packaged superfoods. The conference rooms bear names culled from aughts nostalgia: Messenger Bag, Fixie, South Tower, Tribulations, Australian Meat Pie.

Yesterday Tovah spent five hours in Australian Meat Pie with some members of her team. Cal, the idiot, was worried. He did a worry dump. The big boss, thirty-five-year-old social media tycoon Dieter Delgado, known to the world and his millions of virtual customers as Deets, had shocked everybody on the org chart by taking thirteen seconds out of his day to check on the progress of the dinkiest, most off-grid group in the imperium.

"I've gotten word," Cal said. "Deets is not happy with us."

"Fuck!" said Clytemnestra. Still a teen, she'd worked her way up from pre-tern in less than a year.

"Deets thinks we're deluding ourselves about the launch date."

"I think we're on schedule," said Vincent, handsome even with that dark, fleshy growth on his eyelid. "Why does he think we're deluded?"

"I'm not sure," Cal said. "But we know he's never wrong about this stuff."

"Is there stuff he is sometimes wrong about?" Tovah asked.

"He was right about the internet," Clytemnestra said.

"Right that the internet had already become a central mode of communication and commerce? Right to steal his social media idea from that girl at Yale?"

"Everybody knows that's a load of dook!" Cal said. "That tampon storage unit had her day in court. Deets is a genius."

"Excuse me?"

"What?" Cal said.

"You called the Yalie a tampon storage unit."

"Ah, no," said Clytemnestra. "I don't think he said that."

"Yeah, that's crazy," said Vincent, winked at Tovah. Did he mean to suggest he would cover for Cal now but back Tovah later? The soft, rubbery nodule that jutted from his eyelid made him a hard read.

Tovah clasped her hands together, caught the others staring, perhaps at the recently surfaced liver spot near her knuckle. Hers were elegant, middle-aged hands, but Tovah reckoned they resembled the rheumatoid talons of a leprous crone to this crowd, except maybe, crushingly, to Cal.

Once, a few years ago, in the elevator, she sensed his discreet peep of the drape of her summer dress. After, he coughed. That was about as much as could be signaled in an office elevator without the consultation of lawyers, but she was soon promoted to deputy chief of relational development. That meant she would travel to conferences and trade shows to peddle their growing line of EduToolz. Tovah worried this was some kind of setup for hotel assignations, but Cal never did materialize at her door, with, as Clytemnestra once claimed he always kept at the ready in his Dopp kit, a bottle of poppers and a dental dam. One night, however, he took the staff out for lobster rolls and corporate-themed entertainment. A young Jesus type claiming to be a mindfulness instructor screamed about baby bones mealed in the gears of unfettered capitalism. They booed him off the stage. Booing him seemed part of the act.

"Fuck this smarty-pants dookage," a drunk Cal shouted, dragged the gang to an underground arcade for Skee-Ball. Nobody was that shocked to discover in Cal a fevered, ornery Skee-Ball fanatic. After a few minutes of play, most of their party were ready to quit the company. Whenever it was Tovah's turn to roll, Cal called her "Little Miss Safe Work Environment" or "Lame Summer Dress."

But nobody quit. Nobody could afford to quit.

No grudges, though. Sometimes Tovah pities her tormentors. They have demented souls. They know not what their gruesome ways wreak. She has her poetry, at least, if not the time to write it. Maybe someday she'll make good on what she knows was early promise. Not to be a pro, some prima donna in the verse world. Just to bring that particular music into her life again. To have her song back. And what do scrotes like Cal have, besides whatever is vended in the work lounge? The latest cardio surveillance wristwatches? Even more ancient ancient grains?

Now Tovah hears what sounds like funereal keening coming from the laptop speakers in the twins' room.

"You annihilated my people!" David shouts.

It must be that vile video game Fraz bought without her approval: *Age of Genocide Two*.

"Why did you stay in your village?" Lisa says. "I dropped so many leaflets."

"We've lived there a thousand years!"

Tovah hears familiar grunts outside the front door. Portals confuse Fraz.

"Hey, Tove," he says, slouches in that slight curve in the wall they call the foyer.

"Did you get the good laundry detergent?"

"I couldn't do it," Fraz says.

"What?"

"Seemed extravagant. We're trying to save money."

"It's detergent. I don't care about the money. If I cared about money, I wouldn't be in this marriage. I just don't want my ass to itch."

"Okay, understood."

"Really?"

"Look, I'll go again later. I just need to rest. I'm tired."

"You got up at noon. It's now two. Why do you need to rest?"

"I told you, I'm tired. Can you be a little less aggressive with the settlement-building, please?"

When they were younger, she was the Nazis of the marriage, he was the Jews. If she ever asked him to help out with chores, take out the recycling, scrub the toilet bowl, he'd shoot her an arch *Sig heil*. But now they've progressed to other paradigms. Tovah's tired of the paradigms.

Last night she dreamed that she and a man who may have been Nat Dersh frolicked in a field of lavender. A green, fuzzy stub of horn protruded from the man's chin. Tovah, aroused to recall it, eager for truce, perhaps out of guilt for her dream, dances over to Fraz, kisses him, pinches his tits. She likes to picture herself a frat boy in these moments, pushing vulnerablity against a basement wall. It's better to be the frat boy. They can both be some varsity oinker. Or she'll be Dersh with his jawhorn. She'll jam it in one of Fraz's holes if he wants, but he always lies, pretends he doesn't.

Fraz's desires, in fact, have devolved. He's giving fantasy a bad name. The last time they made love he mumbled something into her neck about how she was a nice girl, and maybe if she loved him good with that baby in her belly, he'd get her work at his shirtwaist factory.

"Do you actually know what a shirtwaist is?"

"Like a lady's belt?"

"You're a moron," she said then.

"Go to the bedroom," she says now.

This time she just lets him grind on her for a while. He's proud of this technique. A friend of his mother, he once told her, taught him sex when he was a teenager.

"I just took to it," he said.

It's tiring, but she'll tap him out soon, slide herself up near his mouth.

He can always make her come that way. Never with his dick. She told him nobody had. It was mostly true. If it ever bothered him, he did not show it. He always had such greed for her body.

These were some of her favorite memories, the years of fucking, laughing, talking, eating, drinking, kissing, rubbing, laughing.

The age of gerunds.

Later something seemed to dim. Dim in her, dim in him.

It was the kids, but also not the kids.

They bought a bed that was too big. They could both spread to their outmost eagle and still not touch.

They bickered, about chores, about the twins, or Fraz's laxity with regard to them, or her obsessive fear for them, projecting from every dumb TV show watched or cupcake devoured their early demise from obesity, crystal meth.

They bickered about his lack of ambition, also, or was it purpose? He'd left his job well-liked. An honorable discharge. He could find more work if he tried. But she'd made peace with all of this before. It just popped up again. Crap pops up. Once, she worshipped the very aspects of his character she now assaulted, saw in his defiance of the normal expectations of adulthood something deeply moral, not to mention fun. She figured Fraz for the best person she knew. Somewhere inside her she must still believe that. But where, exactly? Geographic surveys prove inconclusive.

Sometimes Fraz reminds her of certain photographs, half-starved polar bear cubs cut adrift on ragged chunks of ice. Part of her wants to cuddle these doomed furry babies, maybe die on the ice floe with them. Another part of her wants to turn from the horror, board a plane for Oaxaca, or Rome. She can always almost feel it, the Mexican, the Italian sun, like warm gossamer on the back of her neck.

Near dinnertime they still lie in bed, listen to the twins down the hall. David and Lisa have forsaken virtual war crimes for parallel play. Lisa directs herself in lavish, effects-driven musical comedies produced on her phone. David, Tovah intuits by the clicks and scrapes of a skateboard, performs pop-shove-its on the kitchen Marmoleum. This is forbidden, but Tovah is too weary to remonstrate. She starts to pass out in Fraz's armpit, though she should not fall asleep, as she must enter more revisions to her emendations to the latest EduToolz proposal. This one she has decided to call the Happy Puppy Panopticon. The classroom teacher is a thing of the past. Tomorrow's educator will sit in a control room and monitor the behavior, biorhythms and brain waves of her students on screens while articulated robot hands pass out workbooks, set up lab equipment and tenderly muss little Johnny's hair. It's not Tovah's idea of a textured educational environment, but finding the least scary phrases to describe the future pays the bills.

Fraz snoozes, the parenting book she wants him to read spread on his chest. She finished this popular guide, *Concerning Children: How to Stop Treating Problem Kids as Problems*, over a month ago. David and Lisa aren't really a problem. They make friends, subtly torment more entitled children, do well in school. They just seem a bit cold and peevish at home, as though fundamentally unimpressed with their parents' attempts to provide them with a decent life. Maybe that's the proper attitude.

It beats being the girl she once was, pathological in her servility, by age eleven a harried cook and maid to her father and mother and brothers and sisters, not to mention the prime stoker of familial warmth, a cultivator of cheer, always there to finish her siblings' homework, to fetch her father's drink, to massage her mother's feet, with nary a kind gesture in return. The energy giver, they called her, her mockers, her exploiters, her destroyers, her loving family.

She doesn't visit the fuckers very often.

Seven

Home from her cooler run, Kate surveys her lair. What she once called her gut check gut reno is nearly done. The contractors, the decorators, the designers, have honored her vision.

"You know that bear on the tea box?" she had told them. "You know how he's all snug in that chair by the fire? Now, figure that's all happening, but in a corner of Andy Warhol's Factory. Like Edie might stumble over and fling herself on the sleepy bear's lap. But it's really only half Factory, because the other half is Chateau Marmontish, except for one area that would be, like, Faust's library slash study. Can you do that?"

They proffered solemn nods, did that. They were no less talented than the architects and stonemasons of medieval Europe, though these days the cathedrals tended to be smaller, erected for self-worship.

Kate lights scented candles, jacks the volume on one of the new dirge bands. The vast room gets vaster. She sits at her father's old rolltop desk, uncaps her fountain pen, writes on mint-green parchment: *Shit to Accomplish Like Yesterday.*

She hears footsteps, twists in her chair.

"Oh, you startled me," she says, though it's not quite true.

Hark stands shirtless, pajama-bottomed. He's got smooth skin and a taut bod but he shouldn't be bare-chested in the Faust nook. He's still a guest, even if he's been here almost six months and is her spiritual leader.

"I'm sorry. How was your trip?"

"I wouldn't call it a vacation, thank you very much," Kate says.

"Excuse me?"

"Sorry. I thought you said . . . Forget it."

"Kate, may I get you something from the kitchen?"

"Please."

Hark returns with glasses, a bucket of ice, a bottle of Polish vodka. He pours the vodka over rocks for Kate, tongs a single egg-sized ice cube into his tumbler, frozen water his signature refreshment.

"Are we ready to shoot the new talk?"

"Are you?"

"I think so, Kate. Yes."

"Whatever you need."

"You've been so kind to me, Kate."

"I believe in what we're doing."

"It must be hard for all of you."

"What do you mean?"

"Well, I know what I am. And what this is. But whatever I say, you still must discover it for yourselves."

"Or make it up?"

"What?"

"Hark, you say we are just here to focus."

"In the home or at the office, yes."

"But there must be more."

"Oh, Kate. I'm sure there's more. I'm sure there's much more. But that's beyond us."

Hark sucks his ice cube, spits it back into the glass.

"Kate?"

"Yes?"

"Have you lain with fellow humans?"

" 'Lain'?"

"Do you have a boyfriend or girlfriend?"

"I've had both, and others. But I'm really not interested in that scene right now. What about you?"

"Oh, I had my demon days. But there's no time for flesh and fluids anymore."

"Flesh and fluids. I like that. Hark, can I ask you something?"

"Of course."

"Well, like, we're basically the same age. We're both Americans. Why do you talk so strangely sometimes? No offense."

"We didn't have a TV or a computer growing up. And I didn't have too many friends. Just my bookworm sister. Does that help explain it?"

"Maybe."

"Maybe I'm not really of this time and place. Not the way most people are."

"That's probably a good thing."

"I hope so."

"I'd love to hear about your demon days sometime."

"Sex is a wonderful gift. But it's not focus."

"It can be."

"Maybe, Kate. For a little while. Anyway, I'm glad we could have this chat. Sometimes we get so caught up in the demands of mental archery, we lose each other as people. All of us. You, Teal, Fraz, the others. That cameraman. I can't always remember their names."

"Schnitz."

"Right. Well, I should get some sleep."

"I think I might head out for a moment."

"Really?"

"It's like I put everything into making this the perfect environment for myself but often I can't stand being here. Like it's somebody else's house. A person I detest. But I'm also very conscious of that somebody being me. Have you ever been shot with a real arrow?"

"Ha! Not yet."

"There's still time, though."

Hark's eyes blaze with strange joy.

"Yes, I believe there is!"

Kate wraps herself in fashion-cut oilskins, strolls the neighborhood under a cold night drizzle. She spots the dolphin-green glow of a neon sign in the darkness: THE PEARLESCENT SHOAL. It's the new pub that's taken over the lease from the Chakra Khan. Ale beats kale in this neighborhood now. Where will she procure her cleansing toddies?

The place is nearly empty, a ghost joint, the few patrons mostly alone, or in quiet pairs, huddled under vintage lamps. The décor nods to the golden age of saloon culture without tipping into big-mirrored gaucherie, and it makes her worry that she took her reno's particular themes too far. Or perhaps the Faustian/Warholian bargain was exactly what was required. We are such mysteries to ourselves, how can we decide about anything important, let alone the wallpaper, or matte or shiny finishes for the cherrywood floor?

Years before she accidentally killed the man, Uncle Conrad told her that it wasn't until you owned everything that you really, finally understood that life is just utter shit. She vowed to never become a person who could arrive at such a truth.

She'd become somebody else, but what? Or maybe she'd become a few different people. You couldn't really plan it. When she'd been a revolutionary socialist in college, going to meetings, to rallies, to janitor and librarian strikes, to newspaper sales (because handselling was how you connected with workers), she knew it wasn't her place to make a plan. The people would decide the future, after the day was won, the ruling class crushed. It was 1999. The country was turning the corner. It would happen soon.

But there was The Struggle and there were also certain struggles. Some of her comrades, the judgmental pricks, castigated her for bourgeois individualism. Her penchant for donning heavily stylized factory worker outfits from the Roosevelt era didn't help. She had not meant to mock or take the legacy of labor lightly. She'd just never felt more part of the vanguard than those months spent in fashion-forward factory duds, the silk head-kerchiefs and apple-green satin coveralls.

It was meant as a gentle, running joke, her proletarian wardrobe in brazen palettes, but the cadre did not much appreciate her humor. The Rumplers might have been loaded but she wasn't, not yet, not enough to fund the revolution or foot a typical evening's bar bill. Her comrades voted her out of the branch. Most were teachers and attorneys now. One or two still convened meetings. She used to picture the lot of them, herself included, after the revolution, victims of a party purge, lined up against a stucco (always stucco) wall (should she have ordered stucco for her reno?). Kate would stare into the eyes of the rebel girl about to blow a hole in her sternum, signal her forgiveness with a certain empathic droop of her lips. So long as they weren't tyrants, or ideological clowns, or seasteaders or something, Kate would find it in her soon-to-be-punctured heart to believe in the inherent rectitude of the folks about to snuff her, go to her lime-pit grave referring to them as folks.

Hark is no tyrant. Nor is he an ideologue. There are no ideas in mental archery, or no complex ones, just poses, mini-wisdoms, historical nuggets of dubious accuracy. Pearlescent shoals of the stuff.

Harkism is the answer because it offers none. It's not a philosophy, but a tool to clear ground. True, she's tried other modes for focus, for peace of mind, yoga, transcendental meditation, Buddhism. But even Buddhism has baggage: Buddhists. They've been tyrannical enough in the past, violators, *génocidaires*. Harkism hasn't existed long enough to serve as a platform for mayhem. Perhaps it can carve us all a pocket in which to breathe, away from the chatter, the murder. Let enough people into that pocket to unite and heal, and maybe they'll arrive at an answer together, or at least a feasible way forward.

This must be what Hark believes, whatever time and place he hails from.

Mustn't it?

Eight

The twins scale a steep rock at the park. Fraz supervises their climb from a far-off bench. No parent can prevent The Unimaginable Yet Constantly Imagined Tragedy. You buckle them up in cars and teach them how to cross the street. You train them to wash their hands after pooping, warn them off unbleached needles, jack-off nooses. That's about it. Or there's more, but not much. Not much you can control. The rest is asteroids. Brakeless buses. Brakeless men, with machetes, guns. Besides, kids need to make mistakes. Abrasions and bruises, fractures and sprains, they're just the body's pop quiz stickers, life's gold stars.

Fraz is more or less a free-range father, but of the anxious type. He lets them run loose while his guts knot. Still, it beats cinching them up in his fear. Better to hang back, sip his cortado, nibble his scone. He watches them now as they move across the rock face. Lisa, the acrobat, climbs with blithe joy. Sturdy David studies every crevice. Fraz shouts an encouragement, probably inaudible, scrolls through the news in his hand. The news is this: We will all maul each other for the last tin of peaches fairly soon. You can forget about a wage increase. The cost of living will henceforth be your life.

The ads, the advertorials, pop and roll. The sponsored content. Oh, to be sponsored content. Fraz is, like most people, unsponsored content.

It's moments like this that Fraz knows he's made the right decision. Mental archery is the road back to an original wholeness, if such a thing exists, or at least it's the key to inner relief. He's lived too long in exile from himself, faking his freedom, refusing even to wear a tie, even to family funerals, even a clip-on, extolling the virtues of porn to his wife, hiding out in the gym, stuffing himself with fried pickles and an experimental mix of mint and mango ice cream. He's weary of his contrarian pose, tired of his schemes, the funny T-shirts, the penny stocks, the fantasy bandy. Always the same: lose some cash, some dignity, fold. But it's different now. Fraz feels called. To mental archery, and what may lie beyond, and definitely to Hark, or the idea of Hark, or the radial heat of Hark. Others, it appears, are also pulled. Are they as sad as Fraz? Do they look to the future and see nothing but debt, uncertainty, decay, eternal heeldom?

Do they glimpse the political situation, the economic situation, the grave matrices of situations, the grim and inexorable shift?

Do they know how dire it's all become?

Turn back at what you're running from, Hark says. Draw the bow.

The twins trot over, twerped by the cliff. David bleeds from cuts on his lip, his cheek.

"What happened?"

"Lisa hit me."

"He fell," Lisa says. "Like a bitch."

David punches her hard in the crotch. They both sob, clutch Fraz on the bench.

"My babies," Fraz says. "Daddy loves his babies. It's okay. It's going to be okay."

Fraz gathers them to him. He chokes up whenever he remembers that they're his children and, for all their swagger, just easy marks for the world. Maybe he and Tovah were selfish for having kids, the heat, the melt, the universal fester, but he'll live with the crime. He loves Lisa and David in a desperate way, and to crypto-Malthusians and other critics of reproduction he has this to say: You'll count your blessings when my kids are around to wipe your scabbed and desiccated asses, nursing home attendant the only job to exist in the future, all of civilization reduced, for those few who can afford it, to one vast, plastic palace of deliquescence, everyone else flopped out on final islands of scorched sand, beseeching the sea to take them.

Tip my children well, you bastards.

Nine

In the beginning, Hark just wanted to jest. He took improv classes, hovered near open mics. He'd never been the class cutup, or craved attention, or made anybody laugh, not even his family, certainly not his father.

But one day, Hark told Fraz, he decided to try comedy.

There was something awkward, almost insensate, about his stage persona, but for some reason it worked. Hark's strained gestures toward even the easiest or most clichéd modes of stand-up somehow refreshed them. His struggle, it seemed to the audience, was not with idiom but intent. He told jokes as though they were some alien and deathless gospel and grievous fates awaited those who paid no heed. This made his routines funnier. A hostess at one of the clubs told him there were other "spectrum comics," but he was the real McCoy.

"What spectrum?" Hark said, but the woman only laughed, stroked his cheek.

Whatever she meant, Hark never bombed, not ever.

One night a booker noticed this and gave him slots at a new club in the Valley. Hark did five minutes on the pitfalls of office life even he knew were stale, but the bit gave the booker an idea about how to use Hark for a different kind of gig.

For a semi-ample fee, Hark would attend a corporate gathering, a shareholders' meeting or sales conference or tropical team retreat. The bosses would bill him as an expert in some esoteric practice—knife yoga, reverse hypnosis. Mental archery was an early favorite he cooked up after he found a toy bow sticking out of a curbside garbage can.

Hark's program, the CEO would announce, had quantifiable bearing on the health and productivity of the company. Now would come a pall, interrupted only by the thrums and adagios of unsilenced phones, the rustle of pressed shorts. Nobody wanted to hear another expert's speech. They'd already attended their morning workshops, their mind swap sessions. Folks hankered for a dip in the hotel pool, lunch, a nap, a cocktail, a secret suck-around with Evan from design. Now they'd have to sit through another lecture about stress avoidance by some boring shit in a drab shirt.

Hark would play the part, become drab-shirted shittiness itself, upbeat if vague, apt to toss counterintuitive morsels to the crowd. Did you know that archers are among the fittest athletes in the world? That the bow and arrow has killed more people in history than firearms? And fed more people than any industrial or technological advance in food production since terraced farming? Or that people who take up mental archery actually gain IQ points and lower their bad cholesterol? And that one needn't leave one's living room or own archery equipment to achieve this?

The audience would take him for a second-rater, some ideas festival journeyman, part jack-off, part data spurt, or was that one thing? But a shift would begin. Nobody would notice at first, too distracted by the promise of a mahi mahi club with sweet potato fries or some Jacuzzi nookie. Hark would shepherd the sermon weirdward, the measured language fracturing, his docile flock of reasonable tips for better corporate living driven off the best practices cliff, the crowd in horrified witness.

"You are the arrow!" Hark would shout. "But you are also what it pierces. You are the machine and the poor child ground to chuck in its cogs! Flail skyward and hear your demon rulers cackle! Poor fools, you will never break out of your salary frames!"

But before things got too sacrilegious, somebody—the CEO, the CTO, the CFO, the CSO, the CCO, a serious suit, a senior dragon— would leap to the lectern, escort Hark out, to the hoots of the employees, the family, the claims division clan.

"I don't know what the hell that was!" a vice enchilada might shout. "Putz lost his marbles. Anyway, you don't need some loser to yammer on about stress and productivity. You're the most productive fucking stress cases in the country! You win! Mahi mahi on me!"

Hand thunder, that's what Hark's old booker called applause. The hand thunder would roll in. The suits might not inform their people that Hark was a ringer until the postprandial toasts. Or ever. Not that Hark cared. He snatched the check as soon as he got offstage, dove into the airport shuttle like a contract commando fleeing a failed coup.

Thing was, Hark wasn't the only person who worked this niche. A guy named Cornelius the Corporate Imposter had the gig before Hark. Big Lev from Biz Dev had sewn up Silicon Valley. But they were too broad. Nobody bought their acts after a line or two. Hark twitched with the plausible, which in the end was no surprise.

For Hark had begun to believe his words. Not everything, of course, but he saw the potential for an authentic appeal. He began to write the aphorisms, draw up the poses. He built a small brass pedestal for the cheap blue bow. The joke drained away and Hark retired his jester's bells, his craven prance, shed his fool's skin, slithered out, translucent, sincere.

The world was as funny as starlight, or the corpse of a child, and the pay would be crap, but he now knew his calling. He had no particular message to deliver, just an array of useful techniques. But he could still be a humble messenger. Or maybe, as he'd begun to feel a new, strange potency, a not-so-humble messenger. It was a confusing feeling, almost like another puberty, but without the suicidal ideation and sheet acne. He felt himself drawn past the human

threshold into a fresher realm, an immense and shimmering king-
dom he could not yet countenance.

For now, home or office would suffice.

————————

At Kate's, dozens mill in a sunlit corner of the loft. Some chat, others
unfold stacks of folding chairs. Hark hangs back at the snack table,
leafs through his yellow notebook. Fraz joins him, sticks a wedge of
tangelo in his mouth.

"Looking over some lines for today?"

"Reading some old entries for inspiration. Do you think that's a
bad sign?"

Hark winks, a rarity.

Fraz wants to say something about the notebook, how maybe
someday Hark will allow it to be published so millions might have it
on their shelves, delve into the workings of a world-historical mind,
but he refrains, worried his vision of a grand legacy might insult
Hark's reverence for the now.

Kate swoops in with a clipboard, her hair up in a chopstick twist.

"Hard-charging, wisecracking soundstage gal," Fraz says. "I dig
the look."

"I dig yours: deeply unattractive and absurdly insignificant turd."

"What?"

"That was my hard-charging wisecrack. My gal crack. You like?"

"I guess," Fraz says.

"Anyway, guys, I have some new ideas about the set."

"I don't know about that," Hark says.

"I think it might be worth it to experiment," Kate says.

Traditional Hark videos are shot in a static close-up, but today
Kate steers them toward a more dynamic aesthetic: Pull the camera
back, show the set, the audience, conjure the sense that this is really
happening, a live event.

"Realism," Fraz says. "It's a good trick."

"But it's no trick. There are people here. You will be talking to them."

"I know what Fraz means," Hark says. "But, Kate, I also know
what you mean."

Somehow he can gentle them both with his eyes at once, fierce green, tender gold.

"Okay," Kate says. "Fraz, why don't you go get a glance at the Faust Nook."

Fraz glowers.

"It was a joke. You're not insignificant."

Fraz shrugs, heads across the loft. He finds a stool, slides it in front of the bookshelves. Like library stacks. But what kinds of books should feature in the shot? Kate has lots, mostly about art and design, a few novels, some college textbooks.

Does the stool look foolish? Should he drag the wingback chair over? What next? A briar pipe? A Labrador with respiratory ailments exacerbated by the briar pipe? A simple wooden chair, of course, Shaker plain, bespeaks directness, intensity, ideal forms. Maybe Hark can straddle it, for the homespun effect, though Tovah once told Fraz that only sex criminals straddle chairs.

Perhaps Hark should stand for the presentation, like a celebrity scholar on TV, some plum-cheeked old cherub in a Shetland sweater who sways in the wind beside a ruined keep, prattles on about how feudalism was really just a terribly exciting story, a potboiler full of passion and intrigue. Is that what he tells his pupils at Oxford? Or is such rubbish just for the living room rubes?

Kate arrives, kicks over the stool.

"Any suggestions?"

"Yes," Fraz says. "Forget Faust."

Across the loft, Schnitz the cameraman sets up his tripod and lights, grins over at Kate. He's got rotted teeth, a torn leather car coat.

"You know," Fraz says, "I could film this myself. On my phone."

"That's a good idea. In general. Gather footage for the archives. But these talks should be professional quality."

Hark joins them, rights the stool.

Kate hands him a wardrobe bag.

"Where'd you get this stuff?"

"I ordered it. Go try it on."

"We can't be ostentatious," Hark says. "I have a nice yellow shirt I brought."

"Hark, I have to be honest. The shirt is a liability."

"It's my trademark."

"It trademarks you as a human banana."

"Really? Fraz, come with me."

Fraz follows Hark into the bedroom. Hark unzips the bag, lays out suits, sweaters, shirts, ties on the bed.

"I'm sensing a trace of disrespect from Kate," Hark says. "We can't work that way."

"Listen to her, Hark. Listen to us. On the small things. Sometimes?"

Hark appears to consider it, slips into a white button-down and V-neck sweater.

"Hey, Teach," Kate calls from the door. "When's the midterm?"

Kate pulls a magazine out of her bag. The actor on the cover is a man for whom the majority of American women, according to this issue's poll, would sacrifice the lives of their families in exchange for one amorous evening.

"Let's do this outfit here," Kate says.

"Perfect," Fraz says, though he's not sure why. Fashion remains for him another portal of confusion.

"I don't even look like him," Hark says, taps the magazine cover with his index finger.

"Nobody does," Kate says. "*He* doesn't look like him. That's the point."

"Yes," Hark says. "That's the insanity, isn't it?"

"Ordinary women don't really want to sleep with him," Kate says. "They just want their men to respect their thwarted dreams in general, to maybe try their hair like this guy's, or put on a sexy sports coat. Doesn't take much effort. But men are blind. They are rodents. It's in the article."

"It's the end of men," Fraz says. "Fuck those fucks."

"You're a man," Kate says.

"In some rooms, yes; in some rooms, no."

"Bullshit," Kate says.

"Whatever," Fraz says. "I think you're onto something, though. Also, I think Hark needs an expensive watch. It connotes elegance and control."

"Maybe you're not so bad at this," Kate says.

"Better believe it."

"Look," says Hark. "Before we start, I just want to thank you both. Let's hold hands and close our eyes. That's it. Let us remember this moment. And focus on it. Let us relax and focus even as we accept the distractions at the edges. The change begins now. We shall loose the arrows of our hearts."

"Amen," Fraz says.

"It's not religious," Hark says. "I keep telling you that."

"Namaste," Kate says.

"It's not that, either. We'll discuss it later."

They head back to the set. The milling people have claimed their seats.

"Nice crowd this time," Hark says.

"More and more sign up online. I'm turning droves away."

"They must come for the snacks," Hark says.

"Very funny."

Kate drags a metal chair in front of a plain white wall, sets a glass, a water pitcher and a microphone on a stool beside it, along with a card that reads *Dr. Hark Morner.*

"Hi, everybody," Kate says. "Welcome, and thanks for coming. We're making a movie of this, but we also wanted to give you a chance to hear our special friend in person. We think he's amazing. We think mental archery is amazing. Feel free to applaud and stuff. Act like it's really happening, which it is. Since we're making a movie, we may have to stop if there are technical difficulties. But of course there will be no technical difficulties. Isn't that right, Schnitz?"

"That's right!"

"This is Schnitz, everybody. Revered director of some seminal electro-scuzz videos in the early aughts. Isn't that right, Schnitz?"

"I did a teen douche ad, too."

"Kate?" Hark calls. He's slipped on a blue dress shirt and charcoal blazer. He could be the son of the actor in the magazine.

"Yes?"

"I hate to tell you this," he whispers, "but I'm not a doctor. See, I used to say I was other people. But I don't anymore. Or mostly don't. And why are we pretending this is from a big lecture or panel when it's staged?"

"We're not going to make any definitive claims," Kate says.

"My definitive claim is that I'm not a doctor."

"Who said you were?"

"This card on the table says it."

"I guess the lecture organizers made a mistake," Kate says. "It's not your fault. Now let's get some levels."

"Is this one of the small things?" Hark asks Fraz.

"Yes."

"Okay, then."

Hark stares at the blinking light above the camera lens, begins.

Ten

Kate gets a call from Teal.

"Have you battened the hatches?"

"Teal! Why didn't you tell me you were back home from the funeral?"

"Home is where I just was."

"This city is your home. We are."

"Sounds funny coming from you."

"Where are you now?"

"Some bar. Across the street. The Iridescent Mole?"

"Oh, yeah, that place. They keep changing the name. Just come up."

A few minutes later they take tea in the Faust Nook.

"Gotten around to reading any of these?" Teal says, eyes tilted at the bookshelves.

"Started them."

"I've finished a lot of these."

"You're an intellectual."

"I'm a convicted felon."

"You're Robin Hood. Except you forgot to hide in the forest."

"And you forgot to not kill that fossilized dildo. You ever feel bad about it?"

"Are you crazy? Uncle Conrad groped me."

"My father once told me to never kill a man for being clumsy. Actually, he told my brother that. I was sitting nearby."

"Uncle Conrad wasn't clumsy. And he was already dead."

"Before he hit the floor, right?"

"I never meant for him to cark it," Kate says.

"Well, I meant to take that money."

Kate hauls out the vodka and some pills to crush.

"So, my dad."

"I'm sorry, T. I really am."

"His sweet, fat heart exploded."

Teal's father had been a high school English teacher, a white kid from Cairo, Illinois. Her mother, raised in Memphis, is a chemistry professor, one of the first black women tenured in Tennessee.

Care-oh and Maimphis, Teal said. Her progenitors, the Egyptians.

Kate and Teal had bonded the most in their last semester of college—perhaps, it seemed to Kate, as a way to cut ties with closer chums. They took road trips to the nearest cities, or even smaller rural towns, or hosted Regency-themed coke parties in the woods near campus that earned Kate glares from her political pals, the ones on the right side of history but the wrong side of glamour.

Kate and Teal both ran a little cool in those days, shared a tacit disdain for the emotional spillage of some of their female peers. Those girls had no class analysis, not to mention no class. Teal and and Kate paired well, Kate remembers thinking, like a crisp white wine and a rhubarb tart. She figured herself for the crisp white. It was a refreshing but fleeting companionship. They hadn't really dug a foundation, just coasted on mutual regard. Also, the fact that Kate was rich, or would be, was about to matter.

Despite the vows of eternal friendship, they fell away from each other after graduation, almost as easily as they'd come together. It was not unusual for their set.

That they rekindled years later also did not surprise Kate. Though they had maybe never bonded as much as they pretended,

and there existed, beneath their surface fondness, a vague dislike neither wanted to acknowledge, there was also, underneath the afore-
mentioned subdermal discord, something else, a thicker, spongier,
more durable affection, or love, even. The layers, in fact, were fucking ridiculous. And now, at any rate, they could commiserate over
shared history. They'd each committed a quasi-noble crime.

A few years after college, Teal landed an accounting job with
a major online retailer, rose in the firm to a position of responsi-
bility and independence. The founder, she came to learn, funneled
his profits into a fascist think tank, a sort of finishing school for the
young white men arguing against the poor on TV. Teal wasn't much
of a marcher, but she figured she could do her part for a better world
by diverting certain chunks of the bigot's money to good causes.
Out of some odd ethical impulse she chose recipients that were a
bit too broad or centrist for her taste—a liberal senator's reelection
campaign, an environmental lobby that maybe wasn't tough enough
on coal. Somehow she felt more righteous about her act if she chose
slightly compromised beneficiaries. Otherwise, she reckoned, she'd
just as soon buy chemical weapons for immigrants and people of
color to use at their discretion.

The amounts she siphoned off were generous but not obscene.
She'd been shocked when the fuzz nabbed her. How had it come to
this? She'd been a supreme scholastic achiever, could have put herself in the grad school pipeline with a star-track academic job offer
when she plopped out the other end. The boring accounting job had
just been a temporary bird flip to that overbearing institutional body
in her mind, the Ministry of Expectations. Next thing she was going
to the freaking clink.

The worst part was getting sent up to Smallwood, with authentic,
maybe even artisanal murderers. She never should have booted that
bailiff in the balls, but the verdict really ticked her off.

One day she chose her old buddy Kate for a pen pal, wrote a
batch of funny, disturbing letters about life in Smallwood. Prison
wasn't so bad, she wrote. You just had to stay vigilant. Chicks fucked
you up with sharpened toothbrushes, sharpened sports bras. Cut
you. Contused you. The men in uniform, the women in uniform, not
to mention the men in social work sweaters, must have all checked

the I Occasionally Enjoy Committing Verbal, Physical and Sexual Abuse box on the application form.

When Teal got out a few years later, Kate invited her to stay at her place until she got her plans settled. At first it was a blast. They caroused. They gallivanted. They laughed for hours, staggered stoned around Kate's loft. But Teal realized that she wasn't settling plans but settling in, and maybe it grated on Kate. And maybe Teal resented Kate for urging her into the wilds of a job hunt so soon after release. Teal doubled down on domesticity, watched herself get wifey, waited for Kate each evening with cheese and wine, eager to discuss a novel she'd heard about on public radio. Kate was sweet about it, but Teal knew she didn't give a shit about cheese or novels or public radio. Kate knew Teal knew. Wine was all right. But wither the vodka?

They'd discovered Hark together at a yoga class, or outside one. He stood on the sidewalk near the studio handing out flyers. What made them stop and chat with him they weren't certain. Later they both admitted to an odd, almost ethereal charge when they shook his hand, looked into those weird green-gold eyes. That night they visited his dinky website, got hooked on the videos, the strained, earnest cadences with which Hark demonstrated the sequence of archery-related poses. His Zen serenity sometimes threatened to bubble over into something else. Like there was even more to his system he couldn't yet reveal. For now, the small adjustments were enough.

"Observe this famous photo of a sculpture of Hercules the Archer. See his leg outstretched, his foot braced against that rock? Let's all try it. Feel free to use the arm of a couch. Feel free to couch the use of your arm. Feel free.

"Swivel with your non-bow, and release.

"Now picture the arrow speeding past a stand of trees.

"You are the arrow, and the trees the arrow speeds past, and the past the arrow speeds toward.

"Focus on focus on focus," he'd say. "Pull."

They'd repeat these mantras, koans, whatever they were, to each other while they searched for a lost slipper, the TV remote.

It was a joke between them, until it wasn't funny. When it was no longer funny, it became profound. Nothing could be more natural.

That's how Hark, after all, had described his epiphany. The teach-ings seeped in. A new filter on the world. Even as it happened, Teal wondered how it was happening. Your brain gets tired, brittle. It's a bitch being attuned to the bleakness all the time. You crave a certain stupor, aka belief.

Harkism had started to spark, to gather disparate sorts. Even when the sentiments seemed dubious or unwarranted—"Spare not the sparrow the arrow"—his urgent, sometimes stilted, always forth-right demeanor appealed. His vibe wasn't fucky or vain. His gen-tleness reminded Teal of her father, whom she'd loved, though her mother was her leader, the captain of her life. But Hark also seemed beyond usual categories like man or white man or woodchuck. And mental archery, one had to admit, was a kick-ass workout.

They attended events at yoga studios and wellness centers, vol-unteered for what became increasingly less casual apostlehood. Kate made her funds available to what Hark now called the Institute for Mental Archery. There appeared to be a vacuum around Hark, room for them. Only Fraz Penzig seemed more intimate with Hark, and Kate and Teal could both sense Hark's occasional annoyance with the older man. They hewed close to their hero, drew nearer to each other. After a while, maybe they'd fused too much.

One night Kate returned to find the loft sheeted with oily smoke. Teal had sacrificed the veggie lasagna to the gods of oven grease. The smoke detectors wailed and Teal stood under them, waving a broom. Kate slid into bed. She pictured herself a corpse. Or a person in need of a marrow transplant. Or a lover struck motionless by poison. The alarms cut out. The stench of charred cheese lingered.

Teal crept into the room, knelt on the duvet.

"Lasagna is harder than it looks, K."

"Teal. Teal."

"I'm sorry."

"Stop."

"I'll make it up to you."

"How? By getting a job? A place to live?"

"Whoa. Why don't *you* get a job?"

"Yeah, but I don't have to."

"Really?"

"Teal, it's like you've made a prison for yourself right here. I want you to thrive."

"Are you suggesting that by being here a few months—?"

"Several months. Almost a year."

"And I'm the fool who loves the slam so much I replicate the conditions wherever I can? That's your theory?"

"I don't have a theory. I'm tired. I have to fly to Boston tomorrow. With marrow."

"Fuck your marrow."

Kate found Teal a studio in the Bronx. The new cool frontier, Kate told her. Teal hated that, as well as the apartment, but it didn't matter. Teal got a job in a bakery, paid her own rent, got a scholarship for a social work degree.

The fact that they really did need each other pushed the bitterness down. Neither of them trusted anybody else. After a while, their old fellowship flourished again, but they were careful to avoid the bigger moods, the reckless euphoria of the old days.

"I need to shut myself away," Teal says now, in the Faust Nook with Kate. "Figure things out."

"Figure what out? You're always pressuring yourself to figure everything out. Look, your dad died. You need to process it. That takes time."

"I need to get back to work. I have papers to write. And hours at the bakery."

"And we have a lot of institute work to do. It'll all work out."

"Easy for you to say. You one percenters don't have to worry about every tiny detail of life."

"Well, we have our own problems. And stop it with that ancient Occupy language. One percenters. You didn't last three days in that park."

"You didn't last one hour."

"I had a meeting with a financial adviser. I told you that on the way over."

"If I had the proper tool, I'd saw your head off on the internet right now."

"The tool for sawing would be a saw, I think. But no decapitations tonight."

"You sound like my father. Don't you know anybody who can hire me for something better than the bakery? I hate the nights. None of my other old college friends will help me out with a rec."

"You did do time for embezzlement."

"That company was building fascism in America. And its shipping policies were absurd."

"I agree. But still."

"Just keep me posted."

"Okay," Kate says. "I'm flying to Stockholm in a few days to deliver some marrow. Do you need a loan?"

"No," says Teal, pats her bag. "I went to my brother's house and threatened to expose my nieces to a hardened outlaw. He waved some cash at me."

"That jerk."

"My little brother. I remember I once found him hiding down in the laundry room, reading Ayn Rand. This runty little kid panting down there. I thought he was hiding so he could, you know, pull on his root. Tyler just didn't want any of us to see him with that crap. My mama would have whupped him."

"Really?"

"No. She would have lectured him on the history of capitalism, its genius plan for creating racial divisions in the working class. Her father was a radical shop steward."

"Were words like 'whup' and 'root' prevalent in your home?"

"They didn't have to be," Teal says. "They hovered there, unspoken, ghosts of lost communities, my disconnection."

"Are you quoting from something?"

"My college application essay."

"Nice!"

"I know."

"Maybe your brother will come around."

"He'll come around to my grave. And laugh."

Eleven

A spiny, prehistoric catfish nuzzles up to Hark in sleep, brushes brine-scented whiskers against Hark's ear, speaks in a watery, midtale murmur:

". . . and so after the weaving ruse has been discovered, Penelope reckons all is lost, but Athena tells her to announce a competition. Whosoever can string Odysseus's bow and shoot an arrow through a long channel made of crossed ax heads wins the queen. None of the suitors prove strong enough, and, finally, a mysterious wool-cowled beggar steps out of the crowd. You know the rest, the slaughter of the suitors with that very bow, the hanging by the neck of the servant girls who pleasured the suitors while everyone waited for Penelope to finish weaving. Remember this: Carry the bow that no one can string but you. Your secret technique need not rely on brawn. It is more on the order of a bar code for the soul. Know your bow and your bow will know you. When you aim for your life targets, pour your arrows into them as though they were the hearts of these nasty, supercilious suitors, these highborn rummies who invaded your house and humiliated your wife and debased your son and ate your mutton and shat on your rugs and slavered for your crown while you were gone on a business trip, a twenty-year business trip, to join the fight for Greater Greece, gone to war, ostensibly over a pretty girl, but really to smash a rival, a competing brand, you who are not only a warrior king with boatloads of loyal soldiers but a master tactician, a natural leader, with a real psychological gift (only you, after all, can talk that head case Achilles down) and, finally, yes, it's you who are one of the most celebrated consultants in antiquity (and rightly so, a wooden horse? Fucking genius!). This is not to say, of course, that your life goals are equivalent to Penelope's vile suitors. Your life goals don't wish and think you dead. They don't yearn to bone your life partner or seize your throne. But still, there is no reason not to try a variety of visualization techniques. Achilles, of course, or his notorious heel, will come up later in our discussion."

Hark wakes, shouts: "I have pamphlets for sale!"

The catfish has vanished. The bed bears a slimy stain.

Twelve

Days later, blocks from Kate's loft, a gentleman reposes in a dark gastropub with a plate of pickled emu eggs and a tankard of Upper Peninsula ale. He writes with a felt-tip pen on a napkin: *One gander at her unbelievable peach-shaped derriere terminated the dream of parliamentary democracy, pronto.*

Drivel, the gentleman rejoices.

Unlike his wife, Fraz never dreamed of a wordsmith's fame. He's a visual animal, a natural screen bard. Maybe not natural. He resents, for instance, all the equipment involved in the so-called filmmaking process. Questions of composition, of light and shadow, bore him. Stories, actors, seem tedious. Documentaries, subjects, too ponderous, preachy. Movies are a mammoth drag. He never watched that many. But his desire to be a major director buoyed him for years.

The short he made in college, *Wizened Zach*, explored the suffering of his uncle, a retired high school math teacher with late-onset dyscalculia. Fraz, who dedicated his film to "despair," won a tiny amount of prize money. He ran through it quickly, which is what happens with tiny amounts of prize money.

The output, you could say, has dwindled. But during the last Hark shoot, Fraz watched the scuzz auteur Schnitz snake around the set, pursue Riefenstahlian angles on Hark, not to mention reaction shots from the crowd, the astonishment, the recognition, the nascent faith. Filmmaking looked fun.

This morning, in the shower, attempting to jet wash his anus from a frisk position against the tiles, Fraz had an epiphany. He knows epiphanies are passé, but this one overcame categorical obsolescence: *Triptych: Women and Sadness*. Fraz will make a film in three sections, each about a woman who is beautiful and sad, and how the principles of mental archery might free her from the fetters of anhedonia. His mother will be the first panel, Tovah the second.

The film will employ a rigorous neo-emo sensibility. Warts and all, but also, in parts, wartless. What is beauty? Is it truth, or just random molecularity? Is beauty in the eye of the beholder? Does it crush the beholder's eyeballs? The souls of the beheld? Plus, what is sadness? Plus, what are women? He will take on the tough questions.

Maybe he will learn something about his subjects, or himself. Maybe he will learn how to talk to Tovah again.

He's been working on that, they both have, in their counseling sessions with Teal. This was Hark's idea. After Fraz mentioned that he had a Tovah situation, and that Tovah had a Fraz situation, Hark suggested they embark on some couples therapy with Teal, who had not completed the clinical qualifications for her social work degree, but whose life wisdom and experience with mental archery might compensate. Tovah scoffed, but agreed to one session, after which she was converted. Here was a person, she told Fraz, who could comprehend Tovah's pain with proper nuance. Teal was brilliant, like Tovah, and had done time, which Tovah sometimes felt she was doing with Fraz.

Fraz recalls an exchange from a recent session:

TOVAH: I just feel this distance. Like when Fraz makes a joke. I know even before he's finished that I won't find it funny. Whereas I used to laugh at all his jokes. We laughed so much together. Now, even if we're watching a comic on TV, like an intelligent, funny one, if Fraz laughs, I just shut down. Get distant. Icy. It's me, really.

TEAL: What do you mean, you?

TOVAH: When I'm not happy, I disassociate. I'm somewhere else. For a while.

FRAZ: It's true. It's like she's on another planet. A glaze comes over her face. It's like she's teleported out of her body, left it there to operate on autopilot.

TEAL: Where are you, Tovah? Where do you go?

TOVAH: I don't really know. It's a brightly lit place. Well scrubbed. Kind of rustic. A farmhouse. There's a man there. He's tall and lean, with a beard. We're together and we're safe.

FRAZ: Sounds like your father. I don't know where the farmhouse comes from.

TOVAH: I like farmhouses.

TEAL: Is this man your lover?

TOVAH: I don't think so. It's just that we keep each other safe.

TEAL: Do you have lovers in this rustic place, this safe farmhouse setting?

TOVAH: I'm satisfied. It's like the whole deal, the farmhouse, the field, the trees. They are all my lovers.

FRAZ: She'd rather fuck the scenery than me.

TEAL: Accept it.

FRAZ: What?

TEAL: Or fight for her.

FRAZ: Fight her rural fantasia?

TEAL: You want her back on your dingdong?

FRAZ: Yes.

TEAL: Then string your goddamn bow and declare war on her dumbfuck, bourgeois fantasia.

TOVAH: You have to destroy my fantasia, Fraz!

FRAZ: Is this what couples therapy is normally like?

TEAL: I don't know. I just started.

Now Fraz takes another pull of ale from his pewter mug. The others were heartbroken when the Chakra Khan went out of business and this series of upscale lipids-and-gristle joints opened in its stead, but Fraz rejoiced. It's not like you can't get green juice in this town, and this place, with it's faux colonial décor and oak plank piss troughs, is just more conducive to the kind of manly, Promethean thoughts Fraz wishes to think more.

Thirteen

Teal posts the latest mental archery video to Hark Hub. She's worked hard on the redesign and is proud of the look. The page pops, but not at the expense of grace or clean, soulful lines.

Harkists rally in gratitude. It's been a longer interval than usual and followers are famished for fresh content. There is, however, notable dissent. Somebody with the handle Fart Surgeon calls Hark a "knurd." Another viewer asks: "Does he know how schmucko-normative this is?" A third commentator counters these apostates: "Silence, internet ogres! This is pretty impressive stuff. I mean I've heard these stories before, heard them interpreted by literary and psychological experts, and I'm also familiar with people talking about the mind and brain both, because jerks like you probably don't know this, but they are two distinct things. The speaker here seems tapped into a lot of the newest findings, far as I can tell, and what he's done, which is quite difficult, is to take a whole lot of fascinating, seemingly unrelated material and work it together into something quite practical. It's personal philosophy, maybe a little self-helpish (and damn, can't we all use a little self-help—the fucking corporations and the government and the fascists and the tech lords aren't going to help us, trust me), but it's a really powerful message that uses archery as a metaphor but doesn't just sit there and say, 'Look what a nifty metaphor I am,' but is more like a beautiful house you can enter and walk around and hang out in. And this Hark, I can't tell exactly what he's about, but he makes some very solid points. Like the part where he says your immediate goal is a false but necessary first target. Or when he speaks of aimless shooting, or says that the time between when you shoot the arrow to the moment you retrieve it is the most important duration of your life. Nobody else makes it so clear. I'm glad Hark, if that's even his name, is out there. He's like an advanced creature, a wise man from another dimension, but he's also a very attractive guy living in the metro area. Still, I don't even want to talk like that, because he makes me feel so thoughtful, grown-up. I'm sure, you know, he likes a good time like the rest of us, but he seems stripped of the usual crap. He'd better make a new vid soon!"

It's signed Meg217.

Underneath Meg217's post a reply appears: "Dumbitch: this bow&arow homo makes u squirt, fez up."

Teal deletes it.

Fourteen

Tovah once had a boyfriend named Bob Price. Yes, that one, the writer. They attended the same graduate creative writing program in New York. Those days were thick with arrogant, hothouse chaps, but Price was the dark prince of Tovah's heart. He told her to consider him a downed wire: unpredictable, potentially lethal. Tovah thought him more a lost shoelace, but adorable.

Their connection was just a phase. Tovah wonders if her marriage to Fraz is also a phase. Teal broached that possibility in their last couples session. How many phases are we each allotted? How long until a phase fizzles out?

"Till death do us part," Fraz said.

"Was that in our vows?"

"It was."

"Right. We were trying to do this counterintuitive traditional thing. We were so young and stupid."

"I think it's sweet," Teal said.

Tovah's in bed reading Bob Price's new book, a memoir about the blessings of fatherhood. His prose is no benediction, but, as with all of his books, the trick is to flip to the dust jacket photograph every few pages. Bob is bonny as ever, with distinguished gray streaks in his lush, warlock curls. His pitted cheeks, as on certain movie stars, only deepen his allure, as though acne scars alone prove some authentic acquaintance with life's more charged and vulnerable precincts. Tovah skips back to the paragraph she just read:

> I wasn't scared of being a father, but I was frightened of being a type of father. A mean father, a judgmental father, or even a gentle and supportive father. I swore to myself I would become none of those things. I wouldn't be some stock character my unborn child could one day dismiss. I would be original and demanding and exciting. And I have to say, that's pretty much how things turned out. But I know I'm one of the lucky ones . . .

Tovah has to laugh, does, a high, horsey guffaw that would wake anybody else, but not Fraz, who slumbers on, ensconced, doubtless, in lurid, quasi-historical dreamscapes pregnant with pregnant women and flamboyantly whiskered factory barons.

Bob Price was always just dumb enough to thrive. Tovah hopes for their sakes his children inherit Bob's blunted mind. Clarity is loneliness. She can already tell that the twins, despite their digital cocoons, sense the anguish that awaits. Even their hooliganism bears a melancholy strain. She worries, but carries a secret pride in their bent, prescient minds.

As for Fraz, the mental archery project still sounds absurd, but at least these days he reeks less of defeat. It reminds her of a few years back, when he launched his T-shirt start-up, nearly declared himself the inventor of clothes emblazoned with amusing or provocative phrases. One evening—Tovah's stuck with the image—Fraz acquired this haughty, slightly deranged twist to his face, told her how sorry he was that she had to toil in an office while he was on the verge of mega-wealth. The funny T-shirt business was like that, he said. You couldn't make a living, but you could make a killing. He chucked her under the chin, told her she'd be able to quit her job anytime she wanted. His first day he sold two shirts to a guy in the local coffee shop. One shirt was green and one was red and they both featured a drawing of a Viking berserker brandishing his broadsword at the viewer. The legend beneath read: PROBLEM SOLVING. The joke was a weak rip from an old Australian beer commercial. Tovah mentioned this to Fraz, but he shrugged her off.

"It's like any artistic tradition. We're all building off each other."

He sold no more shirts, and soon they served as fallback gifts for friends and family. A box of them sits wedged away in the closet. Fraz wanted to donate the shirts to a clothing drive, but Tovah refused. She said she couldn't stomach the idea of people parading around in symbols of her husband's failure.

"I would love to stomach that," Fraz had told her, but she saw his eyes well up. His blitheness, she knows, is a myth. Fraz is one of the fragile people.

Sometimes this frightens her. Her kin, the Golds, were chilly providers. In lieu of love, her father, Dead Eddie, as he was known in the diagnostic equipment community for his severely laconic sales style, offered safe, if stiff, haven. Had either Tovah's mother or her father ever heard the phrase "emotionally available," both would have assumed it had something to do with hookers, or was a condition for which people were hospitalized. But Eddie was an apex predator of his business world. No daughter of his would ever know hunger. Unless she was doing, say, Pritikin, or some weird nut-and-prune thing for bikini season.

Fraz is a different sort, though these days there's an unforeseen vitality. He still gropes, vapors about, but there's a semblance of mission.

Folly, perhaps, but at least it's not T-shirts.

"I can't stay angry at Fraz," she told Teal during the same session where they'd discussed the wedding vows. "It's not fair. It's like being mad at sheep crossing the road. You know they are innocent, but something builds up anyway. At a certain point, you want to step on the gas, hear the crackle of struck bones, see blood seep into the dirty wool."

"I thought I was a polar bear," Fraz said.

"Oh, right, I did mention that at some point, didn't I?"

"But at least you're not angry at him," Teal said.

"No. Just impatient."

"Okay," Teal said.

"Okay what?"

"That's it. Our time is up. We'll pick up with the sheep slaughter next week."

"It was an accident!" Tovah said.

"Of course," Teal said. "That's how we know these issues are still worth working on."

"You're good at this," Fraz said.

"But ain't I." Teal smiled.

"I really feel like we're making progress," Tovah said.

"Progress is a dangerous concept at the center of a bankrupt form of humanism."

"Of course."

"That said, you are both doing good work."

"All I know," Fraz said, "is that I plan to cross the road much more quickly. Save Tovah the aggravation and me some pain."

"There you go, sheepy," Teal said.

Fifteen

A wilted purple banner strung across the museum portico announces a final exhibition of nearly forgotten twentieth-century painters: *Minor Whites: Contemplating Canonical Chaff.*

Fraz waits on the museum steps, noshes from a wax pouch of hot nuts. Hark approaches and Fraz holds out the bag.

"No, thanks. Those look disgusting."

"They do, but somehow that's the draw."

"So, why did you ask me to come here, Fraz?"

"I'll show you."

Fraz leads Hark through the lobby and into the gallery, eases him down on a varnished bench.

"Shut your eyes," he says. "Breathe."

Hark breathes.

"Now open your eyes."

Fraz watches Hark stare into the swirl of oils, imagines the picture, or pictures the image, taking shape in Hark's mind, the blond boy in knickers, maybe fifteen, perched on a rock in the woods, a golden shaft in his hand.

"*The Boy with Arrow*," says Fraz. "That's the title. Not *a* boy. *The* boy. He's the painter's son. I cried when I saw it here last week. I think of my kids. David mostly, because it's a son in the painting, but I make sure I think of Lisa, too, because ever since I've become the father of a daughter I—"

"Fraz, why am I here?"

"Don't you see? The boy has an arrow. Is he daydreaming? Perhaps. But he has purpose in his face. He's thinking about the future. He's working on his dreams. He'll be a man soon. Mangrown."

"I think I'm missing your point."

"I'm not making a point. I'm sharing a feeling."

Fraz's eyes water. Hark stands, leans toward the wall plaque.

"Douglas Volk. Are you a Volk fan?"

"Okay," Fraz says. "Maybe this was too much."

"It says here that we should enjoy Volk's work but not forget that he was distant with his family in later years and once considered having an affair with a neighbor."

"They have to put that there. It's the law."

"I haven't been to a museum in a while."

"Let's have some lunch."

They leave, find a table at a nearby dumpling boutique.

"I thought you'd like the painting. It had an arrow in it."

"I did like it. I'm glad you showed it to me."

Hark looks down at the menu.

"You know," Fraz says, "I shot real arrows once. In summer camp."

Now Fraz tells Hark this story: When he was eleven, not long after his parents divorced, he was sent to a camp on a freezing Adirondacks lake. The place was staffed with the typical array of sadists, pederasts, dipsomaniacs, Western European teens and public school gym teachers you might find at a sleepaway camp in upstate New York in the late 1970s. The campers bunked in drafty pinewood cabins, administered the traditional rites of warm finger baths, short sheets, hot feet, wedgies. They persecuted the weak, shared care packages of potato chips, chocolate bars, candy cigarettes, off-brand cologne.

Fraz found his niche among the mediocre many, a bystander, for the most part, or, on rare occasions, a mark. Death was not a master from Germany, as a poem Tovah would later recite to him claimed, but a hulking shit from Nyack. The counselors hewed to the logic of corrections officers, let the beastliest run the bunk, looked away when girls' camp interlopers or a flask of peach brandy slipped through the wire.

One day, an older kid, a counselor in training named Barry Buckman, announced that archery would be offered in the field behind the drama shed. Campers flooded the range, giddy at the chance to skewer squirrels, younger bunkers. None expected an interminable safety lesson from C.I.T. Buckman.

"Don't walk out to the targets until I say it's clear," he concluded. "If you walk out to the targets before I give the signal, I'll shoot you in the ass. If you mess around, or aim an arrow anywhere but down-range, I'll shoot you in the ass. Look at my bow."

Buckman held aloft a foreboding contraption, rigged with cables, pulleys, sights and other serious devices. Was that a protractor fastened to it? A sextant?

Leather finger thimbles dangled off his wrist cuff.

"Do you think my parents would buy me a bow like this if I couldn't hit you in the ass?" Buckman said. "I'm a ranked junior amateur."

Some snickered. Buckman barked the boys into orderly rows. Archery was harder than it looked. Most of these kids were lucky to hit the haystacks behind the targets. Some whined about the equipment, the cheap bows and dull plastic arrows. Buckman offered a proverb about how it's often the same people who slide under the hind parts of farm animals and just lie there with their mouths open who also blame the quality of their archery gear. Fraz hadn't heard this adage before, assumed it was just another one of those worn shards of adult wisdom you acquired over time.

Failure to instantaneously master the sport, and the threat of heatstroke, drove most of the campers away. In flagrant rebuke of Activities Time bylaws, they retired to their bunks for shade, water, indoor shaming.

Fraz and Buckman shot on.

"Not bad," Buckman said, surveyed Fraz's latest grouping.

"Want to see a trick shot?"

"Yes," Fraz said.

"I call it the autorimmer."

"What does that mean?"

"Never mind what it means."

Buckman stepped past his bow with one leg and bent over far enough that from Fraz's vantage it looked like the nocked arrow was about to launch out from between Buckman's butt cheeks. The junior counselor released the bowstring, missed the bull's-eye by inches.

Fraz laughed, clapped.

Buckman righted himself, winked, pointed at Fraz's target.

"That's a damn good start. Go pull those and you can try again."

"Are you going to shoot me in the ass?"

It landed oddly, Fraz could tell right way.

"I could tell right way," he says now to Hark. "It just came out wrong. A little too sly. Coquettish. Anyway, we shot for a while, sweating, and Buckman took off his shirt. He had these puffed, pointy nipples, rich and delicate, tufted with wisps of dark hair. I stared at them. Or that's how I remember it. But can you stare at two nipples at once? Maybe I stared at one and then the other. I'd always thought of bodies as curses, particular, inescapable. You know?"

"I do, Fraz."

"But maybe, and here's my point: because I thought this, a lifetime before even meeting you and hearing your message, that Buckman, or somebody like him, might learn to escape that curse through archery."

"How?"

"I don't know. Some kind of ranked junior magic, maybe."

"What happened then?"

"I must have been zoning out, because Buckman shoved me."

"He did?"

"Knocked me to the ground. Told me to go join my bunk. I walked away. But near the edge of the field, I turned back and looked. Buckman just stood there with his head down. He stared at his nipples. Or his nipple. His one nipple. And the other."

"And then what?"

"That's it."

"I see."

"Look, I know it's not much of a story."

"No, it's not, Fraz. There's nothing instructive in it at all."

"Fair enough. Though I don't believe every story needs to have a moral. Or even a meaning."

"Why tell it, then?"

"I don't know. Just to help people focus?"

Hark looks stricken.

"Hark, please understand. I've wasted a lot of time. But I watch you, and listen to you, and I can't help but think you're something different. I thought so from the night I wandered into that crappy little bookstore. And there you were."

"And here we are."

"Hey, I'm not a total dummy. I'm a man of reason. To a reasonable degree. And I think this: You are the sea change. That game-changing sea change of a change agent I've always sought. I want to help carry your message to millions."

"I know you do, Fraz. But you need to remember that I don't have a message. I just want people to focus."

"I get that."

"Then why do I have to have the same conversation with you guys all the time?"

"Okay, I can see that. How it might be frustrating for you. And I do see the genius in not telling them what to focus on. But I need to ask. Do you have a secret idea of what it should be? When the time comes?"

"There's no secret. It's up to them."

"It can't just be up to them," Fraz says.

Hark draws himself up, stern. Has Fraz finally crossed a theoretical line? But Hark laughs.

"You're funny."

"My wife used to think so."

"No longer?"

"I'm not sure."

"Well, Fraz, you do talk a lot."

"If you annoy death, he goes away."

"But you might annoy all your friends in the process. And then they go away. It's my turn to tell a story. Do you know why my name is Hark?"

"A family name?"

"My mother, bless her, always loved that song 'Hark! The Herald Angels Sing.' But she didn't know 'hark' meant listen. She thought it was somebody's name. English was not her first language. She thought the song was about somebody telling their friend Hark that the herald angels were singing."

"That's nice."

"It's asinine."

"What did your father think?"

"He didn't want me in the first place. He thought it was all hilarious."

"Well, it's a good story."

"No it's not. But at least there's a moral."

"What's that?"

"Don't be born to a stupid mother and a prick dad."

Fraz nods. Hark chews his food.

"Look, over there. It's that actor." Fraz points to a handsome man across the room, a friend, according to celebrity news sites, of the star Kate wanted Hark to dress like at the last shoot.

"Why would he eat here?" Hark says.

"I've read that he's really down-to-earth. Look, he's staring at you, Hark. His whole table is. Guess he can't stand being the second-most-charismatic guy in the room."

"I don't know," Hark says. "I still don't recognize him. Maybe from the magazine you showed me."

"He's from that show."

"Okay."

"He's a jerk. Or so I hear. You know what his big thing is? He goes home with a woman—he can have any woman he wants, obviously—"

"Can he?" Hark asks.

"Well, yeah. That's the deal with these guys. These rich, beautiful, famous guys. I mean the beautiful ones, though. The ones women want to be with. Didn't you know that?"

"I guess I never thought of it like that."

"I don't believe you. Everybody thinks about it like that."

"Really?"

"Please. Anyway, he picks somebody up at a party or whatever and they go home and he goes down on her. With astonishing craft, apparently, until she comes, or at least feels obligated to fake it. But he won't let her pleasure him at all. He says it's because he's a feminist. Because, get this, women have already given enough blow jobs. In history, he means. In human time. But it's really a power thing, if you ask me. Going down on a woman and not giving her a chance to reciprocate is extremely antifeminist. You get that, right?"

"I need to think about it."

"Simple logic. Logicus simplex."

"You're a dirty old man," Hark says.

"I prefer generationally fluid. But it doesn't matter. I've been monogamous my entire marriage. Not necessarily by choice. But probably by inclination. Listen, I'm thinking about our demo. We'll need to hit a wider and more affluent audience. I've been working on this."

"You have?"

"I've been pitching, making phone calls. I'm not bad at this. I once had a job in telephone sales. Sold windows. Sell a window over the phone, that's something, believe me. Would you buy a window over the phone? Just from a cold call at dinnertime? And I mean, the windows you have are fine. None are broken. Of course you wouldn't. And yet . . . people do. Okay? I understand your niche. It's not for the dumb poor, or the smart poor, or the smart rich. It's for the kind-of-dumb rich. And the sad middle. And the corporations. And the students. And single people. And married people. And all the people in workout clothes. Somewhere in that spectrum. Also, the kind of people who refer to themselves as seekers."

"I disagree," Hark says. "I believe mental archery is for everybody. Still, I never thought about it so systematically."

"I know you haven't," Fraz says. "That's what appeals to me."

"How do you know all of this stuff?"

"Books. Television. Some music."

"Do you seek transcendence?"

"I've been reduced, Hark. I've been pinched into a little ball. Fuck that. I cry freedom. I'm taking back the night. We'll build an empire for you."

"An empire?" Hark says. "We don't need an empire."

"We need revenue."

"We're starting to get a little. But it's true. I'm not very good at that part. We are reliant on Kate's generosity."

"Which is wonderful, don't get me wrong. But maybe there's more. Maybe mental archery is merely the tip of the spear."

"You mean arrow."

"Spear!" Fraz shouts.

Diners at other tables turn to look. The actor rises, walks over to Hark with the same ruthless swagger he exhibits in his structurally innovative police procedural. Hark looks up with a tight smile.

"I don't want to bother you," the actor says. "I just want to thank you. You've rescued me from an all-enveloping darkness and allowed my talents to shine."

The actor strikes a series of mental archery poses: Ithaka, Persian Rain, Moonlight Diana Number Three, Wheel of Tartars. He bows to Hark, returns to his party.

"Not spear," Hark whispers. "Arrow. Always arrow."

Sixteen

Fraz walks the twins to school, merges with the stream of other neighborhood fathers and mothers and nannies and kids, all of them bobbing along the avenue, sunlight catching on backpack zippers, briefcase hasps. The twins babble, shout, shove each other to the sidewalk.

"Who are the Illuminati, Daddy?" David says. "Why do they have lizard heads?"

"Who told you about that?"

"My phone told me."

"Daddy," Lisa says. "Can I get a keytar?"

"Daddy, the Illuminati control everything."

"Daddy, I really need a keytar."

"Lisa, please. Didn't we just buy you a gee-tar?"

"That's not funny, Daddy, and I played it already. I need a keytar for my new band. We're called the Nameless Yeast."

"Daddy, tell me about why lizards!"

"Shut up, David! Daddy, keytar!"

"Daddy, wait, you're not listening!"

"Shut it, I'm talking to him!"

"Fine, you fucking—"

"Hey!" Fraz roars. The twins freeze, an infrequent delight. A woman with a stroller watches from across the street. She's been put on Earth to witness his firm, sensitive parenting.

"Listen, guys. You can't do this. I'm going to answer your questions. In order. David, I do believe in certain cabals, but the Illuminati stuff is a hoax. Don't bother with it. The real evil is right in front of you. Just look at the political situation. Not to mention the economic situation. Lisa, did you say the Nameless Yeast?"

"Yes, I did, Daddy."

"Daddy," David says. "You know how in ancient times the nine tower and the eleven tower were exploded? Why did the lizard heads do that?"

"They didn't. And there's no they. I mean, no lizard heads. There is a they. But they have regular heads. I'm pretty sure. And we'll discuss the keytar later."

"What?"

"Look, we're here!"

The witness has vanished. Fraz leaves the twins at the school gate. He used to escort them inside, ease coats from their shoulders, kiss them good-bye. He misses it now, the tenderness before the day's mauling began. But his kids don't want him lurking at the threshold of their homeroom. He'll never know classroom drop-off's flood of fondness and relief again. He's not the type to get divorced and start a new family. If Fraz and Tovah split, he would probably never even get to sleep with another person in his lifetime. Unless he paid for the pleasure. But he'd have to save a lot of money, cut corners, eat cat food for months. Some men do exactly that. Or, no, they don't. But Fraz would. That's the sickness right there.

The twins join the crowd in the doorway, slip inside the building. Each day they are slightly new people, and newly, slightly faded people.

Is it lousy child-rearing to dismiss the existence of the lizard heads outright? What does Fraz know about it? He never got tapped for Skull and Bones, or supped at the Bilderberg. What makes him an authority? Buying them smartphones was his first mistake.

Fraz picks up the rental car at a garage near Kate's. He's driving Hark out to New Jersey for a talk at a tech company. Teal booked it, sent a video to an old accounting acquaintance who works there now. Fraz was impressed. It's time to build the brand, he said. Teal winced at this phrase. Once, not too long ago, Fraz might have winced, too, but why? (Maybe it wasn't a wince at all but a flinch from his potential.)

Capitalism isn't going anywhere. Capitalism's not natural, but at this point, neither is nature. You have to dance with the one you came with, Fraz has heard, even if it's hard to picture escorting a global economic system to a line-dancing barn or a strobe-stabby club. Maybe it's more like Fraz's high school prom, where you pick up capitalism at its house, pin a corsage to its gown, and later have drunk sex in a Lysol-tangy motel room down the shore.

Or should Fraz, in fact, wear the corsage?

The attendant pulls up with the Mercedes Fraz ordered. The import costs the institute—or Kate, really—extra, but the least one should expect of a great prophet is that he arrive in a great car. No more trains. Also, city-stuck, Fraz misses the road. Inside his valise is the motorway getup he's broken out a few times over the years: leather half gloves, cloth motoring cap, Milanese driving moccasins. The voyage will take about an hour round-trip.

Teal sits in Kate's loft, scans the latest email to Hark Hub while Hark stares out the window at rooftops. Hark never sends a text or email himself but dictates replies to the questions of his followers. What are the top focus foods? Which does Hark consider the most anaerobic mental archery pose? It's the task of whoever is on duty to provide an encouraging but nonbinding reply: *Thank you for your question about whether mental archery can eliminate free radicals in the body. While it would be foolish to make any kind of comprehensive claim about the healing powers of Hark's system, there is no doubt that an increased focus on health, a focus perhaps achieved through mastery of the basic poses, could have major beneficial side effects, including an elimination of oxidants.*

There is also a message from a woman that seems rather personal: "Dear Hark, You're welcome. Yours, Meg Kenny. P.S. Todd's back. Turns out flowers die rather quickly after you pluck them. Who knew?"

Teal is confused until she remembers a few months ago that Hark had done that rarest of things: logged on to Hark Hub himself, written a note to a fervid endorser of his teachings.

Who is this Meg woman?

The wall unit beeps and Teal buzzes Fraz up. Hark rises, motions for Teal to join him in the center of the room. When Fraz arrives they spread out in a loose triangle.

"Good," Hark says. "Now, before we leave, let's do a quick session, straighten ourselves out. Come over here into the light. Excellent. You know, Buddhists sometimes talk about the second arrow. The first arrow that hits you, that's the pain you can't control. That's the world doing its damage. But the second arrow, that's the damage you do to yourself, with your fear, your anxiety, with dwelling on precisely that which you can't control."

"I'm a major second arrow dude," Fraz says.

"No need to brag about it," Teal says.

"I'm not bragging."

"Okay, let's stay on track," Hark says. "Hannibal's elephant bowmen used to say an archer's spirit must land a cubit past the shaft. But we'll get to that. For now, just assume a sideways stance. And stick your bow arm straight out. Now rotate your other arm. Very nice. Really stretch it. Now bend your knees a little. That's it."

"I really feel this," Fraz says.

"Don't feel it too much. The hunter's heart is not the hunt. So say certain indigenous North American tribes. The Creek, I think."

"Got it."

Fraz is already wheezing.

"Teal, your form is excellent, as usual."

Teal rises from her Downward Loxley, locks eyes with Fraz, sticks out her middle finger.

"Whoa, what was that for? How can Tovah and I do couples counseling with you if you're going to be so immature?"

"Don't you know what that is?" Teal says, runs her other hand up her arm from the tip of her offending finger to the bottom of her elbow.

"No."

"It's how the ancients measured a cubit. About eighteen inches."

"A cubit is eighteen inches?" Fraz says. "I thought that was a talent."

"A talent is money."

"Too bad you don't have one," Fraz says, hears his tone flick too sharp for innocent teasing.

"And yours would be what? Don't tell me it's fucking with your dick. We know that's not the case."

"Hey, that's privileged information. I'm your couples counseling client!"

"Brittle boy."

"You know what you are, Teal? The fucking *third* arrow!"

"I'll take that as a compliment."

"Children," Hark says. "Breathe."

Seventeen

"Are those driving moccasins?" Teal asks, leans forward from the back seat.

Fraz is hurt Hark has asked her to come. He still burns from her words about his carnal skills. Also, he'd wished for a buddy-film feel to the day, but she did line up this gig.

"These?" Fraz says, peeks down at his toes. "They're from Italy."

"Look comf."

"Super-comf."

They cross the river into New Jersey, cruise south on 9W, pull into a business park. A moat of slate-colored water girdles a tower of black glass.

"Look at the place," Teal says. "A fucking cathedral of evil."

"But a good inroad into an untapped market," Fraz says.

"Market?" Hark says.

"Audience. People in need of your help so they can make better choices, whatever they may be."

"Yes," Hark says.

Teal has been assured by her contact that the talk will be well attended. Cutbacks have been frequent, but every gesture toward company morale counts.

The lobby guards check their IDs and a boyish man in an expensive Japanese suit greets them, hugs Teal hello, leads them up in an elevator to the green room.

"Dr. Morner," the man says. "I'm Seth. It's an honor."

"Thanks, friend."

Friend, Fraz notes. That's new.

Fraz pulls his phone out to shoot some video. Electro-scuzz Schnitz is in rehab again. Kate said he tried to inject ketamine into his forehead and the needle broke off in the bone. Fraz isn't sure he believes her.

"Can I get you something?" Seth asks. "Fruit? Coffee? Muffin?"

"Cup of ice, please," Hark says.

"Coffee and a muffin sound perfect," Teal says.

"Well, Seth," Fraz says, "thanks for asking. I'll have a jigger of wheatgrass juice and an egg white omelet with *fromage à Raclette* and finely diced habanero peppers, wheat toast, goat butter on the side, a few slices of Iberian ham, a kiwi-grapefruit smoothie and some of that super-expensive rare coffee that's shit out of Asian elephants. You know what I'm talking about."

"But we're serving muffins and honeydew."

"Yes. I saw the spread out there. But that's the plebe food. What I just ordered is no doubt easily attainable in the executive cafeteria upstairs. Am I wrong?"

"Not wrong."

"Good. See, Seth, Dr. Hark Morner is about to address your company on a very crucial matter. I don't think a simple, decent breakfast is something you want to quibble over. Because I will report it to Mr. Critchley. Isn't that the boss's name, Teal? Can't imagine he'd be pleased."

"Fine," Seth says, turns to Teal. "You still want a muffin?"

"Fuck no. I want the omelet deal."

"Anything to add to your order, Dr. Morner?"

"Nope."

"Very good," Seth says, disappears.

"I'm not a doctor," Hark says to Fraz.

"Who is, really?"

"Dammit. We talked about this."

"We're making a movie here, remember," Fraz says. "A documentary. We're relying on organic in situ tension."

"But you manufactured the tension," Hark says.

"I was hungry. Don't let this stuff throw you."

"I'm not worried about me, Fraz. I'm worried that your evasive maneuvers will finally trap you, friend. All deception becomes self-deception."

A man peers into the room. He wears, beneath his sports coat, what appears to be a vest of delicate silver chain mail.

"Hark Morner?"

"Yes?"

"Sean Critchley," the man says, sticks out his hand. "Call me Critch. So stoked you decided to come. Your manager here is a real breakfast eater. Anyway, we're amped for this, Hark. We have guests from time to time, but I have a special feeling about what you can offer us. Our designs, our business plans, are sound. But as you may have heard from the briefing your staff received, we've had to make a lot of cuts to stay solvent. I'd be stupid to deny that the painful layoffs have caused a rupture in our company culture. We need a new path, a new way to narrativize our roles and goals, as we like to put it. I'm hard-boiled when it comes to the numbers, Doctor, but not in matters of the heart. We were never the best makers of software. But we were always the most motivated, the most at one with ourselves and our mission. Now we need a fresh song. A vibrant life poem with which to propel ourselves into a succession of profitable quarters. I apologize that I haven't read your books or seen your television shows, but after the description my people conveyed, I was too intrigued to pass up this chance. Knock 'em dead, Doctor. But don't go on too long. We have to get these trogs back to the mines."

Critchley nods, slips out the door.

Seth returns with a tray of food.

"We'll give it another few minutes. The auditorium is jammed."

Fraz forks up egg whites, films himself forking them.

"That Critchley guy is certifiable," Teal says. "Archduke Nutcake."

"Isn't that just what a CEO is like?" Fraz says.

"Been a while. I could tell you all about COs, though."

"What did he mean about books and TV?" Hark says.

"Seriously, Fraz," Teal says. "Did you talk to Seth after I set this up?"

"Answer the question," Hark says.

"I hustled. As I promised I would. Did I exaggerate your achievements a little? To get you in the door? Listen, when Einstein was a boy they thought he was retarded."

"How is that possibly germane?"

"Germane? Everything I do is germane. Everything is for us, don't you get it? You've got to trust me. You have something real to share. Just open your mouth and speak. Tell them about mental archery. That's all you have to do. The rest is vanity."

"Fraz, you need to calm down. Try a few poses."

Fraz rubs his toast in egg grease, folds in a thin slice of ham.

Hark changes into his guru wear. It's Kate's idea, an unflattering cross between a *jalabiya* and a hospital johnny, navy blue with stardust glitter. He tugs it down, charges out to the stage. The light-up heels of his metallic track shoes wink pink in the darkness. Fraz scurries down to the auditorium and sinks into a third-row seat.

"Let's hear it for those dry, tasteless corn muffins!"

The outfit is dog shit, but Hark is alive.

The silence isn't quite hostile. Maybe they just don't find jokes about their cafeteria funny. Maybe they're too frightened for their jobs to laugh. Hark needs a new tack. He purses his lips in the manner of a person about to choose a new tack.

"Ladies and gentlemen, it is a great honor to be here with you this morning. I understand you are all living in a time of dread. Glyph Systems, never a visionary company, as Mr. Critchley just informed me, is running out of the only thing that ever kept it profitable, the pride and precision of its workforce. I'm talking about you. Collective anxiety has caused mental drift. A slackening. Fear does this. You would think it would motivate people, but if things appear too hopeless, there is general collapse. I understand. I sympathize. I empathize. Is there really a difference? But that's a question for some leisurely later. Right now we must counter the trend. Forge a new approach. Think of this building. Is it an office tower? Of course it is. But maybe you should also consider it a castle.

"Now, in many castles there are ramparts, or battlements, with these little niches where an archer would kneel and shoot arrows at the enemy. Some other people would be in charge of dropping rocks on the enemy, the invading army, or pouring boiling oil on them, but let's talk about these archers, these men of the bow. Or women. There can be women of the bow. This is a thought exercise, not a history lesson. And recent research tells us there were many women of the bow, so there it is. Sometimes these bow people, or archers, were all that stood, or squatted, or knelt, between continued existence and certain death for the castle dwellers, which wasn't just stuffy let-them-eat-cake royalty in there, mind you, but more like a good-sized town with different walks of life represented. Anyway, here comes the enemy with their monstrous siege machines and catapults, probably designed by guys like Leonardo da Vinci, not quite the Gandhi-type pacifist some may have assumed, and their fierce wall-scaling soldiers. Not to mention the battering rams. Boy, those things could really batter the shit out of your standard castle gate. Picture it all, hordes of vicious soldiers, mercenaries, really, sociopathic freebooters, trying to batter their way in, or climb their way in, or even—and this was a very popular tactic—tunnel their way in. Meanwhile, at the ramparts, what? Some boiling oil people, some rock throwers, but mainly right now, before the hand-to-hand combat really gets going, which will not end well for the castle people, we have the archers, poised to rain iron-tipped arrows on the enemy. It's villagers versus pillagers. Why am I constructing this picture for you? What does it have to do with the challenges the Glyph Systems workforce faces? Everything, I'd say. You are the bow people, people. Right here in this big black glass castle. Now, do I mean we should all go to the sporting goods store and buy some expensive shooting equipment? No, I don't. I'm here to introduce you to another concept, one that I think will go a long way to making you fearless and, more important, satisfied employees. Because you are not cogs, you are craftspeople, and your crafts vary, your guilds vary, from engineering to marketing to production to human resources. Your crafts and guilds are varied and distinct. But in many medieval societies, like merry old England, for example, it didn't matter your specialty, whether you were a cooper, which for some reason was what they called a barrel maker, or a blacksmith, or a sawyer, which, as you can probably guess, was a person adept at sawing, or if you were a farmer, carpenter, tailor, tinker, brewmaster, kegmeister, it didn't matter, because everybody had to be trained in the longbow from the age of six. Citizen archers all. And that's what all of you can become. Citizen archers of your country, which, let's be honest, is this very corporation. You can be citizen archers of Glyph Systems, saving yourselves and your families by protecting these walls, these glass battlements, from fucking animals like Leonardo da Vinci and his war-pig war machines!"

A shallow growl rises from the seats. Critchley's face is blurred at this distance, but Fraz senses the displeasure as the man chugs up the aisle. Hark begins to speak again, fumbles for the threads he's been weaving, but now, in staggered waves, more Glyphers charge for the doors, early adopters of this new technology called walking-out-on-the-lecture-and-scooping-up-leftover-muffins-and-melon-balls. Hark jogs off toward the wings, passes Fraz, who hunches now at the edge of the stage, pans deserted seats with his phone. Teal and Seth, the last people left in the auditorium, slump in apparent grief.

Fraz trots after Hark to the green room.

"It's a process, Hark."

Now Seth steps in through the door, approaches.

"Dr. Morner."

"I'm sorry, Seth," Hark says.

"For what?"

"I bombed out there."

"Oh, no, they loved it."

"They walked out."

"That's just company culture. We have this motto, 'Turn it around,' meaning a problem, or a habit. We talk at our desks but remain silent at the water cooler. We have half-day Mondays in winter. When we don't like something, we applaud. When we love it, we storm out."

"You guys are fucked," Fraz says.

"But if you turn it around," Seth says, "we're not fucked at all."

"Do you have the check?" Fraz asks.

"We have to recut it."

"Why?"

The kid holds up his phone.

"Critch just told me to double your fee."

"Triple's good, too," Fraz says.

———————

Nobody speaks much on the walk back to the parking lot. Teal peels off from Fraz and Hark to join Seth at his car.

"We're going to grab lunch out here," she tells them. "I'll see you back in the city. Fraz, we have a session with Tovah tomorrow."

Hark tosses his gear, the bow, the old sun-bleached pamphlets he still carries as talismans, into the trunk, waves good-bye to Teal.

"See you, Teal," Fraz says, gets behind the wheel. Hark slides into the passenger seat. They sit in silence for a moment.

"Wilhelm Reich died in prison, you know," Fraz says.

"So they say."

"No, they don't just say it. It's true."

"What's your point?"

"I just mean we've got to go for it."

"I gave them everything today."

"Then why did you apologize?"

"Listen, friend, you're not the one up there."

Fraz backs out of the parking lot, veers onto 9W.

"What are you doing?" Hark says. "The bridge is the other way."

"I want to show you something."

"No, just take me home."

"No, I want to show you something."

Hark pounds the dashboard a few times but stops with his hand still in the air, as though struck by a novel idea. He settles back into his seat, lowers the window, closes his eyes to the breeze.

They take an exit onto a steep road lined with split-level houses shaded by maples, oaks.

"Is this what you want to show me?"

"Almost."

They tool through the main drag of a town, brick-faced shops with quaint awnings, drive past a grim stone keep of a grade school with its concrete barriers (Jersey barriers, Fraz remembers they're called) and a rubber tire playground, into a neighborhood of prim Victorians painted in risqué pastels. Farther from the commercial district, the houses get squat, sided with aluminum. They turn onto a dirt road, root-snaked, bounce beneath a green leaf canopy, bump toward a clearing. Fraz brakes, parks.

"Get out."

"Are you planning on killing me?" Hark says, chuckles.

"Do you want me to?"

"Maybe later."

Fraz leads Hark on a short hike to the rim of a reservoir. Black and gray rocks stipple the shoreline.

"A lot happened here," Fraz says. "This was the magic place."

"Looks like a paradise."

"We had a rowboat we'd take out to that tiny island over there. Those were the best times. We'd fish for carp and crappie. At night we'd go for catfish."

"Catfish?"

"Yeah."

"I know a catfish."

"What?"

"Nothing."

"Fuckers would swallow the hook and we'd swing them around on our poles, slap each other. We were dumb, cruel kids. Our fathers didn't fish. Nobody taught us to respect nature. It wasn't even a natural body of water. When we got older we'd take a bottle out there, some weed. Light a little fire. We carried out old cushions and chairs and a mattress. A radio. We had parties. Got my cherry popped over there near that clump of trees. This is kind of the Disney version I'm giving you. There was weirder stuff. Stupid stuff. One night my friend Pete tried to piss on everybody. Then his girlfriend, Tracy, tried it, too. Another time we convinced this kid Edward that we'd brought him out to the island to murder him. See, you weren't the first to think of that. We even tied him up and waved a knife. We even cut him a little. We even found this sick bird and cut the bird open and dripped the bird blood on him. We even ripped off his pants and stuck the bird under his balls. But that was a dark moment in an otherwise sunnier epoch. We'd go skinny-dipping, come out of the water to dry in the moonlight, drink rum on the cushions and the mattress. The moon not that bright, lots of legs and arms and asses, all this young skin. Together we were one monstrous hormonal creature from the lagoon. The stink of peppermint schnapps and cigarettes. The stink of fish. Blackout drunk, or pretending to be. What was all that? I don't know what it was, but it happened here. Then it all ended. They whispered about us for a few months, but even that died down. I mean, the weird shit only happened a couple of times. It all fades. Our house was right over there. About a hundred yards from where we're standing. Through those trees. My parents sold it a long time ago. Moved to Minnesota, where my mom was from. But what I'm getting to is that that shitty little island over there, that atoll of terror and bliss, you must have a place like that, Hark, a reservoir, a lake, a stairwell, a roof, an alley, an attic. You must have had one."

"I had many," Hark says. "But I was alone. Destroying myself alone. Nothing communal. Never even had a friend to piss on."

"Piss on me, Dr. Morner."

"Yeah, right."

"No, really," Fraz says.

"I think those days are over for all of us."

"No they're not," Fraz says. "It's not sexual, if that's what you're worried about. It's about human connection. And power. And sex."

"That's not what I'm worried about."

"What is it, then?"

"It's not real. You're just reenacting your old enchantment."

Fraz's face tightens.

"Hark, what is the secret?"

"The secret to what?"

"To everything. I've been hustling for you. Out of love and respect. Out of belief. But you've got to tell me the truth. Whatever you're withholding while you watch us all blabber on about what we think mental archery means. My life is falling to shit. I need to see the light. Please."

"What you see is what you get."

"You fucking charlatan," Fraz says. "You're just some jerk with focusing techniques for the masses."

"Yes! That's exactly what I am! I'm this guy from California. A cop's kid. Why are you trying to pump me up into some seer? That's what's ludicrous."

"You like it."

Fraz lays his hand on Hark's shoulder. Warm liquid lashes across Hark's pleats.

"What are you going to do now?" Fraz asks.

"About what?"

"About the fact that I just pissed on you."

"Let it dry?"

"You!" Fraz shouts, dives at Hark. They sprawl to the dirt together. Hark presses Fraz hard into the ground with his knees, punches his nose. Fraz cackles in pain, lifts a leg up for a scissor lock. Hark rises, twists away. Fraz rolls onto his belly, looks up. Hark hovers, fist cocked.

Clouds bull across a sky of silly blue.

"Time," Fraz says.

"Time-out?"

"No, time."

"Uncle?"

"Just time."

"Time for what?"

"Time is a scumbag."

Hark smiles.

Fraz leans up on his elbow in the dirt.

"That's one way of putting it," Hark says.

"You let all of this happen."

"I guess."

"You let me get crazy."

"You had some things to work through."

"You could have stopped me at any time."

"Probably."

"Who do you think you are, Jesus Christ?"

Hark laughs.

"Am I your Judas?"

"No, friend. I think you are somebody who needs to relax."

Eighteen

Kate's plane lands at Arlanda. Stockholm will be her next-to-last run. She's spoken with the clinic, pledged a philanthropic check in lieu of further courier services.

She hires a taxi to take her to the Karolinska University Hospital. The young driver plays ambient music he's composed, he tells Kate, in his father's basement. His phone rings, more ambience. Kate makes out a tense voice on the other end. The driver shouts in what must be Swedish, pounds his phone against the steering wheel.

"What a bitch!"

"Boss?" Kate says.

"Therapist."

She wants to believe this is some common and delightfully perplexing Scandinavian moment, but how can it be? It's anecdotal. Try to relate an anecdote these days and a mob will gather in the lane to stone you. Where are your studies, your statistics? This is Kate's take, anyway. Kate's got takes, notions, hunches, but no stats. It's funny that she volunteers for a medical mission. Today's plan is to deliver the cooler and head straight to her hotel for a hotel nap, a hotel massage, some hotel-smoked fish.

Later, she decides to visit the *Vasa*, the mammoth seventeenth-century warship that sank a thousand meters from the dock on its maiden voyage. Kate strolls the Stockholm waterfront, past the curve of pink and white and yellow palaces, a snaking, imperial cake.

Somebody tails her. It doesn't require a career in espionage to sense it. She veers close to the doors of a busy café, wheels.

"Can I help you?"

A windbreaker, stiff brown hair.

"I'm sorry?" the man says.

"You're following me."

"Of course not."

"Tell the truth."

"Okay, I'm following you. I followed you from the hospital."

His pronunciation is precise, effortful.

"That's alarming."

"I don't mean anything . . . stalking, or weird."

"What do you mean, then?"

"I saw you go in with the case. I know what it is. I work at the hospital."

"What do you want?"

"My daughter has leukemia. She is five and she is on a list. But I don't think she will live long enough. She needs a match now."

Kate walks off. The man jogs up beside her.

"My name is Nels."

Kate pulls up again.

"What do you want from me?"

"I have money," Nels says.

"So do I."

"Oh."

"If you think I can help, you are in serious trouble. I'm just a courier. How would I find the match? Who would do the transplant?"

"I have seen videos online. I could do it. I do not kid you."

"I'm sure you don't," Kate says. "I'm sorry, I can't help. Please go away."

Nels brings out something from his jacket, a photograph of a young girl, thin-faced, luminous. The picture reminds Kate of a snapshot she has of herself from that age, at a summer carnival, a dark storm forming in the sky behind her while she burns with scarlet fever.

"Her name is Blenda," Nels says.

"A lovely name."

"You don't really think that."

"It sounds like an artificial sweetener. One in particular."

"My daughter is named for a heroine. Blenda fought the Danes with an army of village girls. She saved the Swedes. Who will save Blenda?"

"I'm sorry," Kate says.

"Take it."

Nels holds out the photograph.

"I can't."

"My information is on the back. If you change your mind."

Kate looks past him across the harbor.

"Take it, please. Throw it out later if you want. But let me think I tried."

Nels looks about to weep.

"I don't think I could begin to help you," Kate says, hands the photograph back.

"Maybe not," Nels says. "Listen, I will leave you now. If you want to have a nice drink, go in the bar of that hotel."

He points out an old stone building with a cracked staircase.

"Okay."

"Have the rusty nail. Do you like that?"

"I don't think I've ever had one."

"It's good."

Kate watches Nels walk off. Part of her wants to hail a taxi back to the airport. She may have sidestepped an awful complication, or worse. But Nels seems harmless. Deranged by worry, but not a threat.

It's too early for a rusty nail, whatever that is. Kate prefers vodka on ice, and no infusions, thank you, no horseradish or lemon peels or pepper. Only that pure demon luger sliding down her throat. No dregs.

The waterfront bends toward the Vasa Museum. People push bicycles along the promenade or drink on the decks of docked boats. Some sit at café tables with mugs of coffee, sandwiches. The harbor sparkles.

The museum, a modern structure, houses an immense model of a warship the likes of which had never been seen in 1628, when Gustavus Adolphus fought in Poland, during the Thirty Years' War. The *Vasa* was massive, with two gun decks and extra-heavy shot, but its center of gravity wasn't low enough. Minutes after setting off, the ship tipped in the wind and sank, one of the quickest ends to a superpower's supersymbol on record.

Kate learns all this from a Londoner who stands beside her at the balustrade. She'd been studying the painted carvings on the hull when he began, unbidden, to tell her the significance of the figures, the Norse gods and Greek heroes and Roman kings. He's lifted his patter, she supposes, from the free guidebook she glanced through earlier, and his pedantic soliloquy begins to grate. She can sense he thinks he's getting somewhere with her. She tries hard not to picture what she imagines he pictures. She craves, for no reason, a rusty nail. Maybe even with Nels. All he'd desire from her is the commission of an international felony.

The man tells her that underneath their progressive rhetoric the Swedes are all vicious ax murderers.

"What about the English?"

"We're desperate little animals, puffing ourselves up with a highly distorted sense of the rational out of pure terror."

"What about Americans?" Kate asks.

"You're just gun-crazy cunts, aren't you?"

The man smirks, checks his wristwatch.

"Care for a drink?" he says.

"Not with you."

The man shrugs, leaves.

Kate takes a seat on a bench that appears to be fashioned from the same blond wood as the ship. One moment you wave good-bye to the crowds on the pier, the next you are drowned, or drowning, or swimming for your life back to the stunned people who just wished you a happy voyage and had, in many ways, already begun to forget you, for they have pots to scour, dough to knead, goats to milk, babies to suckle, children to scold, lovers to clutch, parents to despise, siblings to deplete. And who were you but a fool on a fool captain's faulty bark?

You were not life anymore.

Nineteen

Teal, in her capacity as Gold-Penzig marriage counselor, has mandated a date night for Tovah and Fraz. When Tovah cannot track down any of the usual sitters, Teal volunteers for the duty herself. It's a break with therapeutic protocol, perhaps, but Harkism is about community, or should be, whether Hark says as much or not.

"We'll fake it till we make it," Teal says. "Because it takes a village. Even if it's a Potemkin village. Which we have to destroy to save."

Tonight is a double-date night, with, of all people, Nat Dersh, and his whore du jour, as Tovah puts it. Nat's awful, but sometimes in his presence something lurid, displacing, courses through Tovah, maybe a version of her old Bob Price vulgarian streak. She's only somewhat ashamed of her secret appreciation for classic assholes and classic asshole aesthetics: cocktails, shrimp cocktails, prime rib, the jizzy insistence of an iceberg wedge with Roquefort dressing. Maybe it's the legacy of her daddy, Dead Eddie. It's all so pathologicial and wrong, and she hates herself, and the piggish men she's sometimes drawn to, for collaborating with her on her bad judgment.

Fraz has confessed his wariness about the dinner. It's not like Dersh to socialize with his pseudo-cousins. What's the hitch? Maybe Dersh is feeling nostalgic, or getting bullied by his late father's rivals. Perhaps the evening is simply the case of a young king reaching out to historically supportive thanes.

"Thane?" Tovah said.

"Like from the Scottish play."

"You can say it."

"I don't want to jinx it."

They're booked at a new Thai-Irish fusion sensation. Fraz will dash over after a work session with Hark at Kate's. They are in pre-production for a new video. Fraz has been there most days, clocking the hours of a Wall Street quant, or a composer with end-stage syphilis desperate to finish his final concerto.

Tovah misses the knock but hears the twins storm the front door. She remains before the dining room mirror, knots a silk scarf she stole from her friend's mother in the ninth grade. She hated the friend, loved the mother, the mother's Parisian scarves.

The TV plays in the living room, the audio muted. The president speaks to the press, swivels to answer a question. The man looks terrible, harried, anemic. Does he wash his hair anymore? Cop the slightest ray of Rose Garden sun? He's not an evil man, this president, nor a good one. He was elected to undo the catastrophic policies of his predecessor, who was herself elected to undo the apocalyptic agenda of the man before her, but it all seems too late for that these days, mostly because it's always been too late, though now, pundits agree, this moment is steeped in a radical and irrevocable lateness, a tardy totality heretofore unseen.

An update flashes: PRESIDENT HAS NOT RULED OUT GROUND FORCES IN BULGARIA.

The twins squeal, yank on Teal's arms.

"Mommy, Mommy," Lisa says. "Her name is Teal. Like the color! But she has light-brown skin!"

"I know!" Teal says, shakes her head. "My parents really got it all wrong, didn't they!"

The twins talk about skin color all the time. All the kids from their progressive public school do, too, and not just the white ones. It makes Tovah nervous. It seems racist, but she knows she's the racist.

"Teal's a good friend," Tovah says. "She's been helping Mommy and Daddy."

"Helping them do what?" Lisa asks.

"Helping them be the awesome people they are!" Teal says.

"They're trash," David says. "They're tragic."

"Well," Tovah says, hands Teal a sheet of paper. "Here's how the evening looks."

Teal glances down:

7:00–7:15—Dinner. Heat frozen pizza according to instructions on box. Salad already in bowl, just dress. One Popsicle each for dessert.
7:15–7:40—Reading, or a quiet game with you.
7:40–7:45—Teeth and Peeps (brushing, urination).
7:45–8:00—Stories and songs.
8:00–8:10—Lights out. Sleep.*

* If they make noise after this, refer to the graduated consequence list below.

"This looks like a fine plan," Teal says.

Tovah is relieved. She has never gotten anywhere close to nailing this timeline. The night always ends much later, with screaming (all of them), halfhearted denunciations of domestic tyranny (the children), too much wine (Tovah), unspeakable fears spoken (Tovah), and a final profusion of hugs and kisses (the gang). Fraz handles them more smoothly, but his strategy is corrupt. He just hangs out like they are all dorm buddies until the kids puke from sleep deprivation, beg for bed. The evening is easy, the twins wrecked for the week.

Tovah will see what Teal can do. The young woman is clearly no slouch, though she does slouch, albeit in a compelling fashion. David and Lisa might, in fact, obey her. They do that on occasion.

Tovah spots Nat at a table near the window. He picks at a plate of stew.

"Take a load off, Tovah."

"You ordered."

"Hyper-famished."

"I guess Fraz is running late. He hasn't texted. Your date's late, too."

"My date canceled."

"I'm sorry."

"It's okay. You wouldn't have been impressed with her. She's not really a reader. She's my shopper."

"I like your jacket, so she must be doing something right."

"She's not as sexy as you are."

"Excuse me?"

"You heard me."

"I'll pretend I didn't. Besides, is it her job to be sexy?"

"Sure, to a degree. We are who we are."

"I thought it is what it is. Isn't that what people like you say?"

"People like me? There are no other people like me."

Dersh pops a lump of Thai basil corned beef into his mouth. A few chili seeds dot his lower lip. It's a plump, lovely lip, she must admit. It appears that even cockroaches like Nat Dersh can possess a modicum of winning male sultriness. Still, it's a sad commentary on her life that she's at all aroused by the way his squash-supple hand strokes her knee beneath the table. Why must it be a toss-up between stale seduction tropes and the sterile sibling routine of a tedious marriage?

Who do you have to fuck to stop getting fucked by false choices?

"You have seeds on your . . . ," she says, signals.

"It should be you."

"Oh, now I'm an it?"

"Be here," he whispers.

"I am. Fraz will be here soon."

"I doubt it."

"What?"

"I guess some wires got crossed. He might think dinner was rain-checked."

"Why would he think that?"

"I hope you don't mind, but I've already ordered the County Cork Curry Delight."

"You're a pig," Tovah says.

"We all share a good deal of genetic material with our porcine cousins," Nat says. "What can I say? I cannot tell a lie. I see what I want and I reach for it. It's called embracing life."

"Yes, you can tell a lie. You do tell lies. All the time. Don't you?"

"Everybody lies."

"Fraz doesn't. Not about important things."

"He doesn't have to. He can live in his little truth hutch because we're out here in the world, every day, lying for him."

"You sound like my father."

"Unless he was your lover, I don't want to sound like your father."

"That's disgusting."

"That's reality."

"No, it's just disgusting. And you're hurting my knee."

"Sorry."

"I don't get it, Nat. I know you grabbed my ass that time, but I figured you did that out of spite. Fraz told me how he and the others used to tease you. Fraz still feels bad about it."

"He should," Nat says, sucks seeds from his lip. "I'll never forgive him. I'm traumatized. But that's not really it. I just don't think he deserves you. And maybe this is arrogant, but I think maybe, in my best moments, I do."

"Nat, you're filthy rich. You can have anybody you want."

"Yes, with expensive meals and fine drink I have coaxed my share of attractive women into my hand-stitched king-plus organic bed. But it gets boring. I've said it before: I crave the wise pussy. It's not just that I feel old, either, or need to be around somebody who knows what 1997 felt like, and not from the vantage of a bassinet.

It's you, Tovah. I want you. Every version of you: the poet, the teacher, the mother, the education technologist. I want loving and sharing. I want to take care of you, Tovah. And the twins."

"God help you, Nat."

"He must be. I'm doing so well."

"I'm leaving."

"Maybe we should order some wine."

"Irish or Thai?"

"See, you're so witty. Total package."

"I'm going home, Nat."

"Think about it."

"I won't."

"Liar."

Twenty

Fraz dusts a mole on Hark's jaw with a makeup brush.

A young man in a suit appears with a bottle of water for Hark. It's the kid from the Glyph Systems gig.

"Everybody, this is Seth," Hark says. "He's here to pitch in."

"Welcome, Seth!" the set crew calls.

"Welcome, Seth," Fraz says, offers a rather territorial nod.

"Excuse me, Dr. Morner . . . ," Seth says.

"Call me Hark."

"Hark. Sorry, I'm just following the new protocol."

Seth points to a cluster of people waiting across the room. The new regulars. The Harkheads.

"Protocol?" Hark says. "Anyway, welcome, Seth."

Seth strikes the pose of an archer, aims for the ceiling.

"I have pamphlets for sale!" he calls out.

It's the latest craze, this salute, but none of the old-timers have cottoned to it.

Teal and Fraz lead Hark across the room to his stool. The crowd cheers. Hark stares into the lights.

"Quiet, everyone," says Teal.

These are the moments that matter to Fraz, watching Hark poised like a diver at the rim of some pristine quarry pool. Hark will pierce the surface, himself the most beautiful arrow, return to his flock slick with wisdom's waters. The everyday Hark may captivate, but he's still a mere man, with his hurts, his flaws. But this quotidian form is just a costume, a swathing that protects not Hark but the rest.

Here, slipped from his usual guise (as much as possible in this dimension, in this density), even Fraz, the old hand, worries Hark's shine will blind him. Do the words of Hark touch Fraz more than they do others? Who can know? But witness these people, seekers one and all, foragers for the nuts and berries of transcendence, the mushrooms and prized truffles of True Focus, gathered here for nourishment in the Forest of Hark.

"Set it free," Fraz whispers.

Hark begins.

"Hello, my friends. May I tell you about the Mongols? I believe it is time for me to tell you about the Mongols. Of yore, I mean. The Mongols, you see, used a short composite bow that took many months to fashion out of horn and hide. They carried three kinds of arrows for myriad tasks, were astonishingly disciplined in their formations, and could shoot from their ponies at full gallop. The Mongols cooked their meat on the move, strapping raw steaks to their buttocks while they rode. They drank mare's milk and naturally occurring small-batch bourbon. Almost everybody on this planet, and certain other planets, descends from a single splash of semen shot into the air by a masturbating Genghis Khan and caught in the vagina of a nude acrobat in mid-somersault. What we learn from the example of the Mongols is that ferocity plus discipline equals victory. Anger is not to be managed. It is to be weaponized. The so-called cold dish. Sup upon the cold dish and know peace. In the workplace or the workspace. In the venue we call home.

"The Korean Peninsula also possesses a mighty archery tradition. How did a Korean warrior begin his archery training? He'd stand in a field with the bow on the ground before him and meditate upon its contours for months. Finally, at the appointed time, he would lift the bow from the earth and spend upwards of a year holding it in his hand. Think about that. Just a year to feel it in his hand. Then another year to practice stringing the bow and drawing it without an arrow. Then another six months drawing the bowstring back with a nocked arrow. You can picture the rate of attrition. It takes a certain commitment, you might say. After four years, those who remained, who had not quit or fallen ill, were approached by a lovely maiden. The maiden would pull out strands of her hair and give them to the warrior, who would fashion a new bowstring from them. The maiden would reach into her robe sleeve and tug from it a specially fletched shaft. The warrior would shoot this arrow at a kind of clay pigeon—in this case a fist-sized dove modeled out of boiled rice—tossed into the air at the edge of the field. If the trainee hit this false bird, the instructor would bestow upon him a quiver of arrows and he'd be free to return to his village, the maiden dropping flowers in his path. When they reached the end of their journey, the warrior and the maiden would wed. But if the warrior missed, he laid his bow back in the grass and stood for another year. He would have three chances at this. If he missed his third shot his throat would be slit and he'd be rolled into a pond. Many of us must stand in the grass for even longer before we take our first shot. We stand and endure the mounting scorn of our family and friends. They flog us, flay us, push thorns in our brows. They make subtly corrosive remarks. But we must hold our ground. Our moment will come. The arrow will fly. *You* will fly. You must meditate on this. It just takes a little sacrifice. The archery is merely a metaphor. I could be talking about backgammon, or Newcomb. No biggie."

They wrap, order kimchi burgers from the newly renamed pub down the street, the Quiescent Prole, in honor of the lecture's theme. The new video is posted to Hark Hub and the surge in traffic is quick.

"People are watching," Seth says. "The message is getting out there."

"There isn't a message, friend," Hark says.

"But sometimes it seems like there is. What was that part about weaponizing anger?"

"I don't know. That just kind of popped out. Are there more comments?"

"Wow," Fraz says, scoops a petal of beef from the take-out carton. "It's true. You really don't check them."

"It's better that way."

"What I love," Seth says, "are the made-up historical facts. Where'd you get the Korean bit? I'm half Korean and that's all baloney."

"It's mythology, Seth. It's part of the collective human imagination."

"Right," Seth says. "But we do know some facts. The Mongols didn't strap steaks to their asses."

"Maybe one did, once. How can we know? But that's not the point."

"Oh, so it's a metaphor, as you have said."

"What's a metaphor, Seth?"

"Is this a trick question?"

"Answer me. What's a metaphor?"

"Please instruct me," Seth says, his tone an earnest hush.

"It's for cows to graze in."

The group chimes in with reverent chuckles.

"I don't get it," Seth says.

"Nobody does," Teal says.

"That's because I don't say it quite right," Hark says. "I don't have the right accent."

"Which is the point!" Seth says.

"Exactly, friend."

"Of course," Seth says. "I didn't mean to be impudent. I hope I haven't overstepped my bounds."

"On the contrary. You have proven your value. We must always ask the questions, always put pressure on our methods, to test them. Seth, you must continue to administer the tests. We shall call you the Proctor."

Fraz wonders if he'll ever get a nickname.

"To the Proctor!" somebody shouts.

"Now," Hark says, "who's hogging the noodles?"

Later, after Hark has gone to bed, a few linger and talk.

"It's funny," Seth says. "He's so commanding when he speaks to a crowd, but he's got a weird sense of humor about it all. Like part of him thinks it's a put-on. But I don't. And all these new followers don't."

"Men like Hark are complex, Seth," Kate says.

Teal laughs.

"I think Fraz is the real tortured soul."

"Excuse me?" Fraz says.

"Fraz's case could fill a book," Teal says. "Not that he's complex. But once you've probed his emotions and babysat his kids, the narrative becomes clear."

"The narrative?" Fraz says. "There are no narratives. Only moments. Only one moment. When the arrow is released and flies into the infinite regress of the future."

"But, Fraz," Teal says, "you like to watch poor pregnant women suck dicks."

"How would you know?"

"From using your computer."

"Snoop. Abuser of therapist-client privilege."

"All babysitters snoop."

"I always clear history."

"Not completely, it seems."

"Well," Fraz says, "you don't know for certain that they're poor."

Hark slips into bed with one of Kate's computer tablets. Mostly he's avoided the voices out there. But tonight he logs on to Hark Hub, the comments section, lifts the lid off the cauldron, glimpses the roil:

> » Can't tell if Hark's serious or not.
> » if he's serious he's a moron
> » Where's the actual archery? Put on some clown pants!
> » I think its interesting
> » its babble
> » It's "it's," not "its."

» he's satan
» Yes, he might be Satan.
» he's satan the stud
» If you like that sort of thing.
» What sort of thing?
» Haggis-faced pseudo-spiritualists.
» I actually like haggis. And I hate Scotland.
» Listen to him and you might learn something about being more than a dumb narcissist. You might find the focus, the light.
» what, are you president of his fan club?
» I'm president of my local Choke-Out Society chapter.
» 4 reels?
» Come over and find out.
» Who filmed that? A drunk badger? That's some of the worst videography I've ever seen.
» That stuff about Korean archers is a crock.
» It's a metaphor
» I'm Korean. And there actually is a very huge tradition of archery in Korea called Gungsul.
» Who cares? He's using these stories as instruction. You're just doing what dumb fundamentalists do, taking it all literally.
» Has he read Herrigel's Zen in the Art of Archery? Sounds like a rip-off.
» Have you read Zen in the Art of Picking Lint Off Your Taint Hairs?
» Herrigel's book was a crock. Awa, Herrigel's instructor, wasn't even talking about Zen. And did you know that in Japanese archery if you split your own arrow with a second arrow it's a source of shame?
» fucked up but hark isn't talking about zen either
» He is, he just doesn't know it.
» Hark plus Zen = Hen. Or Zark.
» herrigel used real arrows—hark is beyond that shit, dude! he uses his crystal vision. u should get one. peace to the Present.
» Some real scholars in this thread.
» Sidenote: if Hark's going to use examples from history he should get the history right.

- » Hey, Sidenote: He never called it history. He's a thinker, and maybe a healer. And maybe that's what we're all afraid of here. Doctor Hark might be onto something that's world-changing, and rather than confront that possibility, we're haggling over some minor details.
- » It's fear-based.
- » Korean warriors did not stand there for a year staring at a bow in the grass!
- » too busy digging holes in the dirt and sticking their bim-bim-baps in there
- » Get nicked, you bloody racist troll.
- » Doctor Hark Morner. That's DHM
- » So?
- » It could mean something.
- » Like what?
- » Dildo Hanseatic Ministry
- » Okay, Himmler. Whatever you say.
- » Not Nazi, numbnuts.
- » I'm with Meg217. I saw this guy talk at my job. Like a little clinic. He kicks ass. My whole life has changed since he came. The guy's a genius. You take his suggestions and they pay off right away. I spend an hour every morning in the "meadow," with my "bow" up and my "string" drawn. I fire one "arrow" at the end. And I'm locked in for the rest of the day. I don't even need coffee anymore. It's not just work, either. It's everything. There's been this simultaneous lightening and deepening. I'm a confirmed atheist so this will sound funny, but it's almost religious. There is something profound going on. I'm sure it's empirically ex-plainable, but I'm not so interested in hearing about that right now. I'm sort of enjoying this mystical clarity, even if it's false. Does that make any sense? I've never felt this way in my life. I won't even get into the newfound sexiness between me and my girlfriend. Or the changed manner of my son, how he seems to respect me now, looks into my eyes as though desirous of advice and leadership. It's fantastic. I want to give that boy advice and leadership. I never thought I'd be able to do so, but now I can, because of Dr. Hark. I used to work as a development officer for

a college arts program, and I'm hoping to donate my skills one day to help his cause. These teachings need to spread. Maybe this could help keep the world from slipping into the pits of hell.

» Thanks for that incredible testimonial.

» Yes, thanks for the wank-o-monial, belief fag.

Twenty-one

Tonight, Fraz is grateful for a quiet meal with Tovah and the twins. Mental archery is not meant to supplant life but to enhance it. It's time for the old domestic rhythms, for the bestowal of tender glances over a bowl of lemon-dressed chard, for nourishing the wee ones with rousing tales of social struggle and a tofu-and-quinoa platter. It's time for Fraz to swirl cold pinot blanc in his mouth and sample life's simple, complex joys, if not quite feel them.

Tovah, though, feels skittish this evening. She's maybe not used to Fraz's attentions. Why that weird leer when he passes the salad? Perhaps she's just distracted. The office is still an awful, ceaseless strain. The twins put up a sophisticated front, but are fundamentally feral. Home life buckles under heaps of needs.

"Lisa, David, how's school?"

"Daddy, I'm glad you asked," Lisa says. "It's a fucking shitshow."

"Lisa, can you be more specific."

"Okay, Daddy. School's like a factory where they make these little cell phone accessories called people."

"It's more like a tool and die factory," David says. "They turn us into tools and then we die."

"I like that," Tovah says. "You're both very creative."

"Like you, Mommy," Lisa says.

Later she can cash in the points she's just won for candy or a sleepover with her friends.

"Hey, what about me?" Fraz says. "I'm creative. I've been creative my whole life."

"Of course, Daddy," says David, always the weak link in the united front against Fraz.

"Anyway," Fraz says, "you're not wrong in your analysis, kiddos. But you still need to learn. And get good grades. If only to create more choice in your lives."

"They get top grades," Tovah says.

"I know they do, sweetie. Which is amazing given how much they play video games or spend time on their phones."

"We're just showing support for the company Mommy works for," David says.

"Well," Fraz says, "I guess we'll all work for Dieter Delgado someday."

"I hope so," David says. "He's got all the money in the world."

"In my day," Fraz says, "that was a strike against you. In my day what mattered was something they used to call soul."

"That was a dumb fucking day, bro," David says.

Maybe he's not such a weak link.

"Don't you ever say 'bro' at my table again, David."

"But is it really your table? Didn't Grandma gift it to us when she got a new one?"

"*Gift* it to us? *Gift* it? I hate that. Where did you get that? School? What's wrong with 'give'? 'Give' isn't good enough? Everyone has to *gift*? Do you like that, Tovah?"

"Like what?"

" 'Gift.' 'Gift' as a . . . what do you call it?"

"A verb?"

"Yeah."

"I don't know, Fraz. I'll have to think about it."

"You're the poet."

"Am I?"

"May we be excused?" Lisa says.

"You may," Fraz says. "You may and you can."

The twins run off down the hall.

"They didn't bus their plates."

"Let them be kids," Fraz says.

"I need some adults around here."

"I'm sorry, Toves."

Fraz stacks the dishes, carries them into the kitchen. Tovah follows with bowls.

"Did you know he's friends with Nat Dersh?" she says.

"Who is?"

"Dieter Delgado."

"No, I did not. Who told you that?"

"Nat did. In passing. He mentioned that Dieter Delgado had reached out to him with some financial opportunities."

"When did Nat tell you that?"

"At that dinner thing, that horrible night. I told you how I stormed out of there."

"We never really talked about that. Did that bastard come on to you? Did he try to gift you his johnson?"

"No. Not really."

"That motherfucker."

"It's okay, Fraz."

"How is it okay?"

"Just leave it alone."

"You want me to leave it alone? He hits on you."

Tovah offers Fraz her "sly eyes," strokes his arm. "What about you? Don't you ever want to hit on me?"

"God, no!" Fraz says. "I mean . . . I didn't mean . . ."

"I know what you meant."

"You don't, Tovah. It just came out funny. I meant I don't want to be like Nat Dersh. Be all weird and slimy about it."

"But you *are* weird and slimy about it. And it's been a while. Do you want me to pretend I'm pregnant?"

"What? How does everybody know about that?"

"You don't clear your history."

"I do! Look, let's not do this right now. I'm going for a walk."

"No," Tovah says. "I'm going for a goddamn walk. You stay here with the kids."

———

Tovah leaves and Fraz dons his enormous, pretentious headphones for the kitchen cleanup, streams nineties alternative rock classics, all those fuzz pedals and alienated plaid.

Somebody tugs at his shirt. It's David. Should he share his music with his boy? What if the kid scoffs at the plaintive wails of white junkies from the Northwest? That could wound a dad. Fraz holds his headphones out. David waves him off, nods at the intercom on the kitchen wall. Tovah must have forgotten her keys.

A moment later there's a knock. Lisa runs to answer it. The visitor's voice is thick, the words garbled. Heavy steps hammer down the hallway. A large figure swoops into the room.

"Major Van Brunt," Fraz says, the consonants caught in his throat.

The old commando smiles.

"Young man."

"Kids," Fraz calls. "Stay in your room. Daddy needs to talk to his friend."

"I do come in friendship."

"Not like before, I hope."

"I don't eat the excrement of prepubescent children anymore, if that's what you are so cleverly alluding to. I cured myself of that obsession."

"How did you do that?"

"Acupuncture, mostly."

"Congrats. So, can I help you with something?"

"I'm here on behalf of Mr. Dersh."

"I assumed as much. Funny, we were just talking about Nat. And Dieter Delgado."

"Well, since you mention it, yes, Mr. Delgado has asked Mr. Dersh to help him on a special project. They both see a lot of potential in mental archery. They want to help. Inject some capital. Create more powerful platforms for the message. Mr. Dersh thinks it could be like a spiritual online academy. Like the ones for kids about math and science. But this would be for everybody. A way for them to link up. And share a belief system. He sees things really taking off in the period right before total collapse and the big die-off. When there are still revenue streams available."

"Aren't we in that period already?"

"Maybe. There are always sub-periods."

"Why is it you telling me this? Aren't you in charge of his security?"

"I wear more hats these days. Besides, I am merely conveying his message. Will you help arrange a meeting between my employers and Hark?"

"No. That's not what Hark's about."

"Perhaps Hark should decide what he's about."

"He just wants to help people focus."

"We want to help him help people focus."

"And make an enormous profit from it."

"Why is that bad?"

"Honestly? I'm not totally sure. But I've always had this feeling that it's really hard to genuinely help people and also make a gigantic profit. You do one or the other. I was just trying to explain this to my son."

"Your ethical model is very outdated."

"Or maybe it's cutting-edge."

"I don't think you have the rigor for resistance. Or the moral drive. Or the intelligence."

"Could be true."

"Might as well be dumb and reasonably well-off."

"Not this way, man."

"It must be nice to be able to afford such principles."

"Believe me, I can't afford them. That's the point of having them."

"Very well, I guess we made a mistake. You're not the man we thought you were."

"Sorry to disappoint you."

Van Brunt reaches into his jacket and takes out a cigarette, lights it, begins to unbuckle his belt.

"What are you doing?" Fraz says. "There's no smoking here."

Van Brunt takes out his wide, pale penis, slaps it into his palm. Fraz is confused, impressed.

"What are you . . . ?"

"I have my guesses," Van Brunt says, "but I don't really know how much you can take if you decide to oppose the interests of Mr. Dersh and Mr. Delgado. But I wish to show you what I can take defending those interests. Now, what I'm about to do, I learned this from my classmate Bill Belichick during my exchange year at Wesleyan. The man was a genius even then."

Van Brunt clenches his teeth, jams the cherry of the cigarette into his cock flesh.

The stink of burnt skin carries across the kitchen.

"What the hell!" a voice calls.

Van Brunt winces, buckles up his pants.

Tovah stares at them from the hall.

"There's no smoking here!" she says. "What's the deal?"

"My apologies," Van Brunt says, tosses his cigarette over Fraz's shoulder into the sink. "Wretched habit."

Van Brunt brushes past Tovah, limps off toward the front door.

"It's not a habit," Tovah calls. "It's an addiction. Take it from me, you have to accept that to quit."

"Sorry," Fraz says.

"What is that smell? Not the smoke. Something else."

"I'll tell you later."

"I take a little walk and you invite a buddy over to suck on cigs? What is going on with you, Fraz? I'm worried."

"You should be, sweetie."

Twenty-two

L egend tells us," Hark says, "that an Austrian reeve, or bailiff, if you will, named Gessler, erected a pole in the village of Altdorf. Upon the pole he hung his cap and ordered all who passed to honor it with a reverent bow.

"One day, celebrated Alpine activist William Tell arrived with his son and made it a public point to ignore the command. Gessler was incensed. He arrested the Tells and sentenced both man and boy to death, with the now notorious caveat: If Tell could split an apple set atop his son's head, they'd both go free.

"Tell was a crossbow specialist, but he must still be counted as one of the great archers in history. He fired a bolt and halved the apple. What was his son thinking in this moment? What dire sensation danced along his scalp? We will never know. When Gessler saw those apple halves tumble to the soon-to-be-Swiss-national grass, he knew he had to keep his promise: spare the Tells. But he noticed that Tell had drawn two bolts from his belt. 'Why two?' asked the brutal, sly, vain, paranoid (though this is all speculative) Gessler.

" 'If I'd missed,' Tell said, 'and killed my son, the second bolt was for you.'

"Whereupon Tell was clapped in irons and sentenced to death, this time with no chance for clemency. The manner of execution decreed is worth noting. Gessler announced that Tell was to be bound and gagged with an apple. Bound with rope, that is, and gagged with an apple. The archer who could 'skewer the fruit,' as Gessler may or may not have phrased it in his diabolical speaking voice—which, according to no document, bore the lush, nasty cadences of an old-fashioned, stereotypically English Hollywood movie villain—would claim ten gold ingots or the equivalent in grain.

"Before the order could be carried out, however, Tell played a now familiar but then novel trick on the jail guard. He feigned a brain tumor and, as the guard approached to assess the aggressiveness of the cancer and suggest a course for treatment, Tell snatched him by the collar and banged his skull against the bars. Plucking a key from the unconscious guard's belt, Tell flung open his cell door and fled into a brisk and stunning snowscape. Gessler and his Europosse made lively pursuit, and when they rounded the last bend on the mountain switchback, the villain spotted Tell.

" 'Surrender yourself!' he exhorted, but in an instant the founding hero of the Swiss confederation fired a bolt into Gessler's cloudy blue eye. This single shot launched a revolution that would birth a nation dedicated to mountain sports and banking.

"Of course, Suisse credit is also due to Arnold Winkelreid, the other hero of that struggle, though nobody plays 'Arnold Winkelreid' at drunken, murderous, Beat Generation parties because his famous act was to sacrifice his life in order to clear a space in a cluster of enemy pikemen. Also, he used a spear. Is this lecture called mental spearwork? That's a trick question, my friends, because, in fact, it *could* be called mental spearwork. We'd go back to the javelins of the pharaohs, quote the Greek warrior-poet Archilochus. You see, as I mentioned earlier today, mental archery is a metaphor. A place for volleyballs to graze in.

"What happened to William Tell's son, you might ask? I have no idea, I would reply. Obviously he didn't live up to his old man's legacy, but who could? Perhaps if William Tell's son had become a modern Swiss tennis legend and endorser of quality wristwatches, he could have achieved filial parity. But I doubt it. It's difficult to be a son. Daughterhood is harder still.

"But I digress. You see, I understand as much as anybody that we're in a business school right now, and you shining newbies want to know but one thing: What is the relationship between successful entrepreneurship and mental archery?

"Well, let me ask you this. When William Tell sighted down his crossbow in that terrible moment, what do you think he thought? Perhaps he thought, 'Please, God, let me hit the fucking apple.' But perhaps he thought instead: 'Please, God, don't let me hit the boy.' He was good enough that it would be one or the other. He was never in danger of missing both. But which thought, do you suppose, thrummed more fiercely along the tautened bowstring of his mind?

"Close your eyes, friends. Take a deep breath. Hold it. Now let it go. Keep your eyes closed. Keep breathing. Let everything fall away. No thoughts. That's it. Keep breathing. Okay now. Hit the apple. Don't hit the boy. Breathe again. Apple, yes. Boy, no. Apple, yes. Boy, no. Apple, yes. Boy, no. That's it. Breathe. Feel your heart slow. Feel it nearly cease to beat. Apple, yes. Boy, no. Your heart is slowing, easing, maybe, to a lovely standstill. There is so much time between each beat. There is so much space between each beat. So much time. So much space. So much time. So much space.

"Apple, time. Space, boy.

"Apple, time, space, boy.

"Apple, time, space, boy. Apple, time, space, boy. Apple. Time. Space. Space. Space. Boy."

PART TWO

PART TWO

Twenty-three

For many of the folks in the front story, and others, this was the golden age of Hark, the rise of mental archery, the gathering of the forces for focus.

Hark roamed the country to address alternative health symposia and wellness centers. His book, *Mental Archery*, peaked at thirteen on the self-help bestseller list. His videos and podcasts won a devoted following. He became a secret celebrity to celebrities. Movie stars flew him out to Italian villas for long, meandering chats that would end with one question: "How can I help the institute?"

"Please just try to focus a little bit," Hark would tell them. They'd chuckle about how much they hated and loved him for that answer.

He wouldn't take their money. But he was always happy to meet.

He even agreed, against Fraz's faint objections, to talk with Dieter Delgado, who had purchased an old French aircraft carrier and converted it into a floating summer lodge. Hark was choppered aboard.

Up close, Deets resembled a baby owl with his shag cut and round granny specs. The tattooed text along his clavicle read *Body of the Message*.

"This idea of focus is revolutionary, you know."

"It's really not," Hark said.

They ate in the hangar deck at a metal table piled with Dieter's favorite foods: caviar, gravlax, pickled carrots, and vintage Little Debbie snack cakes. The tech lord sipped a tart Grüner pressed from grapes grown topside, in troughs.

"Maybe not to you. Or me. But for millions . . . You see, everybody's been handed this impossible situation. They're supposed to be these multitasking device-enslaved zombies most of the time, and then they are told to make this swift transition into some mindful, authentic human for a few hours each day. And is it a warm, inviting home they are returning to? No, more like a mortgaged-up-the-brown-winker firetrap full of mewlers and bratty attention artists. And it's your fault if you can't just center yourself and deal, and heal? But, Hark, you bring something else to the party. A winning strategy. We've lost that over the years. I'm quasi-Buddhist myself, but the problem with life from that perspective is you can't win it. Not in a palpable, convincing way. What I'm trying to say is that to flourish you must believe that life can be won. That there's a trophy out there. And not just the symbolic trophy for achieving freedom from suffering or peace of mind. Mental archery may be relaxing at times, but it's still about victory. It's about the sudden-death touchdown, the walk-off grand salami. Or, since you like volleyball, the big Godzilla mega-spike. I mean, when you're about to kick the bucket, on your deathbed, or death futon, or whatever, do you want to be thinking: Well, good thing I dodged a little bit of suffering by learning to quell my desires, reduce my expectations? Or do you want to be running around in ecstasy on the hoops court of your dying mind, all your teammates and fans screaming your name because you just banged in the winning shot from fifty-eight feet out? For me, it's always going to be the latter. And that's what Harkism is all about, Hark."

"I see what you're getting at," Hark said. "But I definitely don't agree. Could I have more ice?"

Twenty-four

For Fraz and Tovah, it was not the golden age of matrimony.

It was not even the golden age of wanting to be in the apartment at the same time.

Tovah went out at night with friends. Fraz busied himself with work for the institute, wrote supplementary material for Hark Hub, ran errands, booked more corporate appearances. Kate provided small stipends to those closest to Hark. It was nothing like a salary, but now Fraz could cut back on the tutoring jobs, or begging Tovah for cash.

Nights Tovah went out to the movies or a poetry reading, Fraz settled into fresh rhythms with the twins. They explored new freedoms, extra screen time, multiple desserts. He knew he was a lousy father for not teaching them to suffer, to cultivate patience and grit. But he also knew they would suffer later anyway. His father had been strict, and the result was an underachieving slob of a son. His father had also drilled a football into Nat Dersh's testicles for no obvious reason. Fraz did not doubt that story. Frank Penzig had been a decent man but stunted, full of talk but unable to communicate an honest feeling. Was Fraz much better?

What Fraz wanted to communicate to Tovah was how badly he wanted to communicate with her. Also, it had been so long since Tovah resembled a sympathetic audience. Maybe this was part of the problem, but her approval, her belief in his buried worth, had always been his sole source of self-esteem. Lately, without her approbation, he felt like one of those insect husks they were always finding on the windowsill, swiping into the dustpan.

Some nights he left the apartment to walk around the city, eat a cheap snack. There was a tiny bar where women danced. He got to know the owner, an ex-soldier named Toby.

"Married?" Toby asked one night, pointed to Fraz's ring.

"Yes," Fraz said, watched a woman in sneakers and underpants bob on a milk crate.

"You shouldn't come here."

"Why not?"

"It's not going to help."

"Yeah?" Fraz smiled. "Tell me, what will help?"

"Marriage counseling with a certified mental archer," Toby shouted over the music.

"Are you kidding?"

"You know about mental archery?"

"Maybe," Fraz said.

"It works. We got into it in my Special Forces unit. Our focus was unbelievable. I'll tell you, the guy who invented it should get a Pentagon contract. The combat applications are huge. But it's carried over into civilian life. Saved my marriage. See, if you do the poses together you'll learn how to talk. Otherwise your relationship is finished. Toast. Pink mist. Just start with a wound pose, like Festering Philoctetes."

"Seems a little excessive," Fraz said.

"Excessive? You're guzzling well drinks from a plastic cup at twenty-seven dollars a pop. Just so you can look at some chick's bra. Talk to me about excessive."

"Why are you telling me this? Don't you want me as a customer?"

"Not really," Toby said. "We're hoping to bring in more of a young, hip, polyamorous client base."

"But it's a strip club."

"It's post-cis neo-vaudeville burlesque. We're revitalizing the form."

"It's a strip club."

"No, man, you're a fucking strip club."

Twenty-five

Amid the herbalist circulars, office supply catalogues, charge card teasers and stalker missives that even in this digital age still strive to capture Hark's attention with their printed exhortations appears a letter with a name and return address that Fraz, retrieving mail at the institute's PO box, happens to recognize: Meg Kenny, 34 Clark Creek Road, Pickering, New York.

Fraz resists the urge to steam the envelope open, or inquire, via an internet search, into alternative methods of stealth encroachment. Instead, he takes the letter straight to Hark, who at that moment squats, sockless, on Kate's couch. The young master's faraway stare puts Fraz to mind of a sea captain who glimpses a dire churn on the horizon, perhaps the sign of something gigantic, kraken-y, brined with a prehistoric, ship-splintering grudge.

"What's this?" Hark says, takes the envelope.

"Remember the waffle town?"

"Yes. I do."

Hark tugs out the letter. His lips twitch with vowel shapes as his eyes swivel down the page.

"What does old Meg have to say?" Fraz says.

"She's not old."

"No, I don't mean—"

"Shhh," Hark says, motions for Fraz to peer over his shoulder, read along.

Dear Hark,

Thought I'd try something very old-fashioned and write you an actual letter with pen and paper and an envelope and even, when the time comes, a stamp. Is this crazy? I hope you can handle it!

It was thrilling to see you on that TV program, sticking it to that cynical afternoon talk show d-wad. All you did was make him look dumb and gain many new recruits to the beautiful practice of mental archery.

I guess I should tell you I'm freaking out. Todd is dead. I don't know how else to say it. It happened nine months ago. He had a flat on the thruway and while he was changing the tire a bus came along. The driver said he never saw him. It was twilight and Todd didn't even have his hazards on. Idiot. Fuck, it's been awful. He was often a bastard to me but I really loved him. It's been a horrible grieving process. But I did remember something you said, something about a lean dog, a hungry dog, that would take Todd away? Do you remember this? I thought you were just being weird. Because you are kind of weird, even though you are basically my guru. You see, Todd was hit by a Greyhound bus. What the hell? How did you know, Hark? I bet you don't even know how you knew.

I think you are more than even you might suspect.

You guide me in all things these days. And I need guidance. See, Todd knocked me up before he died.

Little Menny (Menelaus) is of course the greatest thing that ever happened to me, but it's hard being up here in this

town all alone (except for Menny, of course), trying to make
ends meet even as the municipality keeps eliminating my jobs.
(I am no longer town historian.) It's been a strange year and
a half, to say the least. I should probably thank you because
I used a lot of your mental archery techniques giving birth. I
had Menny at home (the town cut most of my benefits and I
wanted to save money for when the baby came). I had a friend
from high school who happens to be a midwife and she took
good care of me leading up to the birth and then the nutti-
est thing happened. The night my water broke I called her up
and she told me to chill out for a while, read a book, watch
a movie, she'd be over soon. But she never came. Hour after
hour went by and she never came. I called some other friends
and they weren't around and this midwife still hadn't come.
Turned out she'd swerved away from a box turtle in the road
and totaled her car. She was fine but in the hospital and certainly not well enough to catch a freaking baby. I didn't know
any of this, though, and was about to call the hospital when
my uterus went apeshit.

   I hadn't been really checking my dilation because the
contractions were coming on strong and it was all I could do
to just squat while I held on to the bedpost. Even when the
contractions were over it took me all of that time to recover
from the pain and then another wave would come smashing
in. To be honest, I was kind of out of it and I don't remember
everything but at some point I managed to stagger over to
the bureau and grab a hand mirror and I held it down there
and I could really see how wide I was getting. Soon a little
bit of Menny's head started to appear with each contraction.
I guess they call this crowning, but it didn't feel very royal
at the time. Sorry. What I thought then was that I was really
thirsty, and not just for water but for orange juice. I just had
this overwhelming hankering for a tiny sip of orange juice.
But by now the contractions were crashing in hard and fast
and I realized I had about as good a chance of getting to the
refrigerator for orange juice as I did showering, putting on a
dress, and going dancing at Little Pino's Rave-o-Tek out on

the highway. The contractions came now without breaks, and even while screaming and groaning I'd check the mirror and see that tiny slick head pushing out and I flashed for a moment on the most famous exploit of Captain Hector Pickering, the purported spy, which was to lead the charge of a battering crew against the timber gates of Fort Daltry, near where the old trestles are now. Those gates burst open and Pickering and his irregulars captured a dozen redcoats and a hoard of cannon shot—grape, chain and standard. They also seized a lockbox full of poorly drawn maps. The subsequent thievery of these maps would actually be Pickering's doom, as he was accused of selling them back to the British. But even though I was still town historian at this point, most of this wasn't on my mind, just the part about the gates bursting open, because the pain was tremendous and Menny's head was just maintaining its place, not pushing out anymore, and I started to panic, horrified by the idea that my baby might get stuck there, that I wouldn't be able to make the final push and Menny might die right there in the birth canal. I really started to despair, and I was crying now out of fear and anger and also, of course, this insane agony, that sensation, somebody once said, of trying to shit a pumpkin, and at this point of absolute horror I thought of you, or one of your videos, something you said in one of your videos, and I started chanting it, "Au revoir, Chevalier," I said. "Au revoir, Chevalier. Au revoir, Chevalier. The arrow is already home. The arrow is already home." I was squatting there, chanting that, and my arms were literally up in the goddamn air, the Agincourt pose, just like in the video. And I'm screaming, not the prescribed phrase anymore, but something like "Die, French Fucks!" (and I love France, especially baguettes and Camembert!). I'm not even sure what happened next. I remember throwing my hands down to catch the baby, I remember that final wriggle of his foot shaking free of me and then I guess I don't remember much. I woke up hours later to knocks on my door. I sat on the floor, leaning up against my bed. I heard the honk of geese outside. (Geese honk, right?) The floor planks were slick with heaven knows what fluids.

And something was wrapped up in a damp sheet in my arms. Something had a little mouth and fed at my breast in half sleep. This was how I met Menelaus Hark Kenny. I felt like I'd run a marathon, and then, limping to the water station, been jumped by a violent street gang. But I was so happy. The happy hormones flowed. I spent two weeks in the hospital. (Still owe on a nasty bill.)

So, the meaning of this letter is . . . I don't know. I guess I just wanted to say thank you, and for you to know what happened to me. There is obviously no way Menny is your son, because we never even kissed that time you came to Pickering, but maybe you can think of him sometimes. He might not be here if it weren't for your teachings. Someday I'll come down to the city and buy you a drink. You can buy me an orange juice.

> *Love (In the Purest Sense),*
> *Meg*

"I think she likes you," Fraz says. "In the purest sense."

"People," Hark says. "Words."

Twenty-six

Most weeks Hark travels with his trusted road team, Seth and Teal, who've become a secret item, though perhaps not that secret, as Hark mentioned the "audible bliss" venting through the hotel wall on their last trip. He seemed to approve. Kate's jolts of platonic jealousy surprised her. Teal, of course, could fuck whomever she pleased, but she had no right to authentic emotional intimacy with another human, even if Kate had cut her off.

Kate's pique lingered long enough for her to resort to some advanced poses to regain her equilibrium. She focused on an impossibly long and merrily feathered arrow piercing the Amazonian mist and, soon enough, the emaciated chest of a ragged Portuguese conquistador who also moonlighted as a corporate events programmer and who now, impaled, tipped off his makeshift barge, a welcome buffet for a school of carnivorous, needle-toothed fish.

Shaft Impact Visualization is a key component of psychic healing. Today Kate waits for Fraz at a table outside the lately rechristened

Tumescent Vole, sips her macchiato, nibbles the cakey ridge of her leek-and-cheese tart. She savors the phrase "savory tart."

Teal has asked her to check in on Fraz, get a fresh take on his state of health. He's been acting odd, referred to his wife in his last counseling session as an "affection abatement technician," a "master manipulator of the cryptocurrency known as love" and "the thane-drainer supreme, Lady Macbitch." Most days he jabbers on about something he calls the "situational carousel." A judgment of Hark's was echoed among the first archers: Fraz, lately, wields a warped bow. Those were not quite Hark's words. They weren't Teal's, either, but somehow that's the language that got lodged in Kate, the translation into organizational cliché her consciousness effected. The mind is an unsavory mindfuck.

Some construction workers sit on the curb and drink soda just a few feet from Kate's table, their tan boots coated with honest dust. Do they despise her for lollygagging with her exorbitant snack and shade-grown joe? Or would they fancy a leek-and-cheese tart themselves? Screw them for their ambiguity. Besides, their lives are opulent compared to most on earth. Maybe they should tour the slums of Bangladesh before they judge Kate. Are they even thinking about her, these construction workers? Do they know about mental archery? Do they know how bad soda, both diet and regular, is for your body?

Fraz arrives, grabs a chair, straddles it like a sex criminal. He appears to be experimenting with a new grime aesthetic, as evidenced by his sooty hair and stained shirt, the poo-hued streaks on his chin one might acquire canoodling with a manhole lid. Fraz signals the pigtailed server.

"You new?" he says to her.

"Yeah. I only work days."

"So you don't know me."

"I'm afraid not, sir."

"That's good. I'll have what my friend here is having, plus a shot of your rail rye."

"I'm not sure we have a rail rye."

"Trust me, you do. And, hey, what's your name?"

"Olive."

"Olive. I like it. Stuffed manzilla. Right?"

"Uh, thanks."

"Are you just waiting tables until your stripping career takes off?"

"Excuse me?"

"What the hell are you doing, Fraz?" Kate says. "He's a jerk. Forget him."

"I've seen her, Kate. Down at the Alley Cat. She's great."

"Thanks," says the server. "I'm trying to get more shifts there."

"I'll tell Toby you deserve more shifts."

"Thanks. I'll go put in your order."

Fraz cracks his knuckles, his neck, flashes a sequence of dim grins.

"My marriage isn't so great right now."

"You're an ass," she says.

"What's new with you, Kate?"

"I have to pee, that's what."

Kate rises, walks past the zinc bar, spots the president on the mammoth TV in the corner. The man has a bad case of razor burn and his mouth looks bruised. Text crawls beneath him: WE WILL NOT LOSE LIECHTENSTEIN.

Why even watch anymore? It's all either war news or hate talk. Kate slips back out into the sunshine. Fraz's pasty arms look melted into the table.

"Did you know that America is fighting a massive land war in Europe?" Kate says.

"I saw something about that."

"So, Fraz, how are you doing?"

"Well, it's been a little hard, I admit it. Tovah's very testy with me. Says she's fed up. I'm still living at home but things are, I don't know. Fraught? Freighted? Fraughted? The air is so thick you could butter it with a knife. Is that what they say? Anyway, this place. I come here sometimes."

"It's got a new name again."

"I know. But anyway, let's talk about the St. Louis trip."

"I'm glad you're still on board with it, Fraz. We're making preparations now. Hark is giving the keynote."

"The trip will be good for me. Give Tovah and me space for a few days. I hear you're coming along this time."

"Yes, I am."

"It's been a while."

"What's that supposed to mean?"

"It's just nice is all. The old crew back together. Everything with Hark is bigger now. And the money."

"Actually, the money piece is not really coming together. We're getting more popular, but Hark still turns down everyone's offer of funding. Except mine. He says I'm the only one he can trust. Everybody else has an agenda. He's afraid we'll lose focus on focus."

"He's right," Fraz says, sways a bit in his chair, shuts his eyes, squeezes them back open.

"Fraz, are you okay?"

"Fine, you got me. Maybe I don't look as sharp as I could. But I'm operating on a different plane right now. I'm in a new area of operation, spiritually speaking. The speed of life in what I'm beginning to surmise might be an extra-dimensional situation is such that hygiene is a kind of conundrum. Soap dissolves before I can apply it to my skin. One minute I step into the shower and the next I'm standing on the bath mat, perfectly dry, with a fresh towel in my hand. But look at my hands now. Where'd all that grit come from? Looks like machine grease. Did I take a job as a mechanic at some point this morning? Did I live an entire alternate life in the last three hours?"

"Are you on drugs?"

"That wouldn't explain it."

"It would."

"Nothing dramatic as that. I just feel a little . . . disconnected."

"There's a disconnect."

"No, I'm disconnected. Tovah and I, well, our compromises have always made our thing work. She accepted that I'd always be the disgruntled employee of the marriage. And I accepted that she'd be Boss Nag. She signed off on me being as much of a layabout as I could get away with, and I ceded her the moral and ethical high ground, as well as control of the purse strings. And it all seemed to work."

"Sounds perfect. But I didn't hear anything about love."

"That's because you're not listening. One makes these compromises out of love. This is what I tried to get Teal to understand."

"Interesting. But what's changed?"

"I don't know. I think Tovah is tired of her compromise."

"Have you talked about it?"

"Not so much. Teal's out of town. We don't talk much outside of counseling."

"Sounds stressful."

"I haven't been sleeping. I walk around a lot. I think about the bow. And the arrow. But more often the bow. And the boy. And the apple. And also the legacy of the New York Jets."

"What?"

Fraz points past the open door to the crowd inside the Vole.

"Did you know, Kate, that some of those jerks in there have never heard of Joe Klecko? How can you be in a bar—sorry, a pub—in this city and not know about Joe Fucking Klecko? Or Mark Gastineau, for that matter. Remember Mark Gastineau? He wooed movie stars! He pioneered the sack dance! He was the leader of the New York Sack Exchange, for Pete's sake. Those freaks in there, they don't know anything about American football. New York football. They're a bunch of poseurs in Tottenham Hotspurs jerseys."

"There isn't really a National Football League anymore, is there?"

"You can find games if you look."

"What's the New York Sack Exchange?"

"It was the collective name given to the defensive linemen of the New York Jets for a few years in the 1980s. They did righteous work in the backfield, namely slamming overpaid, entitled quarterbacks to the turf. Klecko and Gastineau were the most famous. A Pole and a Frenchman. Like Pulaski and Lafayette, heroes of the American Revolution. Then you had two dudes equally fearsome, Lyons and Salaam. All four together constituted an ethnic and religious rainbow of butchery. The New York Sack Exchange. It was wonderful while it lasted, the violence of football and the brutality of capitalism captured in a single phrase."

" 'Sack' makes me think of other things."

"That's in there, too!"

"Well, you are an original."

"No, I just seem that way to people outside my niche."

Fraz leans toward Kate, pushes his sunglasses off his eyes.

"But here's the main thing," he says. "I'm okay. I've just been, like, really unstringing my bow. Like, a lot. But it's okay. Don't worry about me."

"It's hard for people not to worry."

"I have mental archery in my life. How bad can things get?"

"I know. I appreciate what Hark has given us more all the time."

"Exactly," Fraz says.

"Though sometimes I feel I'm unworthy of his teachings. I used to think they were, if anything, almost too simple. You could even say a little dumb. Don't get me wrong. They're inspiring and necessary. But I clung to a part of me that could be slightly dubious."

"His lips move when he reads."

"Really?"

"I think maybe they do. Doesn't mean anything. He's the exception that proves the rule."

"What rule?"

"Nothing," Fraz says. "But you're right. There's something a little too uncomplicated in Hark for people like us. Thing is, *we've* got to change, not him."

"Teal has said something similar. She thinks there's something holy about Hark. Not really, but kind of, you know? Look at how many people, smart people, have embraced him. So maybe I'm the dumb one."

"No, the problem is that you are savvy. You need to be just dumb enough. That's the only way to enlightenment."

"Sounds funny coming from you."

"Maybe I'm changing."

"Change or die."

"See, that's it," Fraz says. "Change or die. You're already on the road. You're going to be fine."

"Apple, yes. Boy, no."

"Precisely."

"My love is the arrow. My heart is the bow."

"Right on."

"You can't eat a metaphor. You can't put it in your freezer for the winter."

"What?"

"He said that to me once. We were eating falafel."

Fraz clutches Kate's wrist.

"Say that again. The freezer in winter. I know I've heard that somewhere before."

Twenty-seven

I n St. Louis, Hark's suite features a choice view of the Arch. The group gathers for room service salads. Fraz gnaws on a bison burger with truffle fries.

"The mighty Mississippi," Seth the Proctor proclaims from the window. "Lewis and Clark started their journey here."

"Lewis and Clark," Fraz says. "A classic comedy team. Can't remember who was the straight man."

"Probably both," Teal says. "Straight and white."

"Why can't the Arch be considered a gateway to the East?" Fraz says. "T. S. Eliot was born here. Learned to hate Jews here. Did you know he once had dinner with Groucho Marx? I wrote a short film script about it. Or thought about writing a short film script about it."

"Woulda, coulda, shoulda," Kate says. "Who cares about that stuff?"

"Not with a bang . . . ," Fraz says.

"No, probably with a bang. But either way, it's over. Don't be a fool."

"Fraz isn't a fool," Seth says. "He's a jester. And every smart king needs one."

"I'm not a king," Hark mutters from across the room. "And I'm not a doctor."

"And I'm not a jester," Fraz says with his mouth full. "I'm just a troubled bitch."

With the voiced bilabial stop of the first consonant of the last word comes a spray of half-chewed bison niblets.

"Close your freaking mouth, Fraz!" Kate says.

"Close yours, tyrant."

"Just chill the fuck out."

"Outfuck the chill, you."

"That's meaningless."

"It's Elizabethan."

"Stop!" Hark shouts, and they all go quiet. "Could you all please just shut it!"

"Sorry, Hark," Teal says, glowers at the others. "Guess we've all got the jitters. You know, big night and all."

"Big night? Jitters?"

Hark stands, sways, staggers off to his room.

There's been something amiss ever since Hark agreed to attend Soul Tech at the behest of Dieter Delgado. It was Nat Dersh, in fact, who made initial contact with the institute as Deets's envoy. He apologized for Major Van Brunt's autoerotic auto-da-fé in Fraz's kitchen. Hark accepted the apology on behalf of the Penzigs.

Agnostic silicon barons, evangelical entrepreneurs, representatives from the Vatican's social media wing, internet imams, public atheists and assorted bandwidth hustlers have all gathered to reflect on the various streams of contemporary life—spiritual, ethical, cultural, technological—before robots seize the planet for good, though it's clear most guests have just come for the all-night dance party. Delgado means to spring Hark on the crowd at tonight's keynote, an international mental archery breakthrough.

"Hark's days in the minor leagues are over," Dersh told Teal and Seth in a preliminary meeting. "The archer has come to the Arch. A prophet's moment."

Hark seems put out by the whole affair, as though still ambiva-
lent about the future of his movement. Fraz has heard him question
Delgado's motives in muted ways, but Hark appears officially delighted Deets has added mental archery to the list of free employee
programs, invited Teal and Seth to lead classes on the Manhattan
campus. Cal Kronstadt, Tovah's boss, now carries a tiny bow he
strings and unstrings to calm his nerves. Tovah also reports there's a
new large meeting room called Faux Bow Pose, right between Fixie
and Australian Meat Pie. Still, the more attention Hark receives, the
more sullen he becomes.

His talk is just a few hours away.

"Is he drunk?" Seth asks.

"He's not drunk," Fraz says. "He never drinks."

Seth nods, gestures to Teal to follow him out the door.

"A little pregame nook-nook?" Fraz says.

"They have to go down to the stage and block out their poses,"
Kate says.

"What, they're going to flank him like go-go dancers?"

"Hark may need that."

Later they knock on Hark's door to rouse him. Fraz films the
expedition. For the Harkives.

"Come in."

Hark lies in bed, eyes pitched to the ceiling.

"Howdy, there," Kate says.

"Yes, absolutely," Hark says. "Howdy. Boy, howdy."

"How are you feeling?"

"Much better."

"They always say," Fraz says, "bad dress rehearsal, great opening
night."

"There was no dress rehearsal," Hark says.

"I think Seth and Teal are having one."

"Oh. Who says that anyway?" Hark says.

"Who says what?"

"About dress rehearsals?"

"Theater people," Fraz says. "I did some theater in college and
there were these theater people around. Future theater people. But

they already knew the adages. Like it's not the size of the part, it's the size of the actor."

"I don't get that," Kate says. "Do you mean midgets? Or the obese?"

"It's about what you can do with your role, whatever its size," Fraz says.

"Oh."

"Like Fraz here," Hark says, leans up on an elbow, reaches for a bottle of water on the nightstand.

"What do you mean?"

"How do you feel about the size of your role?"

"Honored."

"And what is the size of your patience?"

"Enormous."

"Don't give me that."

"Hark, what can I say? I'm a Harkist. I just want to be in the circle, contributing."

Fraz almost shudders from his candor, wonders if he won't be believed precisely because he's telling the truth.

"No you don't. You want more. Always grasping for more."

"Not from this. I'm satisfied."

"I'm not satisfied. I want less. I want out."

"Please," Kate says. "You're tired. We're all tired."

"You're right," Hark says. "Get out of here. All of you. I need to nap."

"After," Fraz says. "You can nap after. You just have to go downstairs for a little bit. You want to help people focus, right?"

"I guess. Maybe."

"Well, here's the big chance. They're all waiting."

Hark drains the water bottle, tosses it at Fraz, who whiffs tequila vapors. Did Hark raid the minibar?

"Who's waiting?" Hark asks.

"Everybody. In the auditorium. And around the world. There's a streaming simulcast. Dieter Delgado is hosting it himself."

"I never gave him permission."

"Somebody did."

"The Proctor, I bet."

"Come on, Hark, they want to hear about the arrow."

"Okay, then. Let's tell them about the arrow."

"That's it," Kate says.

"Help me up."

"Here you go. Now let's put your jacket on."

"This is my moment."

"Yes," Kate whispers. "Your shining hour."

"My shining seven minutes."

"That's it!" Fraz says.

Seth and Teal hit the stage, tunics aglint, strike a series of mental archery poses—Priapic Centaur, Roaring Rama, Encircling Sioux, Cantering Hun—to a medley of tunes that alternate between Andean pan flute and intergalactic Celtic.

The crowd hoots, screeches. Fraz and Kate march Hark through the backstage corridor. Kate kneads Hark's shoulders, Fraz whispers into his ear.

"Apple, yes, boy, no, apple, yes, boy, no. Walk in the shadow of the shaft. Sing to the hum of the bow. Arrows of outrageous fortune, baby. Arrows *con pollo*. Bring the bow! Bring the wound!"

Fraz spots Nat Dersh at the end of the corridor. Between up-jabbed thumbs he holds aloft a computer tablet with Dieter Delgado on the screen.

"Tell it, mental archery man!" Dieter whoops, famous for his open office battle cries. "Actuate the world!"

Hark gives a hollow nod.

"Did he hear me? What the fuck?"

Dieter leans out of frame.

"Come up to the suite later," Dersh says.

"We have the best suite in this place," Fraz says.

"You have the best one they advertise. We're in Suite Z. There's no button for it in the elevator. We'll have somebody bring you guys up."

Kate shoves Hark forward.

"That's it, almost there," Fraz says.

Fraz is startled by the figure at the podium. It's a person-sized robot, a model from 1960s TV shows, with shiny, tubular arms, pincer hands, treads for feet. The robot's face is a flat screen on which Dieter warms up the audience, which seems odd to Fraz because it sounds like he's been yukking it up for a while, though he just whooped at Hark from Nat's tablet a few seconds ago.

". . . who with his methodology and philosophy, not to mention his personal grace, has changed my life, and I think will change the lives of many others over the months to come. Ladies and gentlemen, Hark Morner."

Hand thunder.

"Fraz," Hark says. "I'm sorry about before."

"You have nothing to be sorry about."

"Someday you'll remember saying that. You may even chuckle. A gentle, rueful moment in your wheelchair."

"My what?"

Hark shuffles out to the stage. The mandroid swivels to embrace him but Hark stiff-arms the robot away. Dieter laughs on the screen face, but Fraz tracks confusion in the wunderkind's eyes. Dieter recovers, mugs for the crowd, points to Hark.

"Crazy Genius Alert!"

Hark studies the audience for a moment. The applause dies down.

"Greetings, friends!"

"Greetings, Hark!"

"Thanks for your warm welcome. I just want to say . . . hmm, what do I want to say? I'm just a little . . . I don't know. Shit. Sorry. Wait. See, they wanted me to get this down to seven and a half minutes. One of the organizers called me and said that this was going to be a process, me learning how to get my talk done in seven and a half minutes, because everybody at the confab was very busy, that's what she said, you are all incredibly busy, doing what, I don't know, trying to make a buck, get laid, land a new job, have just one fleeting moment of human feeling, perhaps a friendly glance in the glass elevator over there near the fountain; but at any rate you are all fantastically busy, buying an iced cappuccino, checking your messages, buying an iced latte, posting a selfie in front of the glass elevator, trying to compress your presentation into even fewer minutes so you won't, as the organizer put it, waste people's chronocredits. I don't want to waste your chronocredits. I really don't. Anyway, I'm honored to be here. In St. Louis. Where they used to make the beer, right? I remember that old St. Louis beer. I used to drink it in stunning quantities. Tallboys, longnecks, pony cans. I loved to crack open a cold one. I haven't done so in years. Though I had a little something tonight. A little firewater, you know. But, hey, listen. My name is Hark and I say listen. Hark. That's my real name, you know. My mom's idea. She was from somewhere else. Goofy, right? So Hark is my real name. But I'm not the doctor you think I am. It's a heartbreaker, I know, but I'm not a fucking doctor. But I like it when people call me doctor. Who wouldn't? Those cruds I called friends back in my youth, they'd laugh so hard if they knew that people called me doctor, or even listened to what I said. But, anyway, I'm off point right now. On point would be me getting everything all nice and tight so all the busy people can hear my message. But the fact is, as I keep telling everybody, I don't have a message. There is no core philosophy, no Vedic truth, no Confucian wisdom, no grand Western synthesis, no radical breakthrough in the human endeavor. I just have a few techniques to help people focus. At the office or at home. For whatever reason. Maybe just so you hit a few cross-table winners in a weekend Ping-Pong match. Or have a quickie with your lover before your spouse or partner bursts into the bedroom. Or have a quickie with your spouse or partner before your child comes home from choir practice. Or a quickie with your child before . . . just shitting you. Incest jokes. Child abuse jokes. Why do people love them? Because they're true. But maybe, and I'm onto a new thing now, you just want to look focused while achieving nothing in the workplace, or workspace, or the site-specific location wherein the activities that earn your wage are enacted. That's all. Now, see, I'm a fairly intelligent guy when I'm not, well, I keep landing on the word 'unspooling.' I know some of this sounds ridiculous. So make of mental archery what you will. Perhaps there is nothing to it. Maybe I'm a charlatan, a huckster, a pseudo-spiritualist spinning off some old yoga memes. But who isn't? I mean, sometimes it seems like you've got to be a serious con artist just to get your basic needs met. Food, heat in winter. You have to be some moist-lipped carnival barker outside the bright tent of your suffering just to get a fellow human being to care one itty-bitty-assed iota about your pain. Dignity, subtlety, they're dust, kids. Maybe we don't deserve them anymore. Perhaps all we can manage, if we're lucky, is a little fucking focus. Because we're all over the place. All of us. Our brains are gruel. The forest has been cut down, along with the trees. We're just twitchy, reactive, hysterical beasts. We're not connected by technology. Just the opposite. And our natural networks are down. And we've got no fight left in us. That's why, for instance, we have one thieving government after another and why we let rich people—oh, I guess that's a lot of you—mash our souls to a fine, dank paste and why there's an army marching across Europe toward our shores. To destroy us? To liberate us? Is anybody certain? And who's us? Who's anybody? We're too distracted to ever even listen to ourselves enough to find out. Do we know what we're saying? I don't. And I'm the expert. I'm the focus master. But I'm not. But I'm trying. Because maybe there really is something to this. More than you think. I mean, all that history I'm always regurgitating? That stuff is real. Except for what I make up. And maybe I am more of a doctor than a lot of those board-certified bozos. Not for me to say. I give it all up to you. If you have the capacity to love, take it. But if you don't have the love in your heart, that's ball game. Got it, brothers and sisters? Okay, I'm done. Fuck this techpig confab and fuck your hearts. I'm going up for naparooni number two."

Fraz's phone buzzes several minutes after Hark, for his finale, falls to his knees, sticks his ass in the air and crawls off.

"You guys plan all that?" Dersh says. "Just terrific."

"Are you turning it around?" Fraz asks, glances around the suite. Hark's back in bed. Teal and Seth whisper near the window. Kate eats strawberry-yogurt-coated pretzels, stares at a framed poster announcing the Louisiana Purchase Exposition of 1904.

"No, I'm not turning it around. I don't work at fucking Glyph Systems. I'm telling you, your boy is shit and he's done. I can't believe you strung me along like this, Fraz."

"I didn't string you along. I told Van Brunt months ago that this kind of thing wasn't what Hark was about."

"You say a lot of shit, Fraz. First you want to market Hark. Then you want to shield him from commerce. You flip-flop."

"My beliefs evolve."

"Flip-flop."

"Evolve. What about Dieter?"

"He left early. Hark really is finished, Fraz."

"Yeah?"

"We just got word that some scientists are going to announce the discovery of a gene."

"A gene?"

"A focus gene."

"Come on."

"That's right, who needs mental archery now? Doctors will be able to go into your DNA with a goddamn motherfrigging micro-wrench."

"I'm not sure it works quite like that."

"It works exactly like that, you dumb Penzig. A microscopic wrench, or pair of nano-tiny needle-nose pliers. They just go in and tweak your strands. No bull-dinky, no silly pajama poses. Voilà! Focus forever! Take care of yourself, fakey cuz."

Fraz punches the air with his fisted phone.

"Shit!"

"Dersh?" Kate asks.

Fraz sinks down on a cushioned stool.

"Lewis and Clark," he says, after a while. "They were both the bananas. Sacajawea, she was the feed."

"What?" Kate says.

"It's vaudeville. Neo–post-vaudeville."

Kate says nothing. Soon Fraz snoozes on his stool.

Twenty-eight

t's been a while since Fraz left the apartment for more than a school walk, a milk run. He hasn't been to the gym in weeks. He pictures particular barbell plates in lonely repose on foam mats, his old, cold buddies.

Fraz has not forsaken domestic affairs. He'll perk up for food prep or homework help, but seems otherwise stuck in some personal dusk. At his ablutions, he emits porpoise squeaks like a furred, slightly portly man from Atlantis. Dinnertime, he speaks admiringly of the obstinance of kale, but suggests it may suffer from a Masada complex. Tovah can't say she's worried about him. She's never not worried about him. But now the poor guy seems completely spaded out, just a ragged hole in the garden of himself.

Perhaps he secretly awaits his mentor's return. Nobody's heard from Hark Morner since he fled that St. Louis hotel near dawn. You can watch him on the security video—thousands already have—witness a confused-looking Hark stagger through the lobby in mysteriously shredded track pants, curse a departing airport shuttle that stops to pick him up.

Ancient archery remains Fraz's sole topic of interest. He continues to conduct research and compile data, employs a scholastic methodology similar to his master's. The product of his toil is a daring blend of history, myth, rumor, and old-fashioned falsehood. He tells Tovah the stories of Zhou Tong, revered instructor of the Song dynasty. Zhou's tiny, delicate arrows, fletched with honey-stiffened strands of his middle-aged daughter's pubic hair, could clean-split a beetle shell. Or Minamoto no Tametomo, who sank a wooden war galley with one flawless shot to the hull. The other day Tovah found Fraz at the kitchen table reading an article on his phone.

"The Amazon archers of legend," he said, "performed mastectomies on each other."

"Yes, I've read about it."

"They did it for a less cumbersome draw."

"Makes sense, I guess."

"Would you do that?" Fraz said, smiled up at his wife. "Could you?"

"Are you asking me to?" Tovah said. "Most men want their wives to get other kinds of surgery."

"I'm not asking you to do anything. I'm just making a point."

"Which is?"

"Focus is everything."

Tovah senses odd realignments in her husband. He enunciates more, employs awkward or antique figures of speech. "Hang me if I'm wrong, but I do believe we are plumb out of dishwashing pods." He also tests out new walks: a gangland swagger, a street urchin's limp. She thinks maybe he has a tumor, or is sleeping with a prostitute, though where would he get the cash? A guy like him would have to eat cat food for months.

Fraz did tell Tovah he regretted not professing his love more often. She asked what had brought this on and he said a conversation with his new friend Toby. He adored her and wanted things to be good again. They'd slackened off lately, but couldn't they try another round of marriage counseling with Teal?

"Really?"

"Yes, we need to do some work. Especially me."

This wasn't the Fraz she knew. She told him she was touched. She would think about it. He looked disappointed. She couldn't tell him the truth, that she had already begun to beat a path to post-Fraz life, envisioned herself ordering new appliances after letting him keep the wedding toaster, the coffeemaker. She watched the feed from her mind's eye, her inner internet, her MeTube, a clip from the future: Tovah at the laptop with a cup of tea and a vase of tulips on the desk beside her, arranging logistics for the new conditions, deciding which weekends Fraz would get the kids, divvying up school vacations. That was one truth she couldn't bear to divulge. Another was that she'd already been out with Nat Dersh and that they'd done some light Frenching after a late lunch of oysters and Dover sole.

But this winter Saturday feels different, the descent of some heedless good mood. They make pancakes, joke around with the twins, trade shy, playful looks. These past few years, have they been nothing but a glum dream? Here of a sudden is mirth, rounds of Risk, Parcheesi. The sun funnels through the window. Last week's snowfall melts in skinny pools on the fire escape. Renewal beckons, if they'd just throw on their coats, heave themselves out into the day.

They march up to Riverside Park with cheese sandwiches, dried apricots, a soccer ball. It's a throwback excursion. Fraz is warm and loose, defends the twig-marked goal from twin-launched kicks with goofy verve. Every few minutes he runs over to Tovah for hugs, nuzzles. The old affections bubble up. She wants to cradle this frail, tiny feeling, carry it home, feed it cashew milk from an eyedropper.

Later, shoes and socks soaked in spring thaw mud, Tovah announces that it's time to head home. She's loath to spoil high spirits, but the sun's almost down, the park is cold. She's made the wise decision. Does she not possess the wise pussy?

"Yes," Fraz says, "it's getting dark. Just a few more minutes."

Tovah watches Fraz from a few yards off as he grips each twin's ankle, carousels them with a certain reckless-seeming but, of course, utterly safe fun-dad velocity. She considers David and Lisa's view as they giggle and twirl, shards of sky and the darkening green of the trees whirling by them upside-down, a magic movie that will linger in their minds forever, their sprite forms spinning from the spokes of Fraz's powerful arms, the sky a smear of pink above the park, the lights coming on along the avenue to illuminate the wanderings of this fair city's night folk.

Tovah hears a gasp, sees Lisa fly away from Fraz's fingers. Tovah clocks the half-delighted shock in her husband's eyes as he tracks Lisa's ascent, that moment before he perhaps recalls a certain truism about what goes up. Fraz's other hand falls limp, flaps at his hip. David, unlatched, rolls off into moss-fringed mud. Lisa, aloft, sails toward a nearby birch. Her skull smacks the trunk and her body whips around it, flops to the earth.

Tovah's beautiful daughter is a bent, silent heap.

There can be no doubt she is dead.

Twenty-nine

Fraz slouches in the corner of the emergency room, chair turned toward the wall, awaits the blow to the back of his neck, a bolt from the sky.

How long before the deity who doesn't exist smites him for what he's done?

"She's going to have surgery," Tovah says, shakes him. "Tonight."

"Surgery," Fraz says.

"It's okay. They think she's going to be fine. Her brain scans look good. They need to operate on her elbow, actually."

"Her elbow? Her elbow?" Fraz twists in his chair. "That's fantastic!"

"What is?"

"That her elbow is injured and requires surgery."

"She could have problems with it down the line."

"Problems? Are you crazy? She's going to have problems with her fucking elbow?"

"Calm down," Tovah says, points to David, who seems entranced by a window shade, perhaps enjoying a private screening of a film based loosely on his sister's injury.

"Okay, Fraz. I get it. But I've been trying to deal with this while you were doing your catatonia thing. I was really afraid for a while. Now I want to make sure she has full range of motion."

"Me, too. I mean, like, we made that elbow. Didn't we?"

Fraz rises, cups Tovah's chin with his hand, leans in for a kiss. Tovah flinches, wrenches herself free.

"Please, Fraz."

"Please what?"

"Try not to be yourself right now."

"Jesus, what is happening to us?"

"It happened, Fraz. A while ago. Didn't you notice?"

"Of course I noticed. I don't know, I guess I just figured a long marriage has its ups and downs. Joy and suffering. Good runs and rough patches. Look, all things considered, life has been pretty peachy. We haven't even hit our prime cancer years yet. But even when terrible times come, the main thing is to just give all the love you have and soldier on. Right? Am I wrong? Maybe I'm wrong."

"You're wrong. And leave the military out of it. No soldiering."

"What about bivouacking?"

"No jokes, Fraz. They don't work anymore."

"Look, I know I indulge myself, but my love for you, it's still—"

"Tovah," a familiar voice booms. "I came as soon as I could."

Nat Dersh, in road leathers and fawn-colored engineer boots, waves from the door. Fraz recalls mention of a weekend motorcycle club, the Sons of Finance.

"What's he doing here?" Fraz says.

"I called him," Tovah says. "When I was scared and you were out of it. I felt like I needed some backup."

"Backup?"

"Somebody I could count on."

Nat nods to Fraz, takes Tovah's hand.

"I got your last text about Lisa. Thank God."

"Benedict Arnold," Fraz says to Tovah.

"Try holding on to your daughter next time."

Orderlies appear, push Lisa on a gurney, her head and arm wrapped in beige, blood-seeped bandages. Her eyelids flutter and she offers up a weak, stunned grin.

"Oh, sweetie," Fraz says.

A doctor walks over, a lean, pink man with bushy yellow sideburns.

"Hey, everybody," he says.

"You're a different doctor from the one before," Tovah says.

"I'm Dr. Lenz. We're all working together, I assure you."

"Okay."

"So, we took more scans and we think maybe we spoke too soon about being out of the woods, brain trauma–wise."

"What?" Tovah says. "We were talking about her elbow before."

"And there is still elbow talk to be had. But we should prioritize head injury discourse, in my opinion."

"What is your plan, Marty?" Nat says.

Fraz admires Dersh's tone. And how did he suss out the doctor's given name so quickly?

"You're right, I'm sorry, Nat," Dr. Lenz says. "We're going to operate, try to relieve some of the pressure on her brain. We'll also attend to the elbow. We need to prep her for surgery right now. You guys can follow us down. There's a family lounge closer to the OR."

"Oh, poor Lisa," Tovah says, clutches Nat's arm.

"It's okay, baby. They know what they're doing. I brought this guy in. This is the best care possible. I'll make sure of that, I promise."

Fraz lags at the end of the column as they trudge in the gurney's wake. Dersh and Tovah take the lead, fingers laced. Shameless beasts. Fraz revs up for a verbal raid on Nat's morality, but his boy interrupts.

"Daddy, is Lisa going to die?"

"Not today, buddy. Not for a long, long time."

David bursts, a dirty bomb of sorrow. His weeping style is not unlike his father's, up-tempo, puppety.

"What?" Fraz says. "What did I say?"

Tovah turns back to David.

"Sweetie. What's wrong?"

"Daddy says Lisa is going to die."

"What? Fraz!"

"That's not what I meant," Fraz says. "David, stop bullshitting."

"Fraz!"

"Everybody dies, David," Fraz says. "Even Nat here is going to die one day."

"Don't die, Nat!" David says. Nat scoops up David, squeezes him to his chest. David gazes past Nat's ear.

"Hey, Dad," he says, calmer now, a tilt to his head. "Your bald spot is much bigger."

"Is it?"

"Hey, Dad," David says.

"Yep?"

"What's a dolt?"

"A dolt?"

"Yeah."

"Where'd you get that word?"

"I heard Mom call you that on the phone."

"Oh, really? It means a stupid person."

"That's an offensive word."

"What is?"

"Stupid. It's hurt speech."

"Sorry."

"It's okay. Even grown-ups have to learn. At school I'm an ally, not a bystander."

"That's great. We all need to be your sister's ally right now."

"She's a fucking idiot."

"David! No, that's not okay."

"I'm sorry."

"It's okay."

"I thought it was not okay."

"Huh?"

"Daddy?"

"Yes?"

"It's nice to see you."

David reaches out to tousle Fraz's hair. It's bizarre, the boy in his rival's arms. But for a moment the bile subsides. Bile seems silly right now, the four of them shuffling along like some clan of villagers clad in stinky hides, hair caked in blood and vegetable matter, ignorant, afraid, beseeching forces they cannot presume to fathom to spare an innocent child.

Bile is not primordial enough. It's too much of a by-product, a perk. Tonight only the raw states suit, the crazed ones, grave.

What Fraz feels now, like an arrow burrowed in his throat, call it pre-grief.

Thirty

Kate waits for the marrow. Her chair is armless, ugly, its chrome frame stretched with some chemical cloth. It's a chair built to sink into with that sinking feeling, a waiting room chair, bureaucratic, slightly more comfortable—and thus somewhat crueler—than a bench. She imagines her mother or father in such a chair, maybe in the corridor of Kate's old school, summoned for a conference about Kate's problems, or as the headmaster used to put it, her troubles, or even once *the* troubles, as though she spent her extracurricular hours planting pipe bombs in London cafés and not just selling fake ecstasy to prepster goons and writing in her history term paper, "If that pervert Mr. Laigg leers at me again, I'm going to bury my Mont Blanc in his eye jelly."

In another chunk of the multiverse, she could photograph this hideous chair with her phone and text it to her mother and father in a spiteful gesture they would scarcely understand. See, vile guardians, how this furniture harkens (Harkens, ha!) back to the years you destroyed your only child with a no-limit Amex and emotional neglect? But in this sorry sector of existence, Ma and Pa Rumpler are a lost splat on a White Mountains slope.

Kate waits, chats with Nestor, the clinic coordinator, who sits on his desk and picks lint from his smock, taps his clog heel against the desk's wooden modesty panel.

"Katie, where's your friend Teal? The one who came with you a few months ago."

"I don't know, Nes. Why?"

"I liked her. I liked her rage."

"Her rage? How can you tell? She hardly said a word."

"We had our little look-see with each other while you were standing there babbling away. We got real intimate."

"She's been to prison," Kate says.

"She told me."

"With her facial expressions?"

"There are many ways to communicate."

The doors bang open and a nurse sets a cooler on the counter.

"That's you," says Nestor, clipped, official again. "Sign, please. And good luck."

Outside, Kate flags a cab for JFK. She's booked on a red-eye to Lisbon. She can almost taste the *pastel de nata* she will eat in Belém. The café near the beach makes the best in the world, or so the custard tart cognoscenti insist. She hasn't eaten them anywhere else, but it's one of those collective opinions she's willing to abide. The Belém tarts, though not savory, are indeed a scrumptious scandal, as her mother would say of most desserts, as well as some of her lovers, artsy parasites, mostly, like that vigorously untalented sound artist who once applied sunscreen to a twelve-year-old Kate's back with drooling intensity, whispering about ozone depletion and the threat to Kate's "taut, juvey skin."

Men and their guileful trembles, their shudders, their stares. Kate wants to think she's inured herself to these bepenised jackals, to the stab-eyes of strangers, of men, boys, old cruds, cripples, morons, meatheads, nerds. But she knows you never really can. How is it that even the most vulnerable members of the herd moonlight as merciless predators? A withered guy in a wheelchair would rape you if he could. He probably will. It's a technical issue. He'll strive for the solve.

A cab slides up and Kate gets in with her cooler. Somebody already occupies the seat beside her, hoodie'd head tilted away.

This is not how ride-sharing works in this town.

"I'm sorry, I thought this cab was—"

"You are in the right taxi," the person says, with an accent. Though she's only heard this voice once before, a phrase leaps forth.

"Rusty nail," Kate says.

"Hello," Nels says, peels back his hood, reaches past Kate, shuts the door. He grins as though he doesn't grip one of those war knives she's seen in movies, a huge, serrated thing.

Kate looks to the driver. He seems oblivious behind his bullet-proof plastic. The hack license affixed to the separator says the driver's name is Ali Islam. Is that like somebody named Marjorie Judaism or Larry Christianity? She wouldn't know. She wouldn't know how to know. Also, here's this soft-mannered man with a dying daughter nudging her rib cage with the knuckle guard of his knife.

"Please, driver," Nels says. "Take us to Friedrich Douglass and One Hundred and Twenty-third."

"Frederick," the driver says.

"Driver, stop the car. I'm not—!"

Nels clamps his hand over her mouth.

"The driver is part of this, Kate. He's my friend."

The driver stares ahead, his earbud wire trailing over his shoulder. She hears him speak in hushed, kind tones. Is this cabbie on the phone to his therapist as well?

"Your friend, huh?"

"We worked together at a refugee camp."

Kate used to detest those volunteer types she knew in school. They forsook the fabulous to scurry around some ravaged village with bloody diarrhea splashing in their flip-flops, Ebola gibbons screeching overhead. And wasn't the village fucked, basically, by the same forces that allowed their parents to pay half a million so their kids could major in Third World Paternalism at Privilege U? It was more honest to snort club drugs and pretend you were a doomed bohemian starlet. Not that Kate is that person anymore. She carries the marrow. And this gentle, modern sea raider is hijacking the shipment. Is the driver really in on it? Nels cups his hand to let her breathe. Should she bite?

"Be calm and I will let go," Nels says.

He sounds reasonable. Maybe he can be reasoned with.

Kate nods. Nels slides his palm off her mouth.

"When we get out of the taxi," Nels says, "you walk in front and carry the cooler. I will carry the knife. Do you understand?"

"Remember the *Vasa*!"

Kate bites Nels's palm hard. Nels shouts, draws his hand away, punches the seat back near Kate's face.

"Don't be crazy!" Nels says. "I don't want to hurt you!"

"What do you want?"

"The marrow. That's all. And a little time."

Kate leans back against the car seat, tries to breathe.

Islam parks the cab outside a luxury building on Frederick Douglass Boulevard. Nels hustles Kate into the lobby like she's a wounded head of state. They ride an elevator up to a dark corridor. A tall woman meets them, leads them through a door.

Persian rugs and mahogany end tables stacked with papers swerve by Kate as they hurry her into the apartment. Nels guides Kate down to a rocking chair. She watches the driver slip off with the cooler.

The woman from the door approaches. Her hair spills black and silver against her sundress. Eyeglasses swing from a frayed neck cord.

She peers at Kate.

"I'm Shana," she says. "I teach medical ethics at the university. What you're doing here is a brave thing. It's an act of radical empathy. You are exploding the code. Helping those who aren't getting help."

"What if it's against my will?"

"That hardly matters."

"Who are you guys?"

"This is Johnny Islam," Shana says, points to the driver, who has returned to the room.

"It's your dad's cab," Kate says.

"A real sleuth," Shana says.

"You guys are some kind of group?"

"It's pretty vague," Nels says.

"Do you have a name?"

"That would be reckless," Shana says. "Think of us as Doctors Without Borders, but maybe more like doctors without boundaries. And we're not all doctors."

"I'm a doctor," Johnny says.

"That's true," Shana says.

"So, what's the deal?" Kate asks. "You steal from the rich and give to the poor. But instead of money, it's bone marrow and organs?"

"A crude assessment, but not entirely off. And as a lifelong admirer of the rightful Earl of Loxley, I approve. Our organization, a strictly clandestine one, mind you, has many other operations. But Operation Just Harvest is my purview."

"People love that word," Kate says.

" 'Purview'?"

"That, too. But I meant 'harvest.'"

"You know," Shana says, "being attuned to fluctuations in contemporary speech may be amusing and make you feel superior, but it really ain't shit. The tip of the spear is not the tip of the tongue. But a wealthy white American woman wouldn't have any idea of what I'm talking about."

"You're a wealthy white American woman."

"Am I? I'm certainly not wealthy."

"This place isn't cheap."

"It's university housing."

"Shana, she has a point," Johnny says. "You've also got that place upstate."

"Oh, please, you mean the house in Hudson? That's basically a shed with running water, Johnny. That's what that is. Listen, Ms. Rumpler, you look frightened. Don't be. You'll be out of here soon. We're not going to take your organs, if that's what you're worried about. Just what's in the cooler. And you'll be making a large donation to our cause. Off the books, of course. Hark will just have to tighten his belt."

"Hark? What does Hark have to do with it?"

"Everything. Ask Fraz Penzig. Ask him about the archery counselor at his old summer camp."

"You mean ask him right now?"

"Don't be so literal."

"So, there never was a Blenda?" Kate asks Nels.

Nels stands.

"Follow me."

Kate trails Nels into a narrow bedroom. A girl in a purple nightgown lies on a bare mattress, facedown, the cooler and a tray of medical supplies on the table beside her.

"You don't know what you're doing," Kate says. "How do you know it's a match?"

"Nestor made sure," Nels says.

Shana looms from behind, rests a hand on the back of Kate's neck.

"This is a beautiful thing," she says.

They lead Kate back to the living room, the rocker.

Johnny fumbles with a thin vinyl rope.

"I'm better with stitches and stents."

Nels nudges Johnny away, picks up the ends of the rope, ties them into a methodical knot.

"My cousin had a sloop."

The pink marinara, the snazz, the red flag, the crimson lady, the Eric, the tears of the iliac crest, Hematoad punch, Slice of Life, King Gazpacho, the sacred infusion, the marrow arrow.

"You don't have to do this," Kate says.

"Later, you'll be glad," Nels says. "They will ask you if we tied you up. You won't have to lie."

"I get it."

"Johnny, please take the specimen and treat Blenda. We're running out of time."

"May I see her again?" Kate asks. "Blenda? I never saw her face."

Nels looks annoyed but nods his head.

"Blenda!"

The girl edges out of the bedroom. She looks a bit older, but she is the child from the photograph.

"Hello, Blenda," Kate says.

The girl waves.

"You wonder if the weight gain is part of the disease," Nels says.

"What weight gain?" Kate says. "She looks maybe a little under-nourished to me."

"But she is just a fat shit for ordinary reasons."

Nels speaks another sentence in what sounds like Swedish.

"Papa," says the girl.

"I'm sorry, dear. But you sneak candy."

The girl bites her lip, steps back into her room.

"If I'm going to save her life, I need to be honest with her about her obesity."

"Why save her life if you're just going to fat-shame her?"

"Ridiculous Americans."

"Nels," Johnny calls from the door. "I need your assistance."

Nels stands.

"Obviously," he says, "I am very tense."

"I might have some Klonopin in my purse," Kate says.

"I don't do Big Pharma."

"Have you ever tried a Clever Oshosi? Calm you right down."

"A clever what?"

"It's a mental archery pose. Oshosi is a spirit in the Yoruba tra-dition who—"

"Don't let Shana hear you talk that mental bow-and-arrow crap."

"Excuse me?"

Now Shana comes over to Kate, holds up her laptop, a video playing on the screen.

A large man with a dangerous and complicated-looking bow marches toward a lime line in the grass. Spectators in sun hats clap. Kate notes the sour slant of the archer's mouth.

"Looks like he's talking to himself."

"He is."

"Wonder what he's saying."

"He's saying, 'Don't miss, you pathetic shitbag.'"

"You can read his lips?"

"No, I remember. That's me."

"Really? Wow. Did all that self-loathing work?"

"I made the Olympics. Look it up. Barry Buckman."

"I thought you were Shana."

"I was Barry before I made a much-needed change in my life. Do you know what a sin is?"

"Excuse me?"

"In archery?"

"No."

"It means to miss the mark. Maybe we're all sinners sometimes. But I work very hard at not being one."

"Can you untie me?"

"Not yet. You know, many members of our group would like to see Hark dead. They think it would be symbolically fitting if somebody qualified could put a steel-tipped arrow in his left ventricle. But I believe that a series of disbursements could dissuade them."

"What do they have against mental archery? It's a positive message. And pretty harmless, right?"

"It's a sideshow. He's encouraging the consumerist individualism, the navel-gazing, that impedes real change. But we do need cash. So maybe an agreement can be reached."

"An agreement? More like extortion."

"Under the present economic system, the distinction is moot."

Thirty-one

Fraz, asleep on a couch in the hospital lounge, dreams of couches, or one in particular, his home couch, Old Plaid 'n' Scratchy, twin-ruined, torn up from years of leaps, tussles, sneak attacks and bored cushion gnawing, stained by a decade of snack smears and juice box spills. In his dream, the couch spins a few meters above the surface of the moon. Rips mend, splotches lift in granular puffs, the upholstery renewed by low gravity and purifying celestial wavelets.

Tovah pinches Fraz awake.

"What is it?"

Across the room, Nat threatens the doctors with oblique remarks about his connection to the hospital's board of directors.

"She's in a coma," Tovah says, her eyes moist, rimmed red.

"What?"

"Lisa. She has sepsis."

"She has sepsis or she's in a coma?"

"Both!" Tovah says.

"What the hell happened in there!" Nat shouts at one of the doctors, another new one.

"We thought there might be an infection," the doctor says, "but we didn't suspect it could develop that fast. Maybe canine feces on the ground spread into her wounds?"

"Dog shit? You've got to be kidding!"

"I kid you in no way."

The doctor speaks with an Eastern European accent and to Fraz looks young for her profession. But her youthful appearance is probably just a case of good genes, a vegan diet, and Tour de France mountain stage simulations on a stationary bike at dawn. They've always been around, these smiters of mirth, scourge of the carouse-until-your-coronary crowd, who are Fraz's people, though, to be fair, he takes his healthful measures, or at least cultivates his conception of the muscular Jew. Fraz is, after all, a free-weights fiend when he's not washing down Peking duck fat with Trappist ale.

"It is all very curious," the doctor continues.

"Curious?" Nat says.

The doctor may be heart healthy if not exactly heartfelt. Somebody has to wear the white coat.

"Yes, curious. I have seen nothing like it."

"Nothing like it?" Nat says. "And what, in your short career, have you seen? A broken arm? A split lip?"

"Nat," Tovah says. "This is counterproductive."

"Maybe," Nat says. "But I'd still like to counterproduce her ass out of a job. Where's Marty? He was supposed to take care of this."

"Dr. Lenz had another emergency."

"Who the fuck are you anyway?"

"I'm Dr. Musil. We're doing what we must for your daughter."

"You'd better be."

"Hey," Fraz says. "She's not your daughter."

"Mr. Counterproductivity himself rises from his crypt."

Nat stalks off. Tovah lurches in his direction, calls his name.

"You're pathetic," Fraz says.

Tovah rears up, turns.

"No, that would be you."

"Hey, there," Fraz says, ambles over to Dr. Musil. "I hate to have you repeat yourself, but I missed the beginning. Now, I'm sorry for the behavior of . . . that man, but let's try again. I know you guys are busting your buns on this one. Obviously my daughter is going to be okay, but can you give us a general time frame for her recovery? And also, is she in any pain? I hope not."

The doctor studies Fraz, perhaps not quite certain what she sees. Here appears to be a middle-aged American white man with mussed hair, big teeth and a pale, pimpled neck that begs to be cleaved with a voivode's broadsword. He wears shiny basketball shorts, leans over to knead his quad, as though later he might ask her to look at where he tweaked his knee. Why does he apologize for the previous man's ire? Does he believe a polite demeanor will somehow change his child's prognosis?

"I don't know, sir," the doctor says, "whether your daughter will be okay or not."

"What does that mean?"

"It means that nobody knows. We have to wait. But I assure you there is nothing obvious in the situation. She has a high fever and probably her body hurts. We can't put her on painkillers, not yet. Her system is too fragile. We are waiting. We will see. I am sorry I don't have more information."

Fraz returns to the couch, to Tovah.

"Where's David?"

"The sitter's with him."

"Okay."

"One of us should relieve her."

"I'm not leaving."

"Neither am I."

"Nat will do it."

"Really?"

"Of course. Nat loves hanging out with the kids."

"Isn't he too busy actively supporting slavery in the South China Sea and manufacturing cheap pencil boxes? Not to mention trying to co-opt mental archery for global profit?"

"You'd know more about that. He's your cousin."

"He's not my cousin. They were family friends. And lousy ones."

"Let's focus on Lisa. She's the one who needs our energy."

"Of course. You brought it up. Are you sleeping with him?"

"Nat? No."

"Do you want to?"

"I want a lot of things."

"Like what?"

"Like Lisa to get better."

"Good. Yes. Let's concentrate on that."

Fraz takes Tovah's hand.

"I'm letting you hold my hand as a co-parent right now," Tovah says.

"I know."

Fraz thinks about his daughter, her brown curls and dare-you grin, the sharp, elated knowing in her eyes, as though she's seen the future and it's a nonstop birthday party with cakes and prizes, and she's been sworn to secrecy about the coming delights, and also senses, vaguely, the melancholy of a life filled exclusively with prizes and cakes. Okay, sure, he's projecting. Hire a process server, sue him in the court of fatherly love. He recalls Lisa's early crawls more than her first steps, her tiny arms and legs stretched out for exuberant scoots on the hallway carpet, like a baby turtle too quick for her shell. Speaking of animals, a soft menagerie once lived on her bed, dolls collected from every town fair and airport over the years, stuffed pandas, stuffed penguins, stuffed tigers, stuffed moose, her counterpane a glorious, fuzzy preserve of mammal-patterned terry cloth and synthetic fiber batting. But mostly he thinks of what it's like to cuddle together with a book, the moon in the window, the two of them trading off pages, doing the voices of the tree house club or lake raft gang, giggling or tossing the story aside for a moment so they could, in Lisa's words, "just talk." She would ask him questions about planets, oceans, babies, death, drill him on the eating habits of penguins and pandas.

"Apple, yes," Fraz whispers. "Girl, no."

"What?" Tovah says.

"Repeat after me: Apple, yes, girl, no. Apple, yes, girl, no."

"That's absurd."

"Maybe. But how can it hurt? Apple, yes, Lisa, no. Apple, yes, Lisa, no."

"Don't be silly."

"Just say it."

"Really?"

"Really."

"Apple, yes," Tovah says, "my daughter, absolutely, positively, no, you evil goddamn piece-of-shit abyss-pimping fucks."

"Okay," Fraz says. "That's a good start."

Thirty-two

The catfish, who has begun to ooze a viscous turquoise liquid through its dermis, flops on the rostrum, rasps into the microphone. Hark sits beside him, bound with wire to a folding chair, gagged with a candied apple studded with crushed walnuts.

"This guy here," the catfish announces to the darkness. "What a guy. I mean, truly, now and forever, what a fellow. And let me tell you, it was never a picnic, being Hark. Kid came up hard, a wayward youth with predilections. A host of predilections. For powders. For rough sex. Rough on him, I mean. He liked girls to beat the bejesus out of him, which I guess might seem impossible on the face of it, but anyways that was the deal. Poor sap was looped out on plutonium-grade snortables half the time. Sounds fun, maybe, but after a while it wasn't fun, not even for the women, who were, like, believe me, unbelievable, semipro bodybuilders, some of them. He would just loll there, blank-faced, far-off, martyred, with gouges in his chest, blood in his eyes. What a crock! How is that a gas? But I guess he liked it. Or needed it. Might be the only rational reaction to this dung-choked plain of pure suffering we so blithely call the real world. Reminds me, you know, of when I was a young catfish, this time I was swimming with my buddy and we passed by this worm just wriggling there in the water. Yes, Virginia, or whoever the fuck, there is a Santa Claus, and contrary to popular stupidity, even then we knew what fucking water was. Now, of course, I figured out right off that this slimy dangle boy was hooked bait, but my compadre, Pierre, wasn't exactly the Enrico Fermi of the Mississippi flatheads. His folks had been noodled off by yahoos before they had time to teach him much. We were in strange waters, too, a reservoir somewhere in northern New Jersey, don't ask. Pierre, dumb as a sunny, just swam up and swallowed that worm down hard. We both watched the line go taut and Pierre just floated there while the hook tore back up through his guts. He gave me this weepy look, flipped over, died. That's when I realized the world was garbage and human beings were a goddamn plague. Yeah, that's right. Okay. Where was I? Oh, Hark. See, he was a bright kid. Not a scholar, but thoughtful. He'd been through a lot, his father a man-ruin of a cop with shot credit and a nookie addiction, his mother a devout woman, a department store clerk in undousable emotional flames. Like she had a heart wrapped in rayon. His older sister raised him, mostly. His older sister gave him books. Only Connie knew his soul. You can't imagine. The scale of the loss when she died. It was some kind of cancer. The scale of the loss and sadness when she went. And you would not be wrong to think that from that time on the beatings and the powders did increaseth. And so did the despair increaseth. But one day, traipsing down Sunset Boulevard, this Hark, still a child in most ways, spied a little blue bow-and-arrow set sticking out of a trash bin. Hark ran home, did some lines of shitty coke to steady himself, and started to shoot the flimsy arrows around his living room. The bowstring snapped within minutes and most of the arrows lost their tips and fletching. What do you want? The thing was a piece of crap manufactured in a destitute country by slaves. But Hark continued to shoot. He didn't even need the bow. He stumbled around on the carpet, barked and growled and sobbed, a delayed burst of mammal grief. Mental archery, in some sense, was born in that moment. Others, of course, had devised procedures called mental archery before.

But what they did wasn't really mental archery. And don't even start with Buckman and that so-called Rimmer shot.

"So, what do you think, people? Is this a compelling enough origin story? It's a little canned, I admit. But what do you want? I'm not a professional storyteller, or a performer. I don't go around to schools and corporations drumming up business with some derivative, cockamamie rap about the power of narrative. You know what I am. I know you know. Do I have to say it? Okay, I guess I do. *I am a fucking catfish*. Keep that in mind when you judge. Nobody thought I had a chance coming up. Manage your catfish expectations, the cowards told me. Well, I'm here to say—"

Hark jolts up, slams back against the headboard. The bedroom spins. Hark's pinned to the wall, feels the floor drop out, like that old carnival ride—what was it called?

He shouts: "I have pamphlets for sale!"

Hands reach over, stroke his shoulders, ease him down.

"I have pamphlets for sale," Hark sobs.

"I know, baby."

"Where am I?"

"You're home," Meg whispers. "You're home with me in Pickering."

"Good," says Hark. "Please hold me."

"I'm holding you, sweetie."

"I can't feel it."

"I'm right here."

"That smell," Hark says.

"What smell?"

"Smells like river in here."

"Like what?"

"Like rotten river."

"Okay."

"Oh, right."

"Right what, honey?"

"That's what it's called."

"What what's called?"

"The Gravitron," Hark says.

"What's that?"

"It's what pins you to the wall."

"It's okay, baby."

"I know, sweetie. Please hold me."

"I'm holding you."

"I can't feel it."

"I'm here, I'm holding you."

"I believe you."

"Good."

"I don't like him."

"Who?"

"That fish. That catfish."

"What catfish? On the internet, sweetheart?"

"The internet?"

"What kind of catfish?"

"The kind with whiskers. That swims in the fucking . . . Come on, Meg!"

"Okay, Hark. You don't have to yell. I'm right here."

"Hold me."

"I *am* holding you, baby."

"I can't feel it."

"Please, Hark."

"I believe you, Meg. But I just can't feel it."

"Don't you love me, Hark? You said you loved me. You said it was just you, me and Menny."

"I know, Meg. But I'm not . . . I'm not who you think I am."

"But you are, Hark. That's why I love you."

"I don't think so."

"I do, baby. Can you feel me now?"

"Yeah, I'm starting to."

"Do you have pamphlets for sale?"

"I do."

"Tell me."

"I do."

"No, tell me."

"I have pamphlets for sale."

"That's right."

"I have pamphlets for sale."

"Yes, my love."

"Are you holding me?"

"I am."

"I can feel you now. I love you, Meg."

"I love you, too, Hark Morner."

Thirty-three

Lisa does not wake from her coma. Dr. Musil tells Fraz it could mean she is not ready to wake or else that she may never wake again.

"It's up to Lisa now."

"Up to Lisa?" Fraz says.

"Yes."

"Which Lisa is it up to?" Fraz asks. "Lisa the consciousness? Lisa the bruised brain? Lisa who has dog crap in her blood? Lisa the sister, the daughter? Lisa who hates cherry tomatoes and likes pearl onions? Who has two friends named Martha? What could you possibly mean? If it were up to Lisa, I'm pretty sure she'd already be out of this place and playing in the sunshine or watching a lesser Pixar movie and eating popcorn. Up to Lisa?"

Fraz notices the doctor is gone. He turns to Tovah.

"Am I right or am I right?"

Tovah's gone, too. Has she left the hospital? She has, to buy a pack of additive-free cigarettes and smoke a few on the sidewalk. She's been up for days, has decided that if she makes of herself a human sacrifice to Small Tobacco, Lisa will survive. Since she already knows this is magical thinking, she believes she can short-circuit rational critique. Stay alert to the fact that it's illogical, and magical thinking can become magical reality. Also, there is nothing like a thick, additive-free, filter-tip cigarette, like the kind the Native Americans used to puff on during peace talks, to help you stare down whatever sick force in the universe thinks giving a little girl sepsis and a brain injury at the same time is in any fashion whatsoever appropriate.

"What's up?" Tovah says, back in the room.

"What's up is that it's up to Lisa. Not too much pressure, right?" Fraz sniffs his wife.

"Have you been smoking cigarettes?"

"Yeah."

"May I have one?"

"No. It's my self-destructive coping strategy. You have to find your own."

"Lisa can't die."

"I know that."

"It's not up to her."

Somehow Tovah persuades Fraz to show up for the only tutoring job he has scheduled for the month. A little time away from the hospital might refresh him, gird him for more nightmare. Lisa has stabilized, and, frankly, Tovah needs a few hours sans Fraz, requires a break from his chaos, his oppressive anxiety, and since he's the shithead who let go of poor Lisa's foot, he must obey.

Fraz does feel relief to be out of the waiting room. His proximity to his daughter only points up his helplessness. He'd never leave her bedside if only he'd be allowed to keep a constant vigil, but for now the doctors have exiled them all to an adjacent room. He remembers when the twins were babies, and Tovah and Fraz would finally get them to sleep. After an hour or so they'd wonder if the kids were still alive, even as they heard their tiny breaths on the monitor. Fraz would argue against reconnaissance. "Let's not risk waking them," he'd say. "If they're dead, they're dead."

They'd laugh. They loved each other and were tired enough to laugh.

Fraz tutors a middle school kid in Hamilton Heights, a smart girl with no discernible deformities. They do some pre-algebra that Fraz fakes his way through. He's not some fucking Fields Medalist, after all, but at least he charges far less than the smug Ivy League groomers. He's the people's tutor. The session over, Fraz chats with the girl's mother while she chops greens in the kitchen.

"Klecko. Gastineau. Lyons. Salaam," Fraz says. "I'm not trying to get all manstalgic on you. I'm just naming heroes."

" 'Manstalgic'?"

"I had enormous feeling for these men. Now they are forgotten."

"Many extraordinary women have suffered the same fate," the girl's mother says.

"I don't deny that. I'm pretty well versed in that history. Feminism is sort of a hobby of mine."

"Really?"

"Hey, I pay attention. Like, for instance, what do you think about these guys going around, and I mean this is happening on a large scale, these guys that are going around refusing oral sex from women? As, like, a stance. Concept being there have been enough blow jobs, if you'll pardon the expression, given by women throughout recorded history. Not that all these jobs were recorded. Plus, how many of these historical sex acts were even consensual? The codes were different. I mean, I totally get it. It wasn't yes means yes, or no means no. It was yes means 'Suck it, strumpet,' and no means 'Burn, crazy witch.' These guys I'm talking about are aware of this disgusting history and will perform cunnilingus on you all the livelong day, but if you make even a single gesture toward a reciprocal hummer, they will shut you down. Just because you happen to be a woman who happens to want to give head. I mean, what do you think of that? It's confusing, right?"

"Confusing? I think that's wonderful. Are you one of those men? I think that's very cool. Are you a part of this movement?"

"I'm still working it through. I would never expect head. Obviously. I would never even ask for it. But I believe in a woman's right to choose whether or not to go down on me. I'm against any ideological application to the subject. Like, just do it. Or just don't do it."

"So, no ideology but borrowed corporate slogans?"

"Ha."

"Are you married?"

"Yes."

"What does your partner think about all of this?"

"It's never come up."

"Yet you find it natural to broach the subject with a stranger, a woman, who is employing you to tutor her daughter."

"What are you cutting there?" Fraz says.

"Ramps."

"And ramps are . . . do we even know?"

"Of course we know."

"I should just look it up on my phone."

"Here," the woman says, drops one of the soft stalks from her cutting board into his hand. "Now you're holding one."

Fraz studies the plant in his palm, the green leaves, the white and faintly purple stems, the delicate, tentacular bulbs.

"They have other names," she says. "Wild leek. Spring onion."

"Okay. Sure. My mother used to buy these at this farm stand in our town."

"Sounds idyllic."

"It was just the suburbs. But they had a farm stand. From when it was farms, I guess. I want to cry now. But not about the ramps. My daughter is so sick. And the doctors don't know what to do. Nobody does."

"You are the arrow and the bow. Start with that."

"Excuse me?"

"Oh, nothing."

"No, please."

"Are you a Pofer?" the woman says.

"A what?"

"Forget it."

"No, tell me. Apple, yes."

"Oh, so you *are* a Pofer. Like I thought."

"I'm a mental archer. I don't know Pofer."

"Power of Focuser."

"You know he never actually uses that phrase."

"Don't be insane. It's in nearly every other sentence out of his mouth."

"Maybe I *am* insane."

"You must look to Hark. The secret is that he's a traditional healer. He's picked up moves from shamanic rituals and goddess cultures all over the world. A beautiful synthesis. And he's helping people. He's really got something. He's the only man I'd ever listen to. I feel like he could bring back the dead."

"How about the almost dead?"

"That's harder, but sure."

"Will you pose with me now?" Fraz asks. "Just for a moment?"

"Excuse me?"

"I know I was being crazy before. Creepy."

"Yes, you were."

"I'm sorry . . . . I just need . . ."

"Let's do Bond of Bows."

They kneel together on the kitchen floor, face-to-face, palms on each other's shoulders. They hold the pose for several moments, until their breath is perfect breath, the breath of one. The woman smells of sweat and onion and a pear-scented soap. Her spirit hums with calm, honest concern, her heart out at the astral barricades in defense of the molecular formation called Lisa, a girl she's never met, who, for all she knows, given the oddness of this man in her kitchen, might not even exist. Fraz feels a brief surge of love for the world.

Thirty-four

He will look to Hark, Hark the shaman, Hark the healer, Hark the goddess culture synthesizer.

They record the video plea at Kate's. The original disciples have come, along with a few volunteer assistants, young mental archers eager for Hark's return. They prep the set, drag lights around. Schnitz, back from rehab, circles Fraz, searches for his shot.

Fraz brushes croissant crumbs from his shirt.

He's had a quick standing breakfast with Tovah this morning. She wished him the best for his shoot.

"It all seems insane," she said. "But at this point, anything for Lisa."

"I agree."

"Remember when you made that film? About your uncle Zach?"

"I want to make a new one. *Women and Sadness*. I want you in it."

"As a woman, or as sadness?"

"Let's go, let's go!" Schnitz says now.

Seth rises and Fraz takes his place on the hardwood chair they've placed before the white wall.

"Action," calls Kate.

Fraz breathes out, smiles.

"Hi!"

"Cut," Schnitz says.

"I'm the one who says cut," Kate says.

"Okay," Schnitz says, "but he opened with hi. Only liars say hi."

"Action," Kate says.

"Hello," Fraz says.

Schnitz stares at Kate.

"Cut," Kate says.

"What's wrong?" Fraz asks.

"Hello?" Schnitz snarls. "Don't say hello."

"Hark says it."

"It sounds holy coming from him. From you . . . just say what you came to say."

"Kate," Fraz says.

"Action," Kate says.

Fraz sucks in a quick breath.

"I'm Fraz Penzig and my little girl won't wake up. I am a mental archer, a Harkist, perhaps one of the first. I knew Hark Morner before he fully knew himself. Certainly before he ever became a doctor. That's a joke. And it's the last one I will make.

"Hark, if you're watching this, I realize you must blame me for some things. I've screwed up, I admit it, and I'm sorry for anything I said or did that hurt you. Or drove you into silence. I thought I saw the big picture. But it was just a blown-up version of the small picture."

Fraz stands, wipes his eyes.

"Hark, my daughter is in the hospital and I don't know what to do. I thought there was something I could do, but the case turns out to be otherwise. The case, I fear, is about to be closed. I'm not feeling very good about modern medicine right now. But I believe in your ability to help us focus. I realize now that what you meant by focus wasn't just helping us be more efficient at work, or more present at home. It was about transforming our way of being in the world. Maybe this can be a first step. A test run. Maybe we can send the right energy little Lisa's way, make an existential difference for one suffering kid. And if we can, then the only question is: What else can we do? Or what else can't we do?

"Hark, I'm begging you to help. I wish I could say I've never begged anyone for anything until now, but that would be untrue. I've begged people for all sorts of things. But this is begging on the grand scale. I'm begging you for a life. The life of my daughter. I won't say she's innocent. Nobody is innocent. But she's a good kid when she's not being a jerk, and I believe she'll be a generous, bighearted grown-up. Besides, she lights up a room. Isn't that enough? In this dark age? Please, Hark. Come back to us. Lead us. For Lisa's sake, for the sake of mental archery, for the sake of the land! That's all."

"And cut!"

Schnitz takes a tight pull from his flask, offers it to Fraz.

"The land?"

"I kind of liked that," Kate says.

"Won't go down in the annals of oration," Teal says. "But it'll do."

Fraz takes a hit off the flask, coughs.

"What is this?"

Schnitz grins. "Rum. And Xanax. And Adderall. And Saint-John's-wort. And maple water. It's like a health shake."

"It tastes like raspberry cough syrup."

"That's passion fruit. It's passion fruit–flavored maple water."

"Why not maple-flavored maple water?"

"If I knew the answer to that, man . . ."

"If you knew the answer to that, what?"

"Just saying."

"What are you saying?"

"Hey, fucker. Hand over my flask."

"Okay," Fraz says. "Here."

"Schnitz," Teal says. "You need to go back to rehab."

"But I'm doing my best work."

"That's the grandiosity talking."

"Actually it's the *New York Times*. Did you see that feature on me and my long-standing influence on music videos and style?"

"I've been busy."

"It was good. I mean, they got everything wrong, but that's not their fault. The reporter was, like, twelve."

"Well," Teal says, "I'm glad you're getting the attention you deserve, but you're going to die soon if you don't stop all the drinking and drugging."

"Same little fucker will probably write my obituary."

"If you're lucky."

"Lucky? What does luck have to do with it? I worked hard to destroy my body and alienate all the people who ever cared about me."

"You're right, Schnitz. You did."

"But it's okay. Hark will save me."

"Do you even practice mental archery?" Teal asks. "Do you know any poses?"

"Just the one," Schnitz says, squats, twists himself up with a wince.

"What's that?" Fraz says.

"It's Cupid, god of cute herpes."

"That's not a pose," Teal says.

"It's not?"

"No."

"Well, I'm sure I'm not the first to say it should be. Now can I have my flask back?"

"I already gave it to you."

"Good. Then we're done here."

Thirty-five

S hana Buckman stirs her Earl Grey tea with a souvenir spoon
from the Barcelona Olympics, watches late-morning sunlight
splash the lacquered leaves of her umbrella tree. Sometimes, to
be sure, she takes for granted the relentless pleasantness of her apartment. It's all she really needs, plus the place upstate, and everybody
on the planet could have precisely what she has—nothing more,
nothing less—if the super-rich were not such avaricious scum. She'd
like to porcupine them with some Afflictor K2-Hybrid Broadhead
arrow points, designed for expanded blood channels, and maybe one
day she will.

Meanwhile she must continue her work, which can also be a kind
of play.

Ethics, after all, is merely a dance, a daring jig on morality's wire,
high above the lava lake of nihilism. That's what her dissertation
adviser once told her. He also said that women were incapable of
ethical behavior for hormonal reasons, and that the female chair
of their department, who'd grown up in Mexico, had a habanero

chili–coated twat that could liquefy your cock on contact, or so he'd been informed.

Shana was still Barry at the time.

It would be a noble endeavor also to rain a passel of cyanide-tipped shafts on her old adviser, now a provost in the Ivy League, but ethics is also the science of restraint.

What joy to indulge in this meditative, bergamot-infused interlude in her apartment in her new, old, new body. But now her project must take priority over personal transformations. Marrow, organs for the world's poor, that's only a tiny slice of the program pie. Sometimes, for funds, they sell hijacked specimens to moneyed types. Sometimes they do favors for evil swine. It's part of the bargain. This outfit has overhead. The fact that they could help Nels was the only thing that made her agree to this particular mission. That it was all orchestrated by Dieter Delgado's people in an effort to rattle the Hark brain trust, and break their bank, doesn't sit easy, no matter how much she disdains mental archery. But sometimes, when interests converge, you do business with the enemy even as you try to destroy him.

Still, nobody died. Somebody (Blenda) lived.

The money she extorted from that Kate Rumpler girl goes to the Committee, though she's not exactly sure where the Committee is, or whom it comprises, or how they spend the funds. She's heard they have connections to the Army of the Just, which has recently, according to reports, taken Rostov.

The world is a crudfest. The personal, the political, the body, the mind, the brain. The Earth, the moon, the stars. The laws, the codes, the protocols, the conundrums, the dilemmas. The haves, the have-nots, the maybe-have-soons, the heart-shreddingly optimistic never-have-evers. The clinical trials and the preexisting conditions. The heart lists, the liver lists, the kidney lists, the scrolls of the Dead Sea dead.

Shana's tea cools too quickly. She fetches some ice cubes from the freezer. Flexibility is the key to victory. Iced tea is better than lukewarm tea.

Is there any lemon?

She had to laugh when she first heard about Hark and this mental archery scam. The idiocy, the arrogance. Now the fool gathers multitudes under the banner of a narcissistic movement that, after the bloom of false liberation wears off, can lead only to more despair and stasis. She took that girl's money and promised Hark's safety, but it still might be necessary to drop some rods in that mountebank's spleen, if he ever comes out of his hidey-hole.

Ethics is a void in a system designed solely for unethical behavior. Oaths are broken the moment they are sworn.

Thirty-six

Hark's video reply is brief. Meg shoots it on the back porch of the Pickering house.

"Hark here. I know it's been a while, but let's not get into that right now. All will reveal itself in good time. I'll be standing here a week from tomorrow at five p.m. Join me, in the flesh or in the great virtual sanctuary we have created together, and we will focus for little Lisa. Good night."

"There," Meg says, lowers her phone.

"What did you think?"

"It was fine."

"Fine?"

"I'm worried about this, Hark. If the girl dies it will be terrible."

"She has a name, honey. I know her. Sort of. I can't give up on her."

"You're not a miracle worker. You said so yourself. You're not Jesus."

"Says who?"

Hark grins, grabs Meg by the waist.

"Look," she says. "I believe in you, baby. I really believe you can help people. I want to help sustain you, your practice."

"You're doing a terrific job, Meg. You really are. I couldn't do any of this without you. That's why I left the city. Why I came here."

"I thought you loved me."

"Of course, that. That, of course. They are all parts of the same thing."

"But I'm worried you might be losing your sense of what the thing is."

"Don't be crazy."

"I'm not crazy," Meg says. "Please don't ever say that. It's a button for me. Todd used to say that."

"I'm sorry. Of course you're not crazy. Hey, answer me honestly. Do you think it's possible that the power of focus we generate will be strong enough to bring that girl out of a coma?"

"Did you say power of focus?"

"Well, yeah. Whatever. I'm more okay with the phrase now. But do you think it will be strong enough?"

"That's not what mental archery is for."

"But maybe now it has to be," Hark says. "For the future."

"Say Lisa lives, and I truly hope she does. There is still no way to prove that you had anything to do with it."

"Not me. All of us, together. We could stop a train in its tracks if we wanted to."

"Hell, Hark. What happened to just helping people focus? In the office or in the home? I don't know what to say now. You sound like you're changing."

"More like shedding, Meg."

"Shedding what?"

"Habits of thought. Habits of fear."

"Fear? What do you possibly fear?"

"I don't know, Meg. My own possibilities, maybe."

"You sound like somebody on TV. What did you say Fraz called them? Happiness hustlers?"

"I am somebody on TV."

"I didn't mean it like that."

"Look, Meg. Something happened to me after St. Louis."

"I know it's been hard, sweetie."

"No! I don't want pity. Just say you're with me. Don't you get it? You can't do things halfway. You can't pick and choose from various venerated traditions and customize your own warm and cuddly belief system."

"*You* did."

"In the beginning, maybe. But I've grown. I want you to grow with me. Once, long ago, when I was flailing, and desperate, I knew I needed to find some kind of spiritual path. I talked to Buddhists, Muslims, Confucians, Hindus, Catholics, Protestants, atheists, you name it. I met with a rabbi, the father of a kid I'd known in high school. We were talking about Judaism. And I asked him whether, if a man ever converted and happened to have a foreskin, he'd have to get circumcised. The rabbi said that as far as he was concerned, the man would. That it would be a false conversion if he didn't. He admitted it would be terribly painful, but that was the price of admission. That was the leap of faith. That was the covenant, the deal, the agreement. 'But it's so horrible,' I said. 'I agree with you,' said the rabbi. 'It's an awful experience for adult men,' he said, 'and I'm fairly convinced it causes severe lifelong trauma for babies, too. A clear case of genital mutilation.' 'Then why require it?' I asked. 'Because that's what the contract stipulates. That's the promise, that's the vow.' 'But,' I said, nearly screaming at the rabbi, 'that's just really fucked-up!' And you know what the rabbi said? He said, 'Of course it's fucked-up. It's religion!'"

"But you don't have a foreskin," Meg says.

"Exactly. You get the point."

"I don't think I do."

"You look peaked. Wan."

"I'm dropping."

"Get a bar. We'll talk more later."

Thirty-seven

They move Lisa into a new room, grant Fraz permission to resume his vigil beside her bed. He reads her chapter books out loud, rubs moisturizer into the heels and soles of her feet.

"I'm so sorry, baby. Daddy never meant to let you go."

Lisa's eyes are shut, her breathing slow, shallow in the mask.

Hospitals make him think of hospitals. His father rotted in one.

The pink curtain is similar to the rose curtain of his father's room.

Fraz hears voices, looks up. Tovah, David and Dersh tote grocery sacks into the room.

"Party time?" Fraz says.

"Don't even," Tovah says.

"Fraz!" Dersh says. "We've got extra. If you're hungry. Some carpaccio. Fresh mozzarella. Also hummus, Israeli salad."

"Not hungry. And only a fascist would call it Israeli salad."

"That's what the sign in the deli said. Eat it or don't eat it."

"I said I'm not hungry. My daughter is in a coma, sorry if I don't have much of an appetite."

"Stop it, Fraz," Tovah says.

David pulls a chair up to his sister's bedside, whispers to her in what must be some cryptic twin tongue.

"That's good," Dersh says to David, pats the boy's shoulder. "Talk to her. That's what she needs."

"Don't tell my son what to do."

"I'm just trying to help."

"Fraz, why don't you go for a little walk. We'll take the next shift."

"There won't be too many more shifts."

"What?" David says.

"Fraz!" Tovah says. "What the hell are you saying?"

"I'm saying that by this time tomorrow Lisa will be okay."

"Listen," Dersh says, "I'll be there as well. And I think Hark is doing a wonderful thing."

"Wasn't that you in St. Louis telling me Hark was shit, that he was finished? Now you're interested again, huh? Don't think I don't know why. I heard about how that focus gene was a hoax."

"Not a hoax. Inconclusive. That's how science works. Fits and starts. And because of science, of medicine, I believe the doctors will eventually find a way to bring Lisa to full recovery. But maybe Hark can help, too. We don't know everything. In the meantime, there's no reason science and spirituality can't work together. And there's no reason somebody like Hark shouldn't have the chance to redeem himself."

"Especially," Fraz says, "if there's a buck to be made."

"Sorry. I like money, so you can't insult me that way."

"Fine," Fraz says. "Hey, are those egg bagels?"

———

Later, Tovah sits in the hospital cafeteria with a cup of jasmine tea. She's remembering Lisa from not too many months ago. A typical weeknight dinner. Lisa chews some cauliflower, cooked her favorite way, roasted with Parmesan cheese. Tovah carries a pot of soup to the table.

"It's hot, nobody touch it," she says.

Fraz, of course, taps his fingernail against the pot.

"Call that hot, do you?"

David laughs, pretends to touch it.

"Yeah, Mom. Call that hot?"

Tovah realizes that from Lisa's vantage it appears that both Fraz and David have braved the heat. Lisa figures it's her turn, spreads her whole palm against the side of the pot. Tovah watches her daughter register the pain in stages, stifle a howl. Lisa's face crimps up, tears slide down her cheek, but she stays silent, valiantly chews her cruciferous mouthful.

Her courageous sucker of a daughter. Oh, coma gods, wake her up already. I'll never kvetch about how parenthood can engender a loss of creative and personal identity again! Just fucking wake my daughter up!

Thirty-eight

Fraz rents another used Northern European sedan, collects Kate, Teal, Schnitz. Seth the Proctor is already upstate.

Fraz has his driving moccasins, his baby-tush gloves. His being is tuned to the life-pulse of Lisa. It's not up to his daughter, whatever Dr. Musil thinks. It's not up to Tovah or Nat Dersh or Marty Lenz or the Nazarene or Muhammad or Vishnu or Johnny Cash. It's up to Fraz. And one other.

Tovah decides to stay by Lisa's bedside.

"I believe you believe," she tells Fraz. "But I'm staying with my girl."

"Okay, just don't cockblock the focus vibes."

"Get the fuck out now."

Fraz roars northwest toward Waffle Town. Teal navigates, or, rather, provides play-by-play of the cobalt dot's crawl across her phone screen.

Meg Kenny, Hark's new spokeswoman, has confirmed that Hark will present himself at five that evening. A nocking, followed by a loosing. Thousands of imaginary arrows in the sky. The mass betrothal of spine and flex.

Besides his one announcement last week, nobody has heard from Hark. Meg manages all communication. There is much chatter now on the Harkist street about her newfound command. She is a mystery to Fraz, but he surmises from her posts she is passionate, dedicated to mental archery, in love with Hark, and possibly insane. Fraz shares his findings with Teal, who fidgets in the passenger seat, and Schnitz, who sprawls out in back with Kate, digs into a bag of something called SoftChips.

"She's a Svengali's Svengali," Teal says.

"Maybe. Or she's exactly what this thing needs."

"Or both."

"Look at this dumbass nation just flitting by our window," Schnitz says. "Nothing but ignorance, poverty, disease. And Walmart. And Warmart."

"Please," Teal says. "That's the old news."

"Still the only news."

"Hand up some of those shits," Fraz says, bends his palm back.

Fraz bites into a SoftChip. It isn't chewy or crumbly. It's an entirely new texture, with a taste he would describe, if somebody put a gun to his head—though it's hard to picture a scenario where somebody would put a gun to his head to ascertain the flavor profile of a new snack product—as ineffable. SoftChips taste of a superabundant absence of taste. He wonders if SoftChips, even more than climate change, are, in fact, the big one, the all-snuffing meteorite. But that makes little sense. How about all of those other gastric apocalypses he's ingested over the years, from Chocodiles to Pop Rocks to drinks iridescent as factory ponds. The dinosaurs were fucking crybabies. It's not about one big galactic boulder but the ceaseless golden cancer shower. SoftChips is just another smoldering wedge from the stars.

And what is Hark? What category of matter is the anointed one?

Why pose the question if silence means that Fraz can be an arrow coursing through the air with all the others, each shaft angling out in midair to form a single point, a chevron of infinite focus and grace, a singularity, ultimate transcendence, blind, obliterating joy, love to the nth, the multiverse to the max, though Hark has never uttered such phrases? How strange, Fraz muses, to be Fraz, a fairly sharp guy raised by atheists, and still want to believe in this stuff. But it's more than desire. Fraz does believe. Better to believe than accept his mother and father's miserable certainty, their sour invitation to the void. Better to believe than fetishize doubt, that dubious lodestar for all those sweat-bright wrestlers of faith. Doubt is a lout. Besides, Hark is Fraz's destiny, both of their given names born of parental bewilderment. Then again, maybe it's all great heaps of horseshit. Oh, dear. Is it time to don the damp, stinky singlet of consciousness, grapple with the monodude once more?

"How's it going over there, Fraz?" Teal says.

"Okay. Just getting manhandled by a spiritual crisis."

"Too much man fun," Teal says.

"Belief fag," Schnitz snickers.

A sign flicks by: PICKERING, 10 MILES.

"Gentlemen," Fraz says. "Start your waffles."

"What?" Schnitz says.

"You don't remember that?"

"Nah."

"It's 'Gentlemen, start your toasters,'" Teal says.

"How would you know?" Fraz says. "Were you even born?"

"I'm reading about Pickering right now. Named for Priam Pickering in 1753, formerly known as . . . Oh, this is good: His son Hector was hanged as a spy."

"Fucking lobsterbacks did that," Fraz says.

"All of this Revolutionary War stuff used to fascinate me," says Teal, "until I realized it was just a fight among white guys. We were chattel either way."

"Fuck the whites."

"You're white."

"I'm Jewish."

"That's white."

"Tell Leo Frank."

"Who's Leo Frank?" Schnitz asks.

"A Jew in Georgia. They lynched him. Strange kosher fruit."

"I've read about him," Teal says. "But come on. The same guy gets mentioned every time. It's like if Crispus Attucks had been the only black man ever shot by the police in America."

"There is a lot of anti-Semitism in this country," Fraz says.

"It still won't be enough," Schnitz mutters.

"Please, Fraz," Teal says. "I'd worry more about your marriage."

"You still haven't told Tovah and me what the root problem is."

"The root problem? The root problem is that there are no roots. Just destructive anxieties and bad faith."

"When were you going to tell us?"

"I was hoping you'd figure it out for yourselves. It's a more profound discovery that way."

Teal looks out the window, sees the cars parked along the roadside, still a mile clear of Pickering. Clowns, all of them, and she is no exception. Fine, but why must existence be so crushingly personal? She misses the days of middle school algebra, her gifted and talented study group, practice problems on the board. Solve for an x that wasn't you, or your fear, or your damage. She got good at that. But these were not practice lives, no matter how it sometimes felt. Ask little Lisa.

Thirty-nine

They gather in the fields behind Meg's house, Pofers in the thousands, with their hats and their parasols, their mist sprayers, water jugs, giant papier-mâché ice cubes, trail mix. They bear placards lugged here from around the world: *The Arrow Is You*; *Tap the Prune*; *Leonardo da Warpig*; *Citizen Archer*; *Shut Up and Hark!*

Meg stares out the kitchen window at the crowd. Some meditate on picnic blankets, or squat over flat stones, carve imaginary arrowheads with flicks of the forearm a stranger might mistake for gestures spastic or obscene. Others share food and umbrella shade, chase the screeches of children across the grass. Some test phantom bows, fists tilted at the sky. A few loll over wicker baskets and boxed Sancerre, as though at any moment an orchestra might erupt in sound from a painted gazebo. Meg spots a fat man lounging in a low-slung camp chair. He runs his fingers through melted cooler ice, perhaps dreaming of rowboats on a forest lake.

One group joins arms and sways, their Apple Boy invocations like football chants.

Certain veteran mental archers appear to disdain the newcomers, wear the dates of their first focus bull's-eye on ball caps and tattoos, but Meg knows the swelling numbers bode well for the institute.

She rises and walks the fields, greets the crowd as owner of the property and de facto manager of the event. She waves to some of the Harkian (she prefers the softer sonics of this variation) subsets she's been in touch with on the internet, the fetishists who've isolated shards of Hark's history and speech. One contingent has erected a volleyball net, slaps a ball around beneath a banner that reads *Why Not Butterscotch?* Another tends to porcelain tureens of sour-cherry soup. Evangelical strays figure Hark for an archangel, don fluffy white wings. A clique in medieval felt fly flags embossed with crossbows.

Near them Meg notes a tall woman with black and silver hair. She stands with two men inside a low wooden wagon, a gilded horn bow in her hand. The men crouch as the woman, shielded behind them, mimes shooting arrows over their backs. Meg walks over to welcome them, asks about their maneuvers. The woman smiles.

"We're Battle of Asculum buffs."

"Of course," Meg says, shakes her head.

"That was the so-called Pyrrhic victory."

"Oh, interesting."

Now a bald man in pink seersucker approaches. He tells Meg he's a talent agent, begs her to meet his client, an actress, a quirk queen from an earlier era. He lifts a tent flap to reveal her, hunched in a poncho, vaping.

"I want to meet him," the actress whispers. "How is he in bed?"

"That's none of your business."

"Does he refuse blow jobs from women?"

"What?"

"Is he an ally against pole slurping?"

Meg snatches the flap from the agent's hand, lets it drop. She might need more staff to handle such encounters in the future.

Meg returns to the house and finds Hark in the pantry, his study, surrounded by canned tomatoes and artichokes, a book on dark matter in his lap. She tells him about the actress.

"Have I seen her in anything?"

"I don't know," Meg says. "But she's seen you."

"Don't be jealous."

"Now that you're famous, are you going to run off with a famous person?"

"Come here."

Hark tosses the book aside, pulls Meg down to his lap.

"It's just us."

"You promise?"

"Of course."

"What about your friends?"

"Which friends?"

"Fraz and Teal and them."

"It's a new thing now."

"The two of us."

"For the most part, yes."

" 'For the most part'?"

"Meg, you're my rock."

The house rattles with skysuck. Through a window, they watch an enormous gunship wobble down to the edge of the field.

"What's that?" Meg says.

"That's our golden parachute."

"But it's a helicopter."

"Our parachute is inside it."

"Really?"

"Metaphorically. Though I'm sure there are actual parachutes in there, too."

"Say we're going to be okay."

"We're going to be okay, baby."

"Don't try to be funny."

"I'm not."

"Say what you have for sale."

"Come on."

"Say what you have for sale."

"Pamphlets."

"No, say it."

"I said it."

"Say it for real."

"Meg."

"Say it!"

"Meg, honey, you know I will always, always, for you, I swear, I will always have pamphlets for sale. Okay?"

"I don't quite believe you."

"Meg."

"Say it again!"

Forty

Lisa's eyes pop open, hot and scratchy. What a long, wretched dream! A dream in the dark, a dream of sawtooth noises, a screechy murkworld. Car alarms, the ding of microwave clocks, sirens and footsteps and shouts, voices that hissed, whispered, others that floated off, bumped against the rust-blossom dome of the sky. The dream people had wrapped her in mummy strips, bound her to the deck of a metal boat.

But now she's back. To where, she isn't sure. A strange beige room. A man in the chair beside her. She blinks.

"Daddy."

"Hey there. How are you?"

"Daddy, you let go."

"I had to. Sometimes it's best to just let go."

"I went into that tree."

"Just a little booboo. You're good now."

"Where am I?"

"In heaven."

"There is no heaven."

"That what your dumb daddy told you?"

"You're not dumb."

"No?"

"How come nobody else is here?"

"They'll be here soon. I just got a head start. I have to go now."

"Daddy, wait!"

Lisa's eyes pop open again. Or maybe for the first time.

It's a hospital room, flowers thick on the sills, cartons of food on a shelf. Is that a half-gnawed egg bagel? Her face feels pinched by the rim of her mask. Her mouth is crusted shut. She sniffs herself. Puke-sweet. The machine beside her heaves, pings. She gropes for the button on the bed rail. Her hand drops, grazes a warm, plastic bulge. She peers over, spots a bag of pale yellow water, follows the tube to where it leads between her legs.

"Help!" she shouts, her lips stuck. "Help!"

Forty-one

Major Van Brunt and his security detail, ripped young fellows in slim-fit gingham, hop out of the chopper, clear a path for Nat Dersh. They scurry as one squared-away amoebic cluster to Meg's porch, spill into her big country kitchen.

"Where's the talent?" Dersh says.

"The what?"

"Listen, isn't that what his name means? Listen? Where's Listen?"

"It means more than listen. It means pay attention."

"Shit, lady, I *am* paying attention. It's my girl in a coma."

"I thought she was Fraz's."

"He's the bio dad. I'm the dad who makes a difference, if her mother will let me. But none of that matters if she doesn't live. The girl must live."

"We all hope so."

"Oh, I know so."

"You really believe in Hark, do you?"

"I believe in the power of focus. But, more than that, I believe in the power of power."

"That sounds like a business phrase."

"Business is just a metaphor."

"For what?"

"I don't know. Capital dividends? Where is he?"

"He's upstairs. Preparing."

"Get him down here. Deets wants to talk to him."

Dersh holds up the tablet screen and they all glance at the empty beanbag chair on the flight deck of an aircraft carrier.

"He needs a little time," Meg says.

Dersh nods to Major Van Brunt, who signals his men.

"Wait!" Meg says. "I'll get him."

"Riggs, Baby Knob," Van Brunt says to his men. "Stand down."

Somebody bangs on the kitchen window.

"Oh, gee," Dersh says.

Fraz's nose, lips, make a wet mash on the pane.

"Baby Knob," Dersh says. "Door."

Fraz stumbles in, wipes his mouth with his sleeve. Teal, Kate and Schnitz follow, find spots to lean on along the wall.

"Nat," Fraz says.

"Fraz."

"What's happening?"

"You tell me. You sent Hark the message. You put this into play. I hope you know what you're doing."

"What do you mean?" Fraz says.

"Say this power-of-focus thing works, which it won't, because it's your idea, and you are about as intelligent as a giraffe fart. But what if it works too well? What if it's too strong? What if the focus actually drives her into a deeper coma?"

"That doesn't make sense."

"Meg," Dersh says. "Have you met Fraz Penzig?"

"Once. A few years ago. The first time I met Hark. Heard so much about him since then, of course."

"Nice things, I hope."

"Not really. People say you're kind of schmucky. Oh, is that even a word?"

"Sure," Dersh says. "And exactly. He's schmucky. He's a schtarker and a schlemiel and a schnorrer and a luftmensch and a hondler. All rolled up into one krepke."

"I don't know those terms," Meg says.

"I don't, either, really," says Dersh. "I usually just throw my fake Yiddish around in meetings to sound more authentic, trustworthy. We all do it. Japanese, Chinese, Indian, Swiss, whatever. We pretend we are from communities. That we had, like, sage, earthy grandmas. Helps the deal along. Am I right, Deets?"

Now the tablet screen fills with the visage of Dieter Delgado, the pygmy owl, with his deathbird eyes of shiny chartreuse. Some say the effect is not achieved with contact lenses, that he had his irises surgically dyed.

"Well, Nat," Deets says, "my grandmothers were from Guatemala and Austria, and, no, I don't partake in any kind of charade like that."

"Oh. Sorry, Deets."

"Don't be sorry. Just speak for yourself. Now, Meg. I'd really like a word alone with Hark."

"This is bullshit," Teal says. "Fraz is a good guy. And his daughter is the one we're all here for. Who are you people? You have nothing to do with what we started."

Seth edges into the room, winks.

"Thanks, guys," Fraz says. "But I think this is my fight."

"There's no fight," Dersh says. "Riggs, Baby K."

"Sir?"

"Get these people out of here. And find that actress. Meg, I should go check on my camp. We're set up in the adjacent field. Great catering, so please swing by. I've invited some very cool friends, including the former governor."

"Thanks for the invitation, Mr. Dersh," Meg says. "But, with all due respect, that's not my crowd. You're not my crowd."

"Oh, I'll charm you yet, Meg."

"Like you charmed Tovah?" Fraz says.

"Don't you even talk about Tovah."

"I'm her husband. The father of her children."

"What does that even mean?"

"Fascinating discussion, boys," Dieter says from the tablet screen. "But now I really need to see Hark."

"I'm right here."

Hark stands at the foot of the stairs. He hasn't shaved in a while and he wears the old blue robe Kate bought him for the Glyph Systems gig.

"Tip of the spear," Hark says, nods at Fraz.

"Arrow," Fraz says.

"Is there someplace . . . ?" Dieter says.

"There is someplace."

Hark takes the tablet from Dersh, carries it to the pantry, shuts the door.

"How can I help you?" Hark says.

"I just think we're the principals here. It should be us talking. We have the same goals."

"I doubt that very much."

"I bet we like some of the same bands."

"I don't really . . . What are you saying, Mr. Delgado, if I may ask?"

"Did you know I plan to make a lot of money from mental archery? Not that I need money. More to give away. Philanthropy's my only passion."

"Good for you."

"What people like me do, it's not easy. We work in the dark. We do what we can, give what we have."

"Okay."

"You know in the old movies when the villain always asks the hero to join him. And the fucking hero never does. When I was a little kid I would call out, 'Join him!' I was a committed conglomerist."

"I guess that's kind of endearing."

"Don't you want to make money?"

"Not particularly. See, this might be hard to understand, but I'm richer, have more access to resources, can alter the way we live, at a level far beyond you."

"It's all inside you, is that the point? Wealth can't buy happiness?"

"Maybe that's part of it. But I'm really talking about something else. It's not completely clear to me yet. But I'm closing in on some kind of understanding, I'm sure of it."

"Join me."

"Fuck no."

"I'm surprised."

"Why?"

"Well, you could have steered this all toward some kind of revolt against us, the cronies, the owners, the masters, the oligarchs, whatever term is current in your whiny world. But you kept it apolitical. So I figured you wanted to taste the cake. Now I'm not so sure."

"It was never about politics."

"It's always about politics. By which I mean economics. That's where me and my lefty profs at Berkeley agree."

"This was about focus."

"For what? On what?"

"Everybody asks that. It's for the individual to decide."

"Who cares about the individual? That's so bourgeois. Wow, now I'm really sounding like those old fools. Look, people don't want to be individuals. Not in any real way. Oh, sure, they'll do what they can to make a viral video, be a personality online. But only the geriatrics still cling to the idea, if any of them really still do, that they are actual and discrete people who belong to a community and practice, for example, democracy. Nobody else cares. They are happy to be lumps of data points. Just let them download their videos, their games, their porn, and order their drugs, food and clothing online."

"And you make your money off selling information about their numbed-out consumption habits."

"Well, that's one older revenue stream. We're cooking up a lot more. But that's not the point. The point is people still have these big holes in their hearts. And it's hard to get off the couch to fill them. The Hark feed will be huge. Millions will get their nuggets of Harkist wisdom through our filter. And the advertising, only for Hark-approved products, will be mega. But more importantly, if you give them reasons to live, they'll be happier customers. Suicides and junkies don't buy a lot of shit. Except maybe drugs. But only for a time."

"None of this has anything to do with me."

"It can. It's entirely your call."

"I will stop you."

"Dumb idea."

"It's not an idea. It's a vow."

"Okay, we'll leave you out of it. We'll just call it mental archery. That's a generic term, like yoga. And you didn't coin it. We've researched that. We'll rebrand everything without you. The name Hark will be forgotten."

"That could never happen."

"It happens all the time."

There's a loud knock on the pantry door.

"What?" shouts Hark.

"It's me," Fraz says.

"What is it?"

"It's about Lisa."

"Shit," Dieter says. "She better not be dead."

Hark opens the door.

"Oh, Fraz. I'm so sorry."

"No, Hark. It's okay. She woke up."

"She woke up?"

"She woke up!"

"Did you hear that, Delgado? She woke up!"

"Because of mental archery," Dieter says.

"Because she woke up," Hark says, laughs, reaches over and wipes the tears from Fraz's cheek. "Well, Deets, was there anything else?"

"We're not done," Dieter says.

"Yes," Hark says. "We are."

He hands the tablet to Fraz.

"We'll see," Dieter says. "You can't just get rid of me. Pop open your laptop I'll be right in your face, motherfucker. Check your phone: It'll be my beak there, ready to stab your ass."

"I don't use devices that much."

"They'll use you, you fucking monkey."

Fraz swipes Dieter off the screen and they step back into the kitchen. Hark regards the room with a steep, unwavering gaze.

"A house divided," he says, "cannot stand."

"That's Lincoln," Baby Knob whispers to Riggs.

"No shit, shitbird."

Hark strides with regal resignation to the door. The crowd in the field begins to shout, blow horns, ring cowbells. Do they spot his silhouette in the window?

"Lisa's okay," Fraz says. "You don't have to do this."

"I want to say hello to my friends."

"We're all rooting for you, Hark," Seth says.

Hark stops, turns.

"Really? I always thought it was me rooting for all of you."

"Maybe it's both," Fraz says.

"It's odd," Hark says. "I never wanted this. I mean, mental archery. Pretty silly, right? Maybe the whole deal has been an enormous and ludicrous overcompensation for my lack of everything it takes to just be an average guy in America. All I ever wanted were nice friends, maybe some occasional sex. Dull but heartfelt connections with others. A couple of quality cable dramas to watch. You guys didn't really get it, did you? This whole thing. Focus for what? you kept asking me. Well, I'll tell you. The reason we need to focus is . . . oh, forget it."

Hark rests his thumb on the rim of the door latch.

"Remind me again," he says. "It's apple, yes, boy, no. Right?"

Nobody speaks.

"What will finally destroy everything we've done," Hark says, "is the fact that you people have no fucking sense of humor."

Hark opens the door and the noise from the field roars into the kitchen, punches them back on their heels. Fraz watches a slim, dark blur shoot past the doorframe. Hark staggers sideways, crashes into a wall of pegged cookware, slides down in a clatter of saucepans and skillets, a flaked casserole pan.

A long, thick arrow, fletched in shades of neon, juts out of his chest.

Forty-two

Boyd Barron sits front-cuffed in the Pickering holding tank. The metal cot grates his butt. He raises both hands to thumb-tweeze the strand of white hair that curls from a pore in his nose. He plucks it often, but the bastard always pokes back up. It's like a miracle of nature, but a crap one.

He wonders how much damage those uniformed cretins have done to the cams and sights of his Hoyt Spyder hunting bow. Probable answer: cum tons.

About shooting that stupid child Hark Morner, Boyd has minor regrets.

It was never the kid's fault, really. How could Hark have known better, raised in ignorance and with values rooted in the soft faggotry of high expectations? The entitlement generation, duped into thinking they deserve everything just for looking good in their sneakers, moaning about how the whole world should be invited to snout around in the American trough, Paraguayans, Laotians, Syrians, Canadians, Somalis, Dutch, Cameroonian tusk pimps, fat-cat Krauts with spaetzle-burner dealerships on every highway and, of course, the Jews, the Jews, the whole kike cavalcade, the Wall Street Jews, the Suck-the-Baby-Penis Jews, the Hollywood Jews, the Harvard Jews, the Law Jews, the Baseball Jews, the Secret Chinese Jews, the Perpetually Aggrieved Jews, the Actually Dumb Jews, the Formerly Badass Commando Jews, the Lizard-Head Jews, the Elders of Zion, the Youngsters of Zion, the Anti-Zionists of Zion, all of them crowding in, and with the trough itself boasting a thin puddle of gruel at best.

But worse, really, was the way Hark taught those fools to draw imaginary bows. What kind of inanity is that? When this country is finally invaded by the Army of the Just, those nutso motherbangers marauding Europe, are we going to be firing back with fairybook rotary cannon and make-believe cluster bombs? Will the power of focus repulse their navy? Not that there's a Navy of the Just, just yet. But give them time. Half of them are American and European ex-military, fighting their old comrades. Must be some tech-smart sea dogs among them.

Boyd Barron knew back at the Pickering band shell that if this Hark kid ever got traction, he'd have to go bye-bye. Some of the fellows on the Albion Pride Web Forum had tried to dissuade him, but Boyd had perused the world historical sitrep. (Perused it *thoroughly*, because that's what "peruse" means!) The good guys were down a score with the clock running out. That was the goddamn situation. Boyd Barron was the last American quarterback. The play had been called years ago, the squad long assembled at scrimmage.

It just took some time for the snap.

He knows he's done right, though that westerly breeze on release felched elk butt. His arrow shanked and he may only have nicked Hark Morner's heart. Hard to tell from his location. But he did his deadeye best. The hippies had him down in the dirt before he could yank another arrow from his quiver. Those security goons got their licks in, too, as they stuffed him into the sheriff's cruiser. Boyd Barron is still a crack shot, has been since his Delta days, shooting grenade-tipped crossbow bolts at Narco-Leninists in the jungle, but it's been years since he could hand-fight for shit. He's done what he could. Given what he has. His passion was his task. His task was a hard fucking hump up and down the hills of this life.

Now a door slams. Boots bang on the buffed floor. A donut eater, most likely. Or maybe a lawyer, public defender. Some local dunce who can't make it in the world, nurses on state teat. If a screw opens the cell door, Boyd might see daylight again. He'll need one last surge of the old quick-and-nasty. Fake a heart attack, a stroke. Feign a neoplasm in the brainpan. Pop the guard's coconut on the corner of the cot. Get the keys to the cell and evidence cage, his Hoyt back. The right Nuge riff on mind's repeat might jazz Boyd up. He'll make pincushions of the pursuit team, get out past the gates, power his old carcass to the tree line. Never come out of the woods again.

Forty-three

Hark twitches in the Chinook, zooms toward Barr County General.

For the teensiest of intervals, he looks to have a chance to pull through. Riggs, ex-army medic, stanches the blood around the arrow. Hark's pulse stabilizes. Dersh squats behind the pilot with a headset on. Somehow Meg and Fraz have both managed to climb aboard. Dersh studies the tiny tracts of houses far below the gunship's open door, restrains himself from shoving Fraz off his helo. It requires extraordinary willpower, but that's exactly what he's cultivated as a successful entrepreneur.

Fraz cradles Hark's head while Riggs swabs the wound.

"You're going to be fine, honey," Meg says, clutches his hand.

"An actual arrow," Hark says, chuckles up blood. "I'm sorry, Fraz. We didn't get to focus for Lisa."

"It's okay. I told you, she woke up. You didn't have to go out there."

"They were waiting for me."

"Honey, I love you," Meg says. "You're going to make it."

"Hate to leave so soon. There was more to do."

"Hark!" Meg cries.

"Fraz," Hark says. "It's you and Meg now. Meg's in charge, but you have to help her."

"I will."

"Fuck Dersh."

Fraz can't tell if Dersh hears Hark say that or not. Riggs does, raises his eyebrows.

"Meg," Hark rasps. "What I was going to say before. About mental archery. I was wrong. It's not just for home or office. It's got to be more. We must fight the corruption, the hate, the patriarchy, racism, misogyny, oppression. We must focus to forestall the effects of climate change. To take down the ruling class and build a better, fairer world. Maybe not heaven on earth. But something."

"Why didn't you say so before?"

"It wasn't time. It's still not time. But there's no more time."

"You'll lead us, Hark," Meg says.

"Listen," Hark says. "I wrote some stuff down. In a yellow notebook."

"Where?"

"He's going!" Riggs screams.

Baby Knob slides over, lifts a huge needle over his head, plunges it into Hark's breastbone.

"What are you doing!" Meg says.

"Adrenaline," Baby Knob says.

"He's not OD'ing!"

"Idiot!" Riggs shouts.

"I feel fantastic," Hark says, dies.

Dersh pulls Baby Knob away.

"He's gone, sir," Riggs says.

"I can fucking see that," Dersh says, takes a photo of Hark's frozen face. "We need to dump the body. Is there a lake or a river around here?"

"Dump the body?" Fraz says.

"It's protocol."

"For what?"

Hark's head lolls off the edge of the helicopter door.

"Okay," Dersh says. "Forget it."

State troopers greet them at the hospital. It's a murder case, and the police have a suspect in custody, a known Pickering eccentric with archery expertise.

Now they have the body.

———————

Meg catches a ride from some troopers back to Pickering. Her neighbors have Menny safe on their farm. They tell her the Pickering police ordered the crowd around Meg's house to disperse, but they've mostly refused. Rather than resort to pepper spray and riot guns, the cops have let them camp out. Thousands wander, weep, howl, or else gather to moan group-focus dirges. The police leave the people to their grief, ticket their cars.

Fraz rides the last bus back to the city.

"I'm Tommy," the man beside him says. "Were you there, man? You were there, weren't you?"

"No," Fraz says.

Tommy breathes hard through pursed lips, bounces his knee, skims his push broom hair with the flat of his hand.

"I still don't know what really happened," he says. "Some say Hark got beat up, or shot in the back by guys inside the house. There are a lot of rumors already. I'm sure he'll be okay."

Dusk has come. Outside the bus's tinted windows, the roadside houses bend in shadow.

"What if he's not?" Fraz says.

"Not what?"

"Not okay."

"Man, don't even think about that."

"I *have* to think about it."

"Why?"

"Thinking about it might be my job now."

"I know what you mean," Tommy says. "We just need to focus. We need to think of Lisa. That's why we all came here, right? I mean, to tell you the truth, that wasn't the only reason. I came for Hark, to see the man who's transformed my life. I mean, when I couldn't get out of my bartending shift, I just quit my job to come."

Fraz puts his hand on Tommy's knee, stills it.

"You look so familiar," the ex-bartender says.

"I didn't jinx it," Fraz says.

"What?"

"The no-hitter. The ball game. I didn't jinx it, okay? The universe doesn't work that way."

"What? Ball game? Holy shit! Of course. I recognize you from the videos on Hark Hub. I'm sorry, dude. I was really ready to focus for her. Your daughter. Shit, man, I'm so sorry."

Tommy lifts his long body from his seat, calls out to the bus.

"Hey, any Pofers here?"

Dozens of heads turn back.

"You guys there today?"

"Yeah," someone calls.

"Since yesterday," says another. "You know what the hell happened?"

"I don't," Tommy says, "but maybe the guy next to me does."

"Don't!" Fraz whispers.

"Who's that next to you?"

"Just Franz Fucking Penzig!"

"Fraz. Not Franz."

"Fucking Fraz Penzig!" Tommy shouts.

"Fraz!" somebody calls.

"Old Fraz!"

"Old Crust!"

Fraz looks at Tommy.

"Old Crust?"

"That's what Hark calls you."

"No it's not."

"Well, that's how you're known."

"Where?"

"In the community, man. In the studios, in the posing barns, on the internet and whatnot. I mean, that's just what people call you. Old Crust. The Old Man. Old Bow."

"I didn't know that," Fraz says. "I guess I go to the wrong threads."

"Oh, you're a legend, bro," Tommy says. "Along with the Rumpler and Little Seth and Dark Teal."

"Dark Teal?"

"Old Crust," somebody calls out. "Do you bear news of Hark? Is he okay? Is the Focus for Lisa rescheduled? When will Meg post?"

"Soon," Fraz says, steps into the aisle. "Meg will post soon. We're waiting for information. Meantime, let us focus on Hark's well-being together. Let us take fifth position, Mind Nock, and hold it. Given our present location, we will move through the sequence silently after that: Nottingham Surprise, Drunken Kyūdō, Mongol Mare Shot, Lancaster of Lombardy, Shores of Gitche Gumee. Just those rudimentary poses."

Fraz does not mention that those are the only ones he's mastered. Fraz does not mention that Hark is already dead.

"We're with you, Old Pock!"

"But first," Fraz says, "picture yourself floating above a field with a crossbow in your hands. A giant apple rolls through the wheat. You can see it, those flashes of red in the great beige stalks. You load the bolt and raise your weapon."

"Sit down in back!" the bus driver yells.

"Focus!" Fraz says. "They don't want us to focus, but we must! Here's the apple, here's the wheat. Here's the apple, here's the wheat. We are going to shoot an apple off the head of the earth. Are you ready? For Hark. For Lisa. For all of us. Focus. Focus, says Old Crust. Focus."

"I said down in back!"

"Halve the apple and hope will live. Halve the apple and we can save the world!"

Fraz hears Hark's voice, a ghost hiss.

"What the hell are you doing, Fraz? What is this?"

Fraz thinks: This is you, my love.

PART THREE

PART THREE

Forty-four

Every age gets the savior it deserves, Fraz writes on his newly issued DIETER-TECH laptop with Glyph Systems software. It's his first column for the Institute for Mental Archery's online organ, *Hark!*.

This age has been cobbled together with old habits at new speeds—greed, war, oppression, xenophobia, spiritual decay. These miseries are our heritage. But the problem is that many of the traditional countervailing forces, such as decency, altruism, social contracts, civic duty, have disappeared. Or have been disappeared.

Technology was supposed to liberate us, and it does when it comes to things like medicine, but it's also inflicted immense economic and environmental damage around the world. And also psychic damage. We are watched and pitched incessantly. We are addicted to rectangles of light.

Meanwhile many humans are pretty exhausted, tired of

the struggle. The violence drags on. War is everywhere. Europe is about to be conquered by a group many call the Army of the Just, a force made up of the same mix of veterans, conscripts and soldiers of fortune that have filled the ranks of marauding armies for millennia. That this horde claims no particular religious or political ideology beyond the abolition of poverty and oppression, and includes members of diverse races, religions and creeds who have gathered from around the world and sworn to fight both globalist power structures and ethno-nationalist movements across the continents is especially startling. It is clear that our leadership is too decrepit to either stop this juggernaut or engage with it in a manner that would avoid major bloodshed. Even if somebody proposes a wiser course, it would be too late.

We need to look somewhere for guidance. The old modes are dead. More and more people are taking a look at the teachings of the late Hark Morner, a visionary thinker and healer whose system, Mental Archery, might just be the answer. Hark gave his life for his belief that with the right amount of love, dedication and forbearance we could evolve as humans at many levels: as people, as families, as societies, as inheritors and stewards of the earth. In my next column I'll introduce you to some details about Hark's thinking. It could save your life, and the lives of everyone you love.

Fraz sends it to Meg. A few hours later she emails: "Cut all but the last two sentences. It'll read cleaner that way."

Fraz wonders how long his career in flackhood will last.

To say it once more, history hides. It hides inside every new interpretation of an interpretation. It hides, in fact, like the gem stuck up the ass of the flabby young man called history at the outset of this tale. History is both the hidden gem and the man in whom the gem has been noiselessly, perhaps greasily, inserted. "Intelligence" may be defined as the ability to behold both of these word pictures at once, in the way you never could with a pair of nipples.

History is also what didn't happen. What if Hark had lived?

Or maybe that's not history at all.

It is, at any rate, a new epoch in our front story. Hark is dead but mental archery, spawned from his majestic dream, thrives. The rolls of registered mental archers grow. A campus has sprung up around Meg's house in Pickering. Teal and Seth supervise the staff. Fraz telecommutes from the city.

Nat Dersh serves as CFO at the pleasure of Dieter Delgado. The Institute for Mental Archery doesn't tithe, and does not yet qualify for tax-exempt status, though a law firm has been retained to fix this. For today, the operation is a spiritual start-up, with Deets as angel accelerator. The institute, after all, is just another business on his roster. Some wither, some die, some go public, some stay private and still effloresce. Dieter hails from the throw-it-all-at-the-wall school. One war, one earthquake, one tsunami, one pandemic, one dating app and, assuming you are well positioned, you can cover your losses and get mega-rich all over again, ad mega-infinitum. Deets read a book about this that inspired him to seek out more catastrophe. The next hemoclysm may make him the world's first trillionaire.

Fraz has recently read a book about Deets. This unauthorized biography neither explained with unerring exactitude the intractable shittiness of the political situation, nor did it transport him to a magical forest of shittinesslessness, but it covered a lot of the Delgado basics. Impressive guy, really. Came from nothing, or, rather, from a wealthy family in a gated suburb, but was waitlisted at Stanford and the major Ivies, had to battle his way through the elite postgraduate caste system.

Fraz has the TV on mute while he works, but the crawl beneath the anchorwoman catches his eye: BATTLE FOR BRATISLAVA PROVES INDECISIVE . . . PRESIDENT INVOKES THE "POWER OF FOCUS" FOR JOINT MILITARY OPERATIONS . . . IBM SUPERCOMPUTER APPOINTED STATE EXECUTIONER IN TEXAS . . . YOUNGSTOWN FC PUTS MESSI ON WAIVERS . . . PRODUCER SAYS PREPUBESCENT LEAR MORE THAN MERE BID FOR YOUTH MARKET . . .

Kate calls.

"It's been a while," she says. "I was just thinking of you."

"Really?"

"Bringing my story up to date."

"How does it look so far?"

"I'm sitting in the Faust Nook with a beetroot salad and a bottle of Moldovan vodka."

"Sounds like a Schnitz combo."

"Hey, you ever heard of a woman named Shana Buckman?"

"Buckman. I knew a Buckman. But he wasn't a Shana."

"Oh."

"What about her?"

"Well, she's no fan of Hark."

"I see."

"Not at all. I gave her a lot of money to leave Hark alone. Like, kind of almost all my money. Guess it doesn't matter now. I also gave her somebody else's marrow. I'm banned from the clinic. They are considering criminal charges but I think they believe that I was forced, which I was. It's been happening to other couriers lately. But it's still not good."

"Come back to us, Kate."

"There is no us. Hark's gone."

"We have to soldier on. Or carry on."

"With Delgado?"

"It's not like he's around much. And there's no escape. Tovah's been working for him for years. A good percentage of the planet's population does."

"The Army of the Just will take care of that."

"Don't joke. It's just a matter of time before they get here."

"That's what everybody says. But they're stalled in Europe now. NATO's beating them back."

"They're just a bunch of terrorists."

"Maybe. But they're for single payer. They're against Citizens United."

"A lot of people will die, Kate."

"Yeah, but some of them will be rich people."

"Like you, Kate."

"Not anymore. How can you work for Delgado? How can you work for Meg?"

"Meg's nice. Just a little controlling."

"She's warping Hark's message."

"Hark never had a message."

"Hey, Fraz, did you ever think . . . did you ever wonder if maybe that Barron guy is just a pasty?"

"A what?"

"I mean, what's the word? A patsy."

"A patsy? No, Kate. Is this some conspiracy shit? You should talk to my son."

"I know Barron is the shooter, but . . ."

"But what?"

"But nothing. How's life at the institute?"

"Mental Archery flourishes on a global scale. We're opening clinics and spas all over. Seth is our international dealmaker. Dieter is sinking more and more money into a huge online mental archery academy. Everybody's very focused."

"Even Meg?"

"Especially Meg. She wants security and comfort for Menny, I guess. Who can blame her? I'd like the same for my kids. Though I'm just a freelance grunt. I won't be cashing in."

"Then why are you doing it?"

"I'm a Harkist."

"So am I."

"I know you are."

"Did he say anything, Fraz?"

"Who?"

"You know who. Hark."

"Say what?"

"Did he say anything in the helicopter? Any last words? Final pointers? Nothing?"

"He was in a lot of pain."

"Right. Of course."

"It was terrible."

"It must have been. Yeah. How are the kids?"

"Lisa's all healed. But I'm not seeing them much. They've been spending a lot of time with Nat Dersh. Or, rather, Tovah has. And the kids go with her. I'm not sure if we're separated or what. It's all pretty painful and confusing."

"I'm sorry, Fraz."

"Me, too."

"Life takes these pretty severe turns, doesn't it?"

"Is that what this is?"

"A turn, you mean?"

"No. Life, I mean."

———————

Fraz fixes his new favorite cocktail, the B & R, a bourbon and rye on the rocks.

Tovah is still at that stupid writers' conference she insisted on attending. True, she scored her first paid vacation in years, and she'd talked about this trip forever, but doesn't she comprehend the urgency of this post-Hark geopolitical moment? The war in Europe will spread here soon, and it's the ultimate three-way standoff: the Armies of the Markets versus the Army of the Just versus the vast majority of people who just want to be left alone to the vagaries of life and the insults of the body. How will the institute, not to mention ordinary folks, survive? Moreover, as Fraz asked Tovah, how can this be the best time to take a poetry workshop?

"When is it ever a good time for the news that stays news?" Tovah replied.

"Cripes," Fraz said, "the only thing worse than American exceptionalism is artistic exceptionalism."

"I'm still going, Fraz. I've earned it."

"Oh, is that what Nat told you?"

"It's over with me and Nat."

"It is?"

"Fuck you," Tovah said.

It wasn't "I'm sorry," but it would do for now.

He was happy to have the kids to himself. He could inculcate in them the tenets of mental archery without obstruction. Hope hinged on the next generation.

Hark is dead, but that can be an advantage. Once a philosophy is no longer in thrall to the human who produced it, the message becomes more malleable, dynamic. Fraz knows he's treading the line between fidelity to Hark's vision and a continuing role in the new conditions, but he believes a balance can be struck. That's the nice way of putting it. But what would Fraz do if really put to the test? And what is the test? Maybe the test came and went when Fraz decided to lie to people like Kate about Hark's last wishes. But he and Meg have struck a deal to keep Hark's words on the helo secret. Do they really both believe Hark's calls to action were just the ravings of a dying man? Or is that their convenient theory? Crises of conscience seem much simpler in movies. A long gaze out the window, some subdued dialogue with a lover or friend, and the protagonist steels himself for righteous self-abnegation. But movie people don't pay the light bills in their movie houses. Then again, Fraz doesn't pay the light bill in his house.

Tonight the twins watch TV. Fraz pours another B & R, joins them.

"May I have a sip?" Lisa asks.

"No."

"Why?"

"It's a grown-up drink."

"You mean a drunk drink."

"Drunks are people who drink too much. I drink just the right amount."

"How can you tell?"

"When you do it every night, you just can. What is this that you're watching?"

"It's a great show on the Animatoon Channel, Daddy. It's called *The Furthering Continuing Adventures of the Fucktoid Family of Cuntfart Junction.*"

"You still watch that?" Fraz says. "I thought that was for younger kids."

"It is," Lisa says, "but it's also for older kids and adults who can appreciate the surrealism."

"Okay," Fraz says. "It doesn't matter anyway. The world is over. There won't be anything for you out there."

"Why do you have to whine so much?" David says.

"Am I whining?"

"Almost always," Lisa says.

Glazed, Fraz regards his children. They are doomed by history and will soon be stripped of their First World privileges. He loves them all the more for their bad luck.

"Dad, stop crying."

"I'm sorry."

"Don't say you're sorry. Just stop. It's embarrassing."

"You guys are everything to me. Do you know that? Come here."

Fraz gropes for his babies, but the twins squirm away.

"Dad!"

"I'm a man who loves his children. Why is that so wrong?"

"It's not wrong," David says, rubs his father's neck. "It's just intrusive."

"I'm sorry."

"No worries," Lisa says.

"Hey," Fraz says, wipes his eyes, blows a little snot onto his thumb. "I'm so happy you're alive. You don't know what it was like for us when you were under. I'm just so happy. Here you are. After that scary time. What was it like for you?"

"It was weird, Dad. It was like I was in a coma."

Forty-five

Perhaps Fraz had never heard of it before, but the Pine Barrens Writers' Conference in southern New Jersey is a celebrated gathering of some of the leading novelists and poets of the day. They come to give readings and talks and to critique the work of aspirants to the craft—graduate students, mostly—as well as other guests, often people in the midst of lives and careers in the regular world, but willing to pay a not insignificant fee to feed their creative souls for a few weeks in August.

Tovah belongs to this second group. Though she's published her poems in journals in the past, like practically every living American poet who doesn't have a trust fund or university sinecure, she's saddled with a real job and other responsibilities outside the world of letters. But for two weeks she can set those burdens aside, find her sound again.

Tovah has wanted to come for years. The money, and the fact of having to entrust the care of the twins to Fraz for more than an evening, always kept her away. But the kids are older now, and this fortnight, in truth, is Tovah's booby prize, a vestige of her crazy run with Nat Dersh. The tuition check he wrote was the last dime he spent on her before he told her to gather her spawn, scram.

Up until a few months ago, Nat and Tovah had seen each other rather frequently, often with the twins, but also alone, for amorous encounters.

Tovah worried her pussy had not proven wise enough, not that Nat was any kind of pleasure wizard in bed, with his bony twitches and phlegm-flutter grunts, his strange chirps for her to "get it," or "take it," like "it" was an acorn, and he was some exotic and generous blue jay.

For Tovah, sex wasn't the point. Nat's wealth just helped her relax. The knots in her back loosened in his enormous suede chairs. The twins reveled in the décor of his penthouse, the infinitude of square footage. The sectional sofa sat forty with ease. The coffee table could support a shipping container. The television, jumbotronic, was suitable for stadia.

What bloomed in these quarters was not, Tovah now realizes, a love affair but a temporary zone of sensual domesticity. Tovah had begun to picture herself in a long, blissful, sexless marriage with Nat Dersh. She'd let him fuck other people. Who cared? Fact was she still loved Fraz and wanted him in her life as the father of her children, and friend, or even friend with benefits, to borrow from the old-timey lingo, just maybe not as a live-in hump forever bathed in refrigerator light, or flung out across the rug for a nap, his apnea nearly orchestral.

One warm May night at the penthouse Nat hired a ceviche chef and they all had a grand time of it with music (Nat played and sang numbers from his favorite band from the early nineties, Spacklefinger, on the banjo, including their almost generation-defining hit, "Police State Barista") and charades (David did something hilariously inappropriate with his heinie for the first syllable of the second word in *Madame Butterfly*). Later, Tovah put the kids to bed and joined Nat in the roof garden, whose designer, Nat told her, had intended a very hanging and Babylonian eyefeel.

"Nailed it, no?" Nat said, sipped his port.

"It's been a strange time," Tovah said.

"Pardon?"

"Sorry. I was just thinking. It's been a pretty odd time. With Lisa's injury, David's trauma, my job, problems with Fraz. Overwhelming, really. But you've been there for me, Nat. You really have. You've been a dream. And I'm so looking forward to things calming down. Not just for the kids, but so you and I can really be together, sink deeper into each other, without all the distractions."

"There are always distractions," Nat said.

"No, I know. But still."

"Like maybe *you're* a distraction."

"Ha."

"I'm serious."

Something cinched up Tovah like a seat belt, that sudden extra tug.

"I guess I'm so sexy, I must be a distraction, right?"

Tovah heard herself laugh: flirty, alone.

"You're desirable for your age, Tovah, but let's not be irrational."

"Okay, Nat. I'll try not to be irrational."

"Hey, I'm no movie star, either."

"Yeah, but you're a gazillionaire."

"There's that. But you knew about my wealth going in. Maybe it motivated your advances a little?"

"My advances? You came on to me. Several times. You set up the fake double date."

"I don't quite remember it that way. Let's leave it to the mists of memory. The fog of war."

"Nat."

"Tovah," Nat said. "It's clear this isn't working. We need to be adults. I'm not ready to be a father to your children. Or a husband to you. I know I said I wanted those things, or wanted an authentic relationship with a real woman, but I've tried, and now I realize that's not what I want. It's like, say you dream of living the simple life on a farm, but then you finally do move to a farm and you discover that farm life is not what you thought it was at all—that farm life, in fact, is hectic and disgusting. And not simple in the slightest. Livestock, crops, hired help. Feeding and breeding schedules, plagues and droughts. Animals covered with animal feces and weeping sores. It's all quite complicated and strenuous. Not that I've ever experienced life as a farmer, but I can only imagine what it takes to be a really good one. You need to be some weird combination of endurance athlete and scientist. So fuck the farm. That's what I'm feeling. And I can't pretend anymore. It's not right and it's been wearing on me. And it's not fair to Fraz."

Nat poured himself another glass of tawny.

"Not fair to Fraz? You narcissistic, lying, horrible fucking—"

"I know," Nat said. "I know. Listen, I'm going for a stroll. I'll sleep in the guest room tonight. Get yourselves gone in the morning."

"But why?"

"Why? I'm a romantic. I like romance. I like beginnings. I get really antsy when women want to share a life, build a future, be partners, pick your cliché. It's like they're quitting. Surrendering to safety and routine. And why would I want to be with a quitter? How can I be turned on by that?"

"What turns you on, then?"

"Being with a woman who challenges me. By which I mean poses a threat. Being with a woman who is much younger and sexier than I am, and possibly smarter, and a passionate, attentive lover who cares about my ordeals but who also might, without warning, while I'm sleeping, cut off my pecker with a grapefruit knife. Not that she would, really. I don't want a psychotic. Just that the idea, the image, gets her wet."

"You're twisted."

"That's all you have to say? And you're a poet? But you're afraid of the dark. You're a poet of the salad bar, of the quarterly report in PDF, of the kid with the mumps, the gourmet cupcakes."

"I live in the dark, you bastard. All I do is claw for light."

"That's such a drag, Tovah. It really is. Everyday struggle is a fucking bore. Don't you get that?"

"Fraz used to say that rich people were actually better than other people. And that's why we should kill them."

"He was never stupid. Good-bye, darling."

That was the bitter finish, but Dersh did not cancel the tuition check. He'd probably forgotten cutting it, although in her time with him she'd noticed how miserly he could be, tipping 11 percent in restaurants, demanding the kids split one ice cream cone at the park because the prices were a "moral outrage." Dersh picked up pennies from the pavement and once, when a beggar sat on the sidewalk grate with a few bills sticking out of his paper cup, she noticed Nat so absorbed by the sight of the money, as though he'd just discovered a new and ingenious way to earn some, that he nearly crashed into a mailbox. But the Pine Barrens check went through.

She'd left the kids with Fraz. He'd taken her back. She'd allowed him to take her back. It was very nuanced. Nuance is a hallmark of nuanced people.

Here in the Pines, she sits in the cabin she shares with a young woman from Boston who is working on a novel about her Brahmin ancestor, a spirited adventuress, a mistress of Albert Fall of the Teapot Dome scandal, and the first woman on record to kill a tranquilized lion with a Maxim gun. Tovah has already made the mistake of telling her roommate that it sounded like an interesting story.

"'Interesting,'" Sarah had said. "What an interesting word, don't you think?"

The lunch gong rings and Tovah heads over to the dining lodge, finds a seat at one of the long wooden tables. Grad students in aprons serve the meal. It's a highly selective honor to be a server, and a number of these kids have gone on to "make noise in the publishing world," as the Pine Barrens Writers' Conference website phrases it. The waiters swagger and snicker as they serve the customers paying full freight. But the instructors snicker and swagger more, cherish their minor celebrity.

Tovah does not partake in these groupie grotesqueries. She's been around long enough to know that writers are regular people, if not a bit more vain and shallow than most. The only solution is to study the techniques of the good ones but to steer clear of their company. Her time in graduate school only magnified this observation.

Tovah fetches some silverware and napkins and sits alone with her laptop. She'll write some emails to David and Lisa, send them some photos she's taken of lightning-charred trees. She'll also have to check in with work. Cal, in an unexpected burst of largesse, signed off on the vacation, even after so much time away during Lisa's coma, with the caveat that Tovah stay connected with her team, put in a few hard hours a day. Otherwise, he said, she should "poeticize her butt off."

"Write about what a creepy a-hole I am," he added. "I don't care. Or write about that weird growth on Vincent's eyelid. That could be one of those resonant details that really anchor a poem."

"Okay, thanks, Cal."

A server arrives with a plate of pasta, her blond hair up in a lime-green clip, some kind of vintage look, Tovah is certain, though she's lost her place on the fashion gesture timeline. Is this a revival of a trend that mocked an earlier revival?

"Having some alone time today?" the server asks.

"I've got a poem percolating."

"Awesome. I love poets. I should read more poetry. And write it."

"What do you write?"

"Creative nonfiction. Not that these designations mean anything. Fiction, nonfiction, and so forth."

"I always thought that the difference was that in one of them you make stuff up and in the other one you try not to."

"You're a scream," the server says. "You should hang out with us. We're having a 2009-themed party in the south field tonight. Bob Price downloaded all of these, like, excruciatingly egregious, like, you know, super, like, cringy songs from that year. I hope the party's not too late for you! Oh, my God, I hope we don't wake you up! Well, if we do, just come on over."

Tovah stabs a ravioli with her fork. The red sauce is thin, the pasta dough rubbery. The dish resembles a pile of blood-spattered surgical gloves. She saw such a pile once, behind a hospital, wrote a ghazal about it.

"Bob Price is here?" Tovah says.

"Yeah. So?"

"Nobody warned me."

"Why would you need to be warned?"

"Oh, sorry, I just meant that nobody mentioned it. I used to know him. That's cool that he's here. I'll have to surprise him. Bob Price. How funny."

"He's a beautiful freak, the Price. A true free soul. I mean, he's like one of us. Except he's a much better writer. But we'll catch up. That's how it works. Anyway, see you later."

Forty-six

Fraz waits to be received in, or perhaps ejected from, Nat Dersh's reception area. He caresses the Swiss Army knife in his pocket. He's been carrying it since Pickering. It's silly, but he's a little spooked. He's a known Harkist and maybe there are more Boyd Barrons out there, codgers with crackerjack man-killing skills. It's really a knockoff, the knife, a Slovenian army knife, or maybe Nepalese. It's a good knife, with clean folding action, two blades, a tiny saw, a screwdriver, a corkscrew, a can opener, a plastic toothpick. He's not sure how he would defend himself with this device, but he could certainly, if granted mercy, the necessary skills and a small amount of balsa wood, make his would-be assailant a nice chest of doll's house drawers.

The room looks dingier than usual, the glass coffee table smeared with ash, stamped with sticky rings, the magazines crinkled, torn, the air stale. Dersh's niece Vera sits at the reception desk with her phone. Fraz follows the piston action of her thumbs.

"You have a party in here?" Fraz asks.

"Just a few friends."

"Looks like it."

"You the party police?"

"Hardly. Used to party myself."

" 'Party' as a verb. Very alluring."

"What, that's not back yet?"

"Soon, Grampy."

"Sorry. Hope I'm not bothering you."

"I'm not cognizant of you enough for that. But what's your desired outcome in this interaction?"

"Pardon?"

"Do you need something?"

"You kids. I'm just shooting the breeze."

"I don't feel any breeze."

"I want to talk to you so I can get a sense of what the world of a young woman is like. So I can help prepare my daughter for the future."

"Is your daughter hot?"

"Excuse me?"

"You heard."

"I don't think I did. My daughter is ten. And she's my daughter."

"I'm not accusing you of anything. I'm just asking a question. But forget it."

"No, tell me."

"Do you think I'm hot?"

"Look, I'm not some old perv who wants to—"

"Of course you are. It's biology. But all I'm saying is you can't really generalize about the experience of women. If your daughter turns out to be desirable to lots of people, she will have a different life than if not. But only for a while. She'll age out of it. But I know my life has perks based solely on my looks. I have an ugly sister, so I am very aware of this. If your son is hot, things will go a lot more smoothly for him as well. People submit to beauty without even knowing they're doing it. That's just a fact. The world treats you a little better. You have more opportunities, more adventures. Perhaps you become more vulnerable in some ways as well. But it's better to be hot. I also think hot people, if they happen to also be sensitive and kind, have more empathy than any ugly person. In a sense, hot people are usually better people than non-hot people."

"You know," Fraz says, "I have a similar theory about rich people."

"Money is totally different. Anyway, what I'm trying to say is that, contrary to conventional wisdom, hot people are deeper people. Because ugly people, and by 'ugly people' I just mean most people, are twisted up with resentment, traumatized by shame. They can't get past it. But hot people are, like, more emotionally and philosophically expansive. Similar traits and privileges attach to tall people, as long as they are reasonably hot. We've all heard how if you're a male lawyer, a trial lawyer, being six feet or over makes a huge difference. Juries almost always side with a tall man. It's been statistically proven. So I wouldn't worry too much about what you can't control. Just love your daughter with all your heart, give her the best education you can manage and leave it at that."

"You're quite remarkable," Fraz says.

"No. I'm just a smart, sensitive, hot person."

Vera tilts her head, as though an insect has grazed her ear.

"Nat says he's ready for you."

Fraz rises, heads for the door.

"Be careful of them," Vera says.

Fraz pauses.

"They should be careful of me."

———

Nat Dersh leans back on his desk, shoots Fraz a curt wave. Seth and Meg and Sean Critchley from Glyph Systems sit around an obsidian coffee table.

"Hey, it's Mr. Goat Butter!" Critchley calls.

"Ha," Fraz says, notices the presence of another man projected on a wall screen.

"Dieter," Fraz says.

"'Sup," Deets says. "Yeah, I remember this guy."

"Fraz," Seth says. "Have a seat."

"Okay. Mind telling me why you wanted to see me?"

"Well," Seth says, "we've been pretty busy over here."

"Doing what?"

"Designing apps," Critchley says. "Apps and bots. Bots for the human spirit. Bots for humanity. Focus-ware. Call it what you want. I'm a businessman, and I'm greedy for more, but how will I spend it, and how will my descendants spend it, if we tip into a new dark age? Or just die from the weather? It's untenable. And space is a drag. Cryogenesis is a joke. And I don't want to live only on a neural network. I still want my meatworld fun. For a while, at least. So we've got to make this work. But you can't change systems without changing people first. And that's where mental archery comes in."

"And that's also where you come in, Fraz," Meg says. "I know Hark loved you. He'd want you here in this room."

"Meg. What are you doing here with these guys? What are we doing?"

"What do you mean?"

Fraz feels the queasiness as the next words leave him, something akin to a conscience rise, slick and sour, in his throat.

"Remember the helicopter? What Hark said?"

"Who are you to ask that, Fraz?"

"Who am I? I'm a man who once walked into a bookstore. Who listened to a kid babble about some fake archery routine."

"Let's not get too grandiose. You can be part of this or not. We've already made a place for you here. For Old Crust. For the Old Man."

"You know, I'm only forty-seven."

"That's old. You understand that, right?"

"What, you want me to keep writing that column?"

"You can still write the column if you wish," Meg says. "But, no, that's not what we're talking about. See, since that performance on the bus back from Pickering, your reputation has soared. It was remarkable what you did, the way you slipped so authentically into the role of inspiring mental archery leader."

"I wasn't trying to slip into a role. Hark was dead. I had to do something."

"Many are looking to you, right now," Seth says. "Oh, they don't think you're the new Hark or anything. But they want you to be one of the public caretakers of his legacy. They want Old Bow to guide them. The polls and surveys are very clear on this."

"Surveys," Fraz says.

"Basic market research," Critchley says. "Anyway, sorry, Proctor. Proceed."

"I think I've covered the bulk of it. If you agree to work with us, we'd put you on retainer. You'll travel a bit, make promotional videos, give the keynote at conventions, lead retreats. We'll tell you what to say. Also, there is evidence that some of the other early Harkians have become, well, folkloric. Dark Teal, of course, and the Rumpler."

"Seth, you call her Dark Teal, too? Isn't she your girlfriend?"

"Not so much these days. And you can call me Proctor."

"The fuck I will. Were you a spy all along?"

"What's a spy? I'm an information conduit, like anybody else. It's who we are as a species."

"Exactly," Nat says.

"Nat," Fraz says. "You know you really hurt Tovah, dumping her like that."

"Never meant to hurt her, Fraz. How is she? Are you back to-gether?"

"Sort of."

"Make it work, buddy. And make *this* work. We need your help. We need you to bring the others back into the fold. They can be part of your entourage. We don't want them out there siphoning energy or denigrating the brand. We hope you'll talk sense into them. We've already seen a few of them speak harshly about our mission in a leading vegan magazine."

"They have strong views."

"So do we," Nat says. "And we have no qualms about taking strong action."

"You mean lawyers?" Fraz says.

"Now, Nat, let's calm down a little," Critchley says.

"Yeah!" Nat laughs. "Lawyers. Sure."

"You're crazy if you think I'm going to go out there and distort Hark's vision so you can make a buck. And drag my friends into it to boot."

"Who said anything about distorting his vision?" Meg says. "If the vision gets distorted, that's on you."

"We don't want you to distort anything," Dieter says from the screen. "We are going to make money by selling the genuine article. The real message. More efficient that way."

"I'm not sure you want to sell the genuine article," Fraz says. "Because I can tell you that right before he died, Hark said some things. You heard him, Meg. He said we should help lead the fight."

"The fight for better focus?" Dieter Delgado says.

"No, Deets."

"Then what did he want to fight?"

"Well, bascially, you, Deets. Meg, you remember. You were there."

"I don't remember anything of the sort, Fraz. Were we in the same helicopter?"

"She's got you there, Fraz."

"Anyway, guys," Dieter says, "I've got to scram. We're about to launch Mercystream."

"So exciting, Deets," Critchley says.

"Mercystream?" Fraz says.

"It's amazing," Meg says. "Instead of letting refugees into the country, we can give them laptops and listen to their stories as they stream them from their camps. It's all about empathy."

"Later, taters," Dieter says, going dark.

"Look," Fraz says, "Meg is lying. I don't know why. But Hark told us he was wrong, that this wasn't just for home or office. That we had to do something with this energy."

"The man was bleeding out!" Nat says. "Are we going to dishonor the legacy he built over years over something only you claim he said in his last, distraught moments?"

"He never said anything," Meg says.

"What happened to you?" Fraz asks. "You used to be the devout one."

"My savior kicked the bucket. I have a kid."

"I have two."

"I don't know how you do it."

"He doesn't do it, really," Nat says. "I've seen him in action. Anyway, are you with us, Fraz?"

Fraz freezes again. What he's with, in fact, is taking out his mystery army blade and slipping it into Nat Dersh's eye. Julienne his brain. Maybe it's an Army of the Just knife. Beats that Swiss shit. The tweezers alone, an amazement.

"But I stick to the spirit of Hark," Fraz says.

"Look, really, if you want to push a social justice version of Hark," Critchley says, "I don't have a big problem with that. I don't think Deets will, either. We're pretty flexible. Just don't knock innovation. Or money."

"That's right," Dersh says. "The fact is, like Deets, I myself spend a lot of money on philanthropy. As does my company. But we're not interested in any large-scale, systemic shift in how things are done on the planet. For that, the downtrodden are really just going to have to come and take our fucking shit and kill us. And so far they are too scared to try. Actually, it's getting kind of boring."

"I'll have high salary requirements."

"Of course you will. You're a self-respecting fellow."

"I want to talk to some friends."

"Say yes, then talk to them."

Fraz knows you can't stop the rot from the inside. That's the oldest canard. They'll toss him on the slag heap when he's no longer needed. And whatever they pay him, it won't be enough to buy his freedom. There really is no choice.

"Okay, I'm in," Fraz says.

"Excellent," Critchley says.

"Hooray for Old Pock," Meg says.

"Hey, I've got a 1985 Richebourg to celebrate with," Dersh says. "Let me just find my wine opener."

Fraz digs out his knife, unfolds the corkscrew.

"The Crusted One," says Critchley, "to the rescue."

At the recently reopened Candescent Boll, Fraz chews his bacon condor burger. A froth of ground bird chuck gathers on his lips. Teal and Kate sip their iced oolongs, listen to Fraz's pitch.

"It really makes more sense this way. We'll carry the message to so many more people if we work with Dieter and Meg and Dersh and the Glyph Systems bunch. Great guys. Teal, you were there that day in New Jersey. Remember when Critchley led everyone out and we thought it was because he hated Hark? That whole turn-it-around thing? There's a certain elegance to it all."

"There's a certain betrayal to it all," Teal says. "It's why Seth and I broke up. This kind of bullshit."

"Oh, please," Fraz says.

"She's right," Kate says.

"Harkism is alive," Fraz says. "I can't help it that Hark isn't. We're all doing our best. I won't lie to you. Tovah and I, we're over-extended. We're in a lot of debt."

"Everybody's hurting," Kate says. "Most of my inheritance is gone. Shana Buckman took it. Or maybe the Army of the Just. Who knows?"

"I told you, Kate," Teal says. "Your maintenance bill is way too high. Dump that place. Stay with me for a while. No more arguments."

"Fraz," Kate says, "doesn't your wife make good money?"

"With the kids, it's not enough."

"Who told you to have kids?" Kate says.

"My wiring."

"Your wiring told you to shoot a load, not raise twins in a major metropolis."

"Fine. You guys win. But what's your plan? Start your own mental archery spin-off?"

"We're thinking butterscotch," Teal says.

"Seriously."

"We're going to live our lives."

"What do you mean, live your lives?"

"We're going to work, eat, sleep, read books, watch TV, go for runs, bake scones and practice mental archery and wait," Kate says.

"Wait for what?"

Teal and Kate flick looks at each other, reach for their teas.

"Hold on," Fraz says, picks up a french fry, waves it. "Hold up. You don't think . . . wait . . . you believe he's coming back?"

Teal and Kate stare down at the table.

"Wow," Fraz says. "Unfuckingreal."

"It's not quite what you think," Teal says.

"Oh, no, it's exactly what I think. You've just cooked up some stupid messiah story. You're fucking idiots."

"It's eternal recurrence."

"Like hell it is. You know, Teal, it's you I don't understand. You're supposed to be the calm and collected intellectual. What are you guys thinking? He was a guy who just wanted people to focus. And, yes, maybe at the end he had a grander vision, but he was no fucking deity."

"It's not like that," Teal says.

"What's it like?"

"You never felt it, did you?" Teal says.

"What do you mean, felt it? Mental archery? I felt it."

"You felt yourself getting important. Maybe you felt a sense of community. You felt Hark's embrace, when he was up for giving one. But you never felt it."

"What?"

"You were never an arrow," Kate says. "You never felt yourself in flight, yet also at rest. You were never delivered by the bow to your ownmost self. You never plucked fruit off the head of the boy."

"Never even been accused of that, no," Fraz says. "You guys aren't joking, are you?"

"I don't think we are," Teal says.

"What if I told you that Hark never felt those things, either?"

"It wouldn't matter. Hark is not perfect. He has his foibles. Like you say, he isn't a deity."

"*Wasn't* a deity. He's dead, remember?"

"Yes," Kate says. "In a certain sense he is."

"Okay," Fraz says. "I'm going to pretend you guys haven't lost your minds. Do what you want. But I'm telling you, it's really best if we at least pretend to be working together."

"What are you talking about?" Teal asks.

"Dersh really wants to make sure you guys aren't going to subvert his big plans. He's talking about lawyers."

"Screw lawyers. We can handle ourselves, Fraz. Why don't you run off to your bosses now."

Fraz nods, stands, fishes in his pocket.

"Let me get this."

"Sure thing. That'll be thirty pieces of silver."

Fraz searches for a retort, how after taxes it was really more like seventeen pieces of silver, but his thoughts are a gas marsh. He walks to the door, which is sheathed in studded leather, notices a photograph on the wall, a face he knows from television, and dreams derived from television. You can just make out the top of the green football jersey. The inscription reads: *To my pals at the Magniloquent Troll, Stay great in the sack, Mark Gastineau.*

It's got to be a fake.

Forty-seven

Meg discovers the notebook in a cellar crate in Pickering. It's hardbound, yellow, with a red ribbon bookmark glued into the spine. The husks of insects molder on the cover, sift to dust with a swipe of her hand.

On the first page there's a sketch of Meg, nude, as she reaches for a can of soup on a shelf. She doesn't recall posing for this picture, though she reckons Hark had seen both her and the pantry enough times to draw from memory. She'd never known Hark to sketch, wants to be moved by these soft, dark charcoal strokes, the tenderness of the rendering, but maybe feels ambushed, coming upon it like this, a bit too seen, though of course she's the one digging through Hark's effects.

She reads Hark's crimped, ballpoint script:

What is the Nature of the Arrow?

> *1. An instrument, a tool. In short, a projectile.*
> *2. But, symbolically? Many things. The soul? Or whatever*

> *we mean when we say soul? (Soul Brother? Soul Mate?*
> *Oversoul? Heart and Soul?)*
>
> *How are we to get from "here" to "there"? Here being*
> *here, and there being there.*
> *How does focus work? What does focus mean? Energy is*
> *the water and focus is the hose. What about "pulling" focus?*
> *Keep your eyes on the prize. What is the prize? It's been many*
> *things, but what about now? Not happiness. Emptiness. And*
> *then: How do you empty emptiness? The garbage truck of*
> *emptiness pulls up to the curb. What is the task of these "gar-*
> *bage men"? Do they wear "empty" smiles? What color are*
> *their coveralls?*

It's much more meandering, and, she must admit, simple-minded, than those early pamphlets. But the pamphlets were stripped down, mystically efficient, mostly diagrams, a few nearly pithy phrases. Maybe this journal is juvenilia, not worth sharing with the community. She wants to shut the book, but reads on:

> *If an arrow that never existed flies through imaginary space*
> *and hits nothing, do I exist? Who am I? Brain and face. Arms*
> *and legs. Penis and balls and ball sack. More? If not, then yes.*
> *Memory: Dad, Detective Morner, his gun. Cleaning and*
> *oiling. Cleaning and oiling. That oily rag. The philosopher cop.*
> *Reading Augustine, going downtown to break heads. Reading*
> *Chesterton, beating a perp with a phone book, or The Best of*
> *Chesterton. Home, suspended on assault charges, kicks a hole*
> *in the wall. Cracks Mom in the jaw. Throws a dish at my head.*
> *Catches me in the neck. I'm on the linoleum. "You little fuck!*
> *Focus! Focus!" Later, another dish. I duck it. "That's it! See*
> *everything, son! That's the power of focus!"*
> *The power of focus.*
> *He wanted to name me Castaneda. But Mom insisted on*
> *Hark. Both names ridiculous. For a ridiculous boy.*
> *Do I talk enough about Robin Hood? Who was he really?*
> *Did he actually give to the poor? Who are you, Robin Hood?*

Memory: Dad and Constanza, always his favorite, strolling ahead of me and Mom on the Santa Monica pier. They laugh, hold hands, like a couple. They are talking about books. It's all they ever talk about. They are the smart ones. I am the dummy. Mom's got her psalms. But I read. Constanza, she's not mean about it. She brings me books. I don't let Dad know. I keep it secret, like the drugs. I read Dante under the covers with the dope-sick shakes. I read Homer, Voltaire. I go cop some tar. I read Shakespeare, the beatniks. I read the magical realists. I read the unmagical realists. I'm not a smart reader, like Conzi, but I read. I should be dead from what I'm doing out on the streets. I want to write, but I don't know how. Not really. Especially then. But I see what a story is. I see that everything is a story. All religions, all science, every theory of the universe. Freud told a story. Jung told another story. Einstein told a story. Marx told a story. People get upset by this because they think that means what they said wasn't true. Some stories are true and some aren't. Some are powerful because they are clearly true. Others are powerful because they speak to what we want to be true. Gravity is real. Peter Pan is not real. Both are great stories. Constanza told me to tell a story. I had the story before I had mental archery. She was the angel. She was the real future. Then the cancer in her brain. She could have freed us. I'm a fraud. Sooner or later people will find out. They'll find out just from reading this dumb fucking diary.

Meg clutches the book to her chest. No, you weren't a fraud, my love. You were brilliant, traumatized. I was wrong. All the major teachers and healers move through the simple and the complex, the visceral and the abstract. Consciousness is a slalom course.

Meg pages through the rest of the notebook. More dire, aching questioning. More strange and salient connections. It needs an edit, some polish, heavy revision in places. But the community must see some version of this. It's not about Hark's insurrectionary mutterings on the chopper. It's about this side of the man. The quest for self-knowledge. She's not as cynical as Fraz would suppose. She just sees the furthest, past stopgaps like bloody revolt. We'll all be fighting our laptops soon.

Now she turns another page and reads from the top:

Can't believe I never got closer to Kate. She is so beautiful. Sometimes she seems so distanced from the movement, or me. Meg is a decent, maternal person. But tough. She's stringy-hearted, like a pioneer woman. She understands what I'm doing. (Way more than me!) She will honor the legacy. She won't let Delgado take over and sell the whole thing out. Meg is like a sister—well, not like my sister. Meg is nice, but too plain. She just doesn't inspire me. We need people like her, plain Jane apostles. The big problem with Meg, though, besides her personality, is that snotty kid she has. I can't stand him. I love kids, but Menny is annoying and selfish and I think also a little slow. He's a big, bawling nothing. I'll be out of here first chance I get. Meg can still work for the organization, but at a very low level and without contact with me. I miss the old gang, Teal, Kate, even Fraz in his way, even though he's such an idiot. It's time to go back to the source. It's time to renew the bow. Maybe I am what some of them think. Tens of thousands claim me as their spiritual leader. Maybe the whole point is it's not going to be a superior being. A special person. If everybody is special, then it's going to be the one who isn't, the ordinary guy. But not ordinary like Meg, or ordinary enough to keep fucking Meg and putting up with that runty dunce she dotes on . . .

Meg climbs out of the cellar and stands in the afternoon light. She looks again at the sketch at the beginning of the notebook, tears the page out, folds it, slips it into her pocket. She takes the journal into the kitchen, opens the woodstove, peers into that orange and burning world. There is much to say, but sometimes fire is the only required utterance. She tosses the notebook into the stove, lets the flames have a few words on the topic of Hark Morner.

Forty-eight

Roomie Sarah drives off to Philly for the day. Tovah has the cabin to herself. She drinks from a thermos of thin coffee, a weak brew that maybe approximates what the French call "sock juice," tweaks a new poem before workshop. She's too nervous to eat breakfast, which is a shame, because the morning spread—muesli, fresh fruit, perfectly poached eggs—is the best meal of the day. But her stomach hurts. She's sick with risk. The sock juice doesn't help.

She knows she's written her best poem yet. She's not worried about its worth. But she knows herself, and if the instructor doesn't recognize its quality, tries to quash her again, she might never write another. She doesn't pretend this will have savage consequences for humankind. But it will depress the shit out of her, for sure.

She hears the afternoon workshop gong, revises the final line.

The poem is called "The Cruising Cloud." The title is from Dickinson and, yes, the entire workshop can screw themselves if they're too cool for Emily.

She runs to the dining lodge, refills her thermos, heads for the trees.

The class meets in a clearing in the woods. There are beach chairs and cracked wooden cable spools for tables. Everybody clutches water bottles, nontoxic bug spray, out-of-range cell phones, luxury pencils.

"Tovah!" Veronica, the workshop leader, calls. She's about ten years younger than Tovah, lectures at Yale. "Please join us."

Tovah takes a spot between a moist little guy named Davey and an extremely tall woman named Julie, a self-indentified "southern giantess."

"Okay, Davey," Veronica says. "Why don't you read your poem?"

They are doing cold readings. Probably to save Veronica prep work. This is, after all, her summer break.

Davey reads his poem. Reads it again. Reads it once more.

Discussion begins.

"I like the phrase 'blue hell,'" somebody says. "Would that be the ocean?"

"The ocean inside you," another offers.

"Maybe I'm biased because I love the ocean," Julie says, "but what's hellish about it? Nothing hellish about the surf at Myrtle Beach."

"May I say something?" Davey asks.

"You know the rules," Veronica tells him. "You may speak at the end. Let's talk about some of the internal rhymes here. It's always going to be a tightrope walk: How much is too much, right?"

"Too much is too much," offers a skinny kid asquat a tree stump. He's one of the servers. An up-and-coming noisemaker. "Everything is too much in this poem. And also not enough. Davey's really straining here. This poem is like an obese kid running up a hill. No offense. And there's nothing dangerous here. Nothing dire. 'Blue hell'? 'Let the tide wash mother moon'? Is this a detergent commercial? There's nothing there. Or maybe we've been there already and we know it sucks. I'm sorry to be rough, but, to be honest, Veronica, you've been using kid gloves all session. We need to rip each other to goddamn shreds to get better. Constructive criticism is crap. We've got to burn it down and build it again. You think there are more than a few thousand people in the country, if that, who read or care about this stuff? There are more poets than poetry readers. Are we ever going to matter again? The smart money says no. But I'm all about the long shot. And if we are going to take it, we have to stop hugging and validating each other and start getting tough. Your poem is shit, Davey. And you know what? The one I brought yesterday was also shit. And I'm sure Tovah's is shit. God knows, most of Veronica's are shit, and she's the prizewinning pro. Let's not settle. Let's be ruthless. Let's be fucking commandos. Let's be midwives. Let's be heroes."

"Are you finished, Fisk?" Veronica says.

Fisk looks around, breaks into a sweet smile.

"Sure."

"Davey, should we resume the discussion?"

"Ah, I don't think so. I'm good."

"I hope Fisk's little speech didn't shut you down."

Davey stares at Veronica.

"No, I'm sure that had nothing to do with it."

"Tovah? What do you say? Are you ready to be a heroic midwife to your poetry?"

Tovah studies her Tevas.

"I think I need to work on this one more. Burn it down and build it again."

"Are you sure?"

"I don't know. I really wanted to read it, but maybe it's pointless. I don't even know why I came here. I'm not knocking the program. It's just been hard for me. I've been through some bad stuff lately. I think I came here to reclaim something I thought was mine. But maybe that was a pathetic story I told myself. I guess I'm no poet after all."

"We're all poets when we're writing poetry," Veronica says.

"That's just bullshit, Veronica," Fisk says.

"Come on," says Davey. "I want to hear it."

"Me, too," Julie says.

"Yeah," another adds.

"We all want to hear it," Veronica says. "This is a place of trust. We're here for each other."

"That's true," Fisk says. "Come on, Tovah."

"Okay. It's called 'The Cruising Cloud.'"

"Dickinson," Veronica says.

"Good choice," Julie whispers.

Thanks, thinks Tovah, but still, screw you.

Tovah begins to read her poem, and the more she reads, the more she feels herself spiraling up and away from her words, her voice. The more she reads her poem, the more it sounds like another person has written it, a stranger, a fool, some ludicrous, fleshly occlusion. Her thoughts wander back to the 2009 party a few days ago, which did, in fact, wake her and where, after she belted her robe and hiked out to the East Field under a blood-pink moon, she found Bob Price, the old skunk, holding court with these smug little sprouts (Fisk was there, and Veronica), regaling them with tales of New York, the old days of publishing he never witnessed himself, the feuds, the donnybrooks, the imbroglios, the fandangos (fandangos?), all that cocky trash talk about when writers and painters drank together in bars, when everyone misbehaved or was a genuine freak, when only third-raters grubbed around for academic posts, when the world was on fire and the literature was real and the fucking was freedom, at least for the men.

Sometimes Tovah enjoyed these rants, despite—or maybe because of—the antiquated posturing. She had her own fantasies about the literary past, though hers had a more flushed New England glow. But Bob sickened and saddened her that night. They'd gone to grad school together, shared a bed, dreamed similar dreams, and look where they'd wound up. He was the one who'd supposedly made it, and he seemed far worse off, stuck in a stupid and fairly unremunerative loop. His books were negligible, too, except for a couple of early stories. She'd supplied the ending for one of them—or, rather, suggested he cut the last paragraph to create a startling stop critics noted.

Toward the end of the party, he stumbled over, put his arm around her. He stank of some kind of candied booze.

"Hey, girl," he said. "I've been waiting for the right time to talk. It's amazing to see you."

"Nice to see you, too, Bob. Looks like you're having fun."

"I love this place. My favorite gig. I always have a blast. But I don't always get to see the one that got away."

"Me?"

"Of course. Don't think I got over you."

"If that's true, it's beyond sad."

"It's true," Bob said, leaned over her, on her.

Tovah let him tongue kiss her for a cold five seconds. He spread his hand across her ass and she shoved him off, partly out of repulsion, she realized later, but also an odd, fierce jolt of fidelity to Fraz, or perhaps not fidelity, as she'd already cheated on him with Nat Dersh, but a kind of perverse nostalgia, a yearning for the known affronts, the home spoilage. Bob's kiss, his grope, charged a dormant circuit. She found herself wishing it were Fraz's tongue swirled up in hers, making her sick.

"Sorry," Bob slurred. "Too fast?"

"No," Tovah said. "Wrong direction."

"That was always your problem," Bob said, broke away. "Your desire never figured out how to outmaneuver your fear."

"Oh, was that the problem?"

"Yeah," Bob said, ducked back into the crowd.

The weakness of that last exchange hurt the most. They were supposed to be language artists. The consolation of acute bitterness is the biting retort. Fraz would not have fizzled that badly. Back in her cabin, Tovah rejoiced. Bob Price, the concept, had been pried neatly out of her. She climbed into her cot much lighter, ready for wide, cool sleep.

There is silence now, and Tovah realizes that she has just finished reading her poem. Her fellow workshoppers, framed by the pines, observe her. She's not sure if she's supposed to say something more, or if maybe she just did. She experiments with a sigh.

"Holy shit," somebody says.

Veronica's eyes stay shut.

"Wow," Julie whispers.

Fisk rises, greasy, alive.

"That's what I'm fucking talking about!" he shouts to the trees. "That's why we still have a shot!"

Tovah breathes out, giggles. He's just an arrogant brat, but maybe he's right.

Forty-nine

The pilgrims come to Pickering for the anniversary of Hark's death. Fraz watches from Meg's porch.

"Nice turnout."

"Why do you think I had you come up from the city?" Meg says. "Did you write anything down?"

"I'm better off the cuff."

"You're not very good either way."

"So why worry?"

They come in clusters, in tribal formations, like the subsets that gathered the day Hark died, but even more diffuse. Tealers wear wooden amulets painted to resemble black-and-white cookies. Rumpler Girls tote medical coolers full of vodka. There are Meg-Bars, and two factions in fierce rivalry, the Frazzers and the Crustifarians. But the majority remain, of course, simple Harkists, or Harkians. For most, it's still about basic Poferism, the fifty-two original positions, the tenets of mental archery.

There is a new parking lot in the meadow, an information kiosk near the well. Construction has begun on a hotel, a restaurant carved into the hillside, a day spa, a small stadium for mass posing. They've already built such centers in major cities, why not at this holy site?

The pilgrims come to visit Hark's grave at the end of the meadow, where the forest begins, the last stop on the tour. Atop a marble plinth stands a steel statue of an archer taking aim at the sky. But there is no bow, no arrow. If one did not know of Hark, of mental archery, the statue would seem to depict a man shaking his fist at the sun. Near his foot, a quiver brims with bronze flowers. A plaque reads: *"The power of focus can actuate the world."—Hark Morner, as told to Dieter Delgado.* The pilgrims leave toy bows, knife-notched arrows, bouquets of daisies and blank, stapled pages that resemble Hark's first texts, as seen in the Mental Archery Museum in Montreal.

Kate and Teal arrive around noon, stride hand in hand across the meadow. Others drift with them, but keep a reverent distance. They know these legends, what they mean to the legacy. Kate and Teal reach the grave, kneel before the statue.

" 'Actuate the world'?" Kate says. "That's new."

"Pricks," Teal says.

They've been here many times. Teal used to work in the office in the main house before everything went corporate. But today Teal senses something in the air, a pulse of unburdening, a reckoning.

"Feel that?" Teal whispers.

"Yes," says Kate.

"Master," comes a voice. "May we kneel with you?"

A group has gathered, some Tealers among them. They hold out their amulets.

"It's not my place to give permission," Teal says. "And take off those stupid fucking necklaces."

The pilgrims toss their amulets away, fall to their knees. Kate spots Meg in the crowd with two bulked-up white men in Tattersall dress shirts.

"Security," she tells Teal.

"I know."

They watch another man, older, pasty, jog up behind Meg and her entourage. He's got a piece of paper in his hand, wears a baseball cap with the new institute emblem on it, an *H* made of arrows.

"For fuck's sake," Kate says.

Fraz passes Meg, Riggs and Baby Knob, plops down next to Kate and Teal at Hark's marker.

"Hey, guys."

"Fraz." Kate nods. "Nice hat. What's the *H* for?"

"Funny. What are you two up to?"

"Just here to pay our respects," Teal says.

"Okay, that's fine. See, I told Meg you weren't here to make trouble."

"We're here to acknowledge our loss."

"Of course. Good. Well, I guess I'm on."

Fraz nods to Meg, glances at his paper, rises.

"Greetings, brothers and sisters of the bow," he says. "How wonderful to see you all. You know who I am, don't you? I'm Old Fraz. The Old Man."

"The Crust!"

"Old Toilet Crust!"

"And I'm here to join you on this special day. To weep with sadness and joy both. Sadness for what might have been had Hark lived. Joy for all that he managed in his short life to accomplish for us."

"Wait!"

Teal stands, faces the crowd.

"Teal!" somebody shouts.

"Don't do it," Fraz says.

"Let's hear Teal!"

"Teal is all colors!"

"People!" Teal says.

"Please," Fraz says. "You don't understand what Meg will—"

"My beautiful mental archers!" Teal calls out.

"We're here!" one of her acolytes says.

"A year ago today," Teal says, "we stood in this very place, waiting for Hark to come and speak, to help a little girl and maybe heal parts of us, too, through the energy we could create together. The energy is not gone. We can retrieve it. But remember, it comes from us, our hearts. It's got nothing to do with resorts, with franchised mental archery centers. With these business maggots feeding on the corpse of a visionary."

"That's not really true," Fraz shouts. "I mean, he wanted to help people, sure, but he was all for commerce."

"Spend the silver yet?" Kate says.

"I'm not Judas," Fraz says. "I'm really not."

"Who could possibly care what you think you are?" Kate says.

"Boo!" shouts an Old Crust lover.

"Teal and Kate are traitors!" calls Meg, edges close. "They want to destroy what we've worked so hard to build!"

"Teal, maybe," calls one of the Rumpler Girls, a middle-aged man. "But not Our Lady of the Marrow!"

"He's coming back!" Teal says. "Don't you fools understand? He's not really dead. He's coming. The Final Focus will be upon us."

"That's a bunch of crypto-Christian bullshit," Fraz says. "You guys are regressing."

"What if it's all true?" Kate asks.

Baby Knob and Riggs wedge their way through the gathering.

Kate and Teal turn to run. Baby Knob snatches Teal's elbow, twists her to the grass. Riggs locks Kate's head in the crook of his arm. Soft blond hairs on his freckled wrist tickle her nose. Riggs flexes his biceps like he means to pinch off Kate's head.

"Ow! Fuck!"

Meg squats beside them.

"Don't be martyrs. We're all on the same side."

"How can you pimp his memory like this?" Kate says. "Didn't you love him?"

"I loved something."

Teal strains upward, peers past the edge of the meadow, into the woods. She must be losing blood flow to her brain, because off in the distance she swears she can make out a figure, a naked man sheathed in dirt, with shaggy mud-sodden hair, piercing gold-green eyes. He nods, smiles, mimes serving a volleyball, darts into the bushes.

"Wait," Teal moans, crushed by the khaki knees on her back. "Wait!"

Fifty

The president is dead. Boyd Barron watches his fellow prisoners watch the news on TVs bolted to cell walls, soak in the deadness of the president. Does anyone still care about the son of a bitch?

We're deep in the shitmire. Thousands of NATO troops killed in the Battle of Antwerp alone. We'll be eating people soon, we don't get some decent leadership. Gets to where you're even missing that skinny mulatto from all those years ago, catastrophic as it seemed at the time. At least he could move around, hit a jumper, smoke a cig. Had that spade cool down tight. Too bad he served only one term. Then that rickety war hero strokes out in the Oval Office. Then we get that stooge from the money gang, though weren't they all? Then we get the commie broad. Feisty bitch, like Pol Pot in a pencil skirt. That was no simple car wreck that took her out, either. Who ever heard of a motorcade crash? Her replacement, the just-dead moron, he was the worst of them. A handsome cement-head. Wouldn't have lasted a day in the field. Or the stream. Forget about a bow hunt. Couldn't hit a barn, or a giant three-legged beaver.

But there's nothing for it. The world's a runaway train, lost, sleeping at the bus station. Our only hope is the weather wipes us out. What was Noah's flood but a climate change event brought on by human depravity? Better believe those tree-hugging labial warts on that score. They're just quoting the Good Book. We'll reap the whirlwind. It'll come and reap everything to shit and tear all the money out of the little Jew paws, strip the black sheets off the Arab ladies. See some good desert ass.

Nothing happening on the TV. People in Washington standing around on the streets, the plazas, waiting for more statements. Waiting for the new president, the widow of that general killed in Liechtenstein.

Should never have greased Hark. Would not be wallowing in this shitpen. Should have shot the selectman of Pickering instead. Bastard said he'd collect those hunting fines come hell or high water. How about come a field point arrow up your fudge pipe? Too late. Screw the Nuge, too. Just a narcissistic string picker. Never took a human life. Never spared one.

The other prisoners watch the chaos on the screen. Boyd is glad for the diversion. He tugs out the long, skinny strip of denim from a slit in his mattress. Bought it from a Nazi Lowrider for the gold in his mouth. He loops it around a corroded bolt he's loosened in the wall. Used to be a TV there, before he told the bastards to take that death box away. He stands on the bunk to reach it. He's still not sure the bolt will hold, but it should. There's a reason prisons make this kind of deed difficult but not impossible. The state is telling you: If you really want it, you can have it. One less hole to feed.

Boyd knots the other end of the strip around his neck, pushes off the bunk with his foot. For a sliver of a minute, it's beautiful. He's high in the rare air, striding across the tops of clouds, nostrils pinched for frost-stab. The bolt holds and now he sways, swings back, bounces off the wall. The marvelous moment is gone. He claws at the cloth at his throat. His legs kick, panic's outsized strut. The cell light shrivels. Boyd spins slow, strangled, a roar in his ears, a crack, a rip, a crash.

His cheek mashed into the floor drain, the question occurs to him: Is he dead? Can a dead man still sniff the stench of his floor drain? What's tight around his throat, it's still too tight. He can't see anything but the wall, and now a shadow falls upon it, or is that a singe? Boyd turns and here's a man, naked, torn, befouled, but somehow more than a man, a spray of light, a platinum shimmer. More-Than-a-Man stretches out his palm.

"Come, friend."

Boyd reaches for the muddy hand, but his fingers pass through it. A mirage?

"Try again," the man says, and his gold-green eyes drill Boyd into the back of himself.

Boyd reaches out, gasps.

"Your hand, it's not there."

"Of course it is. Try harder."

Boyd swipes once more.

"It's not there!"

Boyd is in his baby mind, his beige tunic dark with tears.

"Take it!" the man says. "Take it now!"

Boyd hurls himself at the hand, tumbles into the metal leg of his bunk.

"I can't!" he sobs.

"You can. Just . . . focus."

"What?"

"Focus! Repeat after me. Apple. Boy. Space. Time. Apple. Boy. Space. Time."

Boyd says the words, feels something supple, rough, squirm inside his loosened fist. The ghost hand grows bone, skin. Copper light ignites the man's hair. Is this what they mean by the halo effect?

"Now," the man says. "Can you focus? Do you feel the power of it?"

"Yes."

"No distractions?"

"No."

"And do you know who I am?"

"Yes," Boyd says. "Yes, my Lord."

The man plucks a silken hair from the middle of Boyd's nose.

"That hurts."

"As did the arrow in my chest."

"I'm sorry."

"I know you are, wretch. That's why I'm here."

"Is this a dream?"

"No. But I could make you think it is. Do you want that? Or do you want the truth revealed to you in all its killing splendor?"

"Dream."

"Wrong answer."

"Okay, killing splendor."

"Good. That's better. But I must go now. I'll be back."

"I'll wait for you."

"Could be ten minutes. Could be ten thousand years."

"I can live with that."

"Sure you can."

The cell fills with swirls of light, of diamond-shine. Boyd scuttles across the concrete, yanks himself up on his cot. The man has vanished. The TVs drone on. Boyd can see the screen through the bars of the cell across the corridor. In the capital, flags snap at half-mast in the mist. Police goons in body armor mill beneath high spiked gates. They have sealed the perimeter, but how can they know that every perimeter is about to disappear? In ten minutes. Or ten thousand years. Boyd won't live much longer, he's stage IV in the pancreas, and nobody will ever believe him, but he saw what he fucking saw, held Hark's hand in his hand.

He heard the risen kid speak.

Fifty-one

Fraz rents a new Teutonic chariot, tobacco brown, charges it to the institute. The account at the garage, dormant after Kate's funds dried up, has been renewed. Fraz works for Dieter Delgado, after all, just like his wife. Someday, if jobs, economies, still exist, his children will, too.

Tovah's at an EduToolz conference for a few more days. No need to disturb her. About anything. No more pokes and prods when she gets back. No more bored provocations. Keep it light. Keep it fun. Watch a family movie. Snazz up the evening with white Zinfandel. Maybe they'll have an outside chance.

Sunday the twins beg to tool around in the rental. They range the boroughs, gorge themselves on Salvadoran chicken in Jackson Heights, cruise down to Brighton for Siberian dumplings. They hit Arthur Avenue in the Bronx, scoot up the Hudson River to one of the quaint river strongholds. The twins love to antique, or, rather, enjoy barging into junk shops to knock over junk.

The next morning, Fraz drops them off at school and drives

through the Lincoln Tunnel to New Jersey. Traffic is light. Soon he's parked outside the old house on Pierce Street. He sits behind the wheel, watches movement in the bay window. He's not sure what he expects. The house looks good, fresh paint on the shutters, the lawn mown, a mint-green compact in the driveway.

He knocks on the door. A dog barks, a woman in tennis togs answers.

"Yes?"

"Hi!" Fraz says, but ever since Schnitz the word is ruined for him.

"Yes?"

"You know, I was passing through, and, well, this is funny, but I used to live here. Right in this house. This is my house. I mean, it's your house now. But I grew up in it. I don't want to impose, but could I come in for a minute, have a look around? I'll be quick."

The woman looks off down the street, back at Fraz.

"Absolutely not. Get out of here, asshole."

The woman slams the door, throws a bolt.

He's almost at his car when he decides to double back, slip behind the house. He zags from tree to tree in the backyard, keeps an eye on the window curtains. He trots to the edge of the property.

There's a new security fence, more formidable than the model of his youth, but he sees that the old, rotted toolshed still stands near the chain links, a miracle. He's only somewhat surprised to discover the same groove in the dirt beneath the fence. It's well maintained, smooth and shiny from generations of children slinging themselves under. He wants to slide through himself, worries his gut will snag. If he gets stuck it could be worse than mere embarrassment. The woman in togs seems like an ardent caller of constables.

This is not the only route to the reservoir. He could loop around in his car, take the rutted road he once drove Hark down, but he wants to travel this way, the path of the ancients.

While he sizes up the groove, a young, large-bellied woman in a drab olive tank top walks up from the house.

"Hey," Fraz says.

"What are you doing back here?"

"You're not going to believe it," Fraz says, "but my dad built this shed."

"Why wouldn't I believe it?"

"I don't know."

"You freaked my mom out. She sees you back here, I wouldn't mess with her. She's got a sidearm and she's . . . antsy."

"I don't want to mess with anybody. I just want to get past the fence. Get a closer look at the island."

"Island?"

"The island. Right over there."

Fraz pokes his finger through the fence, points to the hillock that juts up from the water.

"Oh, that. Yeah. You want to go there?"

"Go there? How?"

"I don't know. Paddle?"

The woman walks past Fraz, waddles a bit, and Fraz sees now that she's pregnant. She kicks open the shed door, her strong body engorged with life, more vibrant than any woman he's glimpsed on his websites, though that's not a surprise.

Fraz watches her taut, corded arms drag a metal canoe from the shed. Fraz peels up the fence and the woman slides the slim boat under. She follows, and Fraz strains to make sure her belly clears. Her movements are practiced, liquid. Now it's Fraz's turn. He has to ease himself down, push his spine into the gouge. The sharp steel ends of the fence scrape his stomach, draw threads of blood, but somehow he shimmies through. Only after, as he stands now on the other side, does it occur to him how curious it is that she's initiated this expedition.

"You do this a lot?" Fraz asks.

"Do what?"

"Drag canoes around with strangers."

"First time."

"You're very beautiful. You're a very beautiful pregnant woman."

"Don't make me regret this. Just pick up your end."

"My name's Fraz, by the way."

"Denise."

They carry the canoe down to the water. Fraz rolls his pants up, leaves his shoes and socks on the shore. They walk the canoe a few yards into the reservoir and climb in, dig at the dark water with rubber paddles. A hard current turns them, but they correct course, and soon they reach landfall, which Fraz realizes now is more undistinguished hump of clay than sacred atoll. Soil erosion? Or a childhood memory's error of scale? Even with Hark that time it looked bigger.

They beach the canoe, climb to the tiny plateau, sit on jags of driftwood.

"Ah," Fraz says.

Denise gazes out on the water.

"We used to have furniture," Fraz says.

"Yeah?"

Fraz hears a shrill whistle. A train crosses the iron bridge at the far end of the reservoir. His whole boyhood he listened to the trains from his bed, daydreaming half the night about his future. He already knew he couldn't be an astronaut (bad at math) or a professional athlete (bad at sports), but everything else looked wide-open. He could be a cowboy, a rock star drummer, a spy (information conduit never occurred to him), or a pimp running a string of sexbots on an off-world mining colony.

"We had," Fraz says, "a couch."

"No shit," the woman says, pulls out a vape pen, offers it to Fraz.

"We had a mattress also," Fraz continues, takes a long draw. "Whole gang of us used to come out here and drink and go crazy. Well, only a few times, really. We did some disgusting things with catfish. Once, I came out alone at dusk and jacked off."

"Thanks for the details."

"You sure it's okay to do this when you're pregnant?"

"My mom is always on my ass about getting high. Says the THC is bad for the baby. That's why I come out here."

"Good thing I showed up to give you an excuse."

"What the hell, I figured. Let me go get crinkled with the weird old man. Maybe he's got something to say."

"How am I doing?"

"I don't know. This stuff is like an instant head wound."

Denise spits on a rock. The sun starts to slide behind some clouds.

"Couch is a nice idea," she says. "Just got a crib for when the baby comes. I can't believe I'm actually doing this. And alone. Daddy's MIA."

"Happens a lot," Fraz says.

Denise is right about the weed. Fraz feels half decapitated.

"What happens?" Denise says.

"Dads disappear, can't handle the pressure."

"No, he's really fucking missing in action. He's with the 1st Marines in Lisbon."

"Oh, I'm sorry. That's terrible. But you have to hold out hope, right? For the child?"

"You got kids?"

"Yeah. Boy and a girl."

"What are you doing here? You should be with them."

"They're in school."

"Yeah, but still. Here you are getting high with a stranger on a rock in the middle of a reservoir. What gives?"

"It's kind of a complex situation."

"Is it? You're a deadbeat loser."

"Yeah, what about you?"

"Eat shit. I'm a vet. I was in Ibiza. Saw the deathpits. I was on a nuke squad in Mallorca. I'm just trying to get through the day."

"Hey," Fraz says. "I hear you."

"You have no idea what I'm talking about."

"Maybe."

"Definitely."

"Okay."

"All I know is I'm going to hell. For some of the shit I did over there? I'm going to hell."

"It's war, isn't it?"

"Like I said, you don't know what you are talking about."

"There is no hell."

"You just can't imagine it."

"Okay, sorry. You were the one fighting those maniacs. That must have been horrible. They want to destroy the world."

"No, they want to run it. Just like we do. They'll be here soon. We're losing big-time. Shit, when I first left this town, I swore I would never come back. Never return to this cesspit. Now look at me. A basket case living with my mother."

"It's not a cesspit."

"What?"

"I grew up here, too. It's not a cesspit. It's a decent suburb. Pretty good schools."

"Maybe when you lived here."

"You ever heard of mental archery?"

"Strange that you say that. My mom's boyfriend does it. It's really fucking stupid."

"It's not," Fraz says. "It's really not."

"It's not?" Denise says. She has tears in her eyes and Fraz sees in this moment how he will free himself of Dersh and Meg and the binds of the institute, help people like Denise with his own message, distilled from Hark's teachings, shorn of base motive.

"It's not," he says. "It can save your life."

"I'm beyond saving," Denise says.

"No, that's wrong."

Fraz lays his hand on her arm.

"I'm afraid I am. And you are a fucking sleazy huckster if I ever met one. And a predator. Preying on the walking wounded, no less. Get your paw off me!"

"What?"

The kick in the liver hurts the most, but it's the karate chop to the trachea that does the damage. Fraz sprawls in the dirt, wheezes through his windpipe. He watches Denise rise, walk down to the canoe, push off the bank and paddle away. Her pink, muscled shoulders ripple with each stroke.

Fraz gazes up at the sky. A goshawk glides past. Or is it just a hawk? Where did he get "goshawk"? A word in a book. A guess. Could have learned for real. Could have been a bird-watcher. Happy in a floppy hat. Happy just to study those colorful, flying disease pouches through high-grade nocs.

Could be a vulture, the goshawk, a crow.

"Tovah," he moans, through the shredded reeds of his throat. Maybe Denise's mother will come down to the shore. If she doesn't shoot him, she might have mercy, might feel a stream of mercy course through her, call an ambulance.

"Tovah . . ."

He was wrong. You can't keep it light. Zinfandel won't do the trick. The music, at some point, ceases. The dance dies down and the day grows dark. Tovah and Fraz must hold each other close, grope their way through the depths of night. And when the sun rises again, they must be tender, attentive, refuse surrender to the heart's entropy, the blank drift. Maybe humans are, in fact, a cancer on this earth. Still, we must huddle in our tiny carcinogenic clusters, for the last of the nubby warmth, the last of our love.

Tumors don't swim, but Fraz does. He learned at freezing summer camp. You can't be your metaphor forever. Let the cows graze. Time for a dip. His brain is a fetid sponge, his mind a cannibal orgy. Return to the beginning. The boy with the arrow. The apple and the boy. For home or at the office. For the salvation of human feeling.

Fraz wades into the reservoir.

His arms cut the cold water, his legs churn. He swims hard for a minute, but soon his strength hollows out, his joints burn, his throat throbs from the neck chop. Breathing has become what they call a nonstarter. Except there is no they. Except there is. But also not.

Now he senses it, finally, maybe what Teal and Kate had talked about, just as his legs cramp, seize. He starts to thrash, to sink, but at the same time he feels a certain burden lift away. Fraz's heart hums free and clean. Everything is light and the end of light. Here it comes now, a crystal shaft. Watch it bend from a crease in the sky.

Whether it's an arrow of death, or one of reprieve, he cannot yet know.

"Tovah . . . ," he says, his mouth so wide with filthy water.

Fifty-two

Kate comes to in a beech tree, her arms stretched out, braided into branches. Beneath her spreads a golf course strewn with debris. Hunks of smoking metal and torn suitcases and shreds of clothing and pieces of people, polymers, litter the turf. She spots what is maybe her cooler, upturned, in a sand trap, beside a serrated twist of painted steel.

Nothing moves. She cannot move herself. Most of her clothing has been scorched away. She's a charred one. Blood pools in her burns. She thinks maybe an important part of her face has melted off. Should she not feel unspeakable pain?

An afternoon flight to Canada. She recalls the ticket code on her phone. Wherefore Canada? A mission for Shana. Delivering a kidney, a pair of corneas. Her old gig with new employers.

But planes. What was she thinking? All those years of frequent flyerdom. Her mother and father smeared into that cliffside. Some folks would never have left the earth's surface after that. But Kate spent a good deal of her inheritance flying around with her cooler.

That's why the clinics always called. She paid her own way. Should have spent the money on better shrinks.

But at least she's not alone. She's embedded in a tree. That's sweet. She's a big nature fan.

"Hey, lady!"

Kate peers down through leaves. A naked man, furry, grimy, golden, scampers up the trunk. He's quick and he's here, perched on a branch a few feet from where Kate hangs, woven into bark.

"Kate, it's good to see you."

Hark looks even younger than before. He wears a soft-looking loin wrap, like a saggy satin diaper.

"Monkey man."

"That's me," Hark chuckles. "It's weird. You're, like, totally crucified up here. I empathize."

"Am I alive?"

"Yes, definitely."

"Why doesn't it hurt?"

"The human body is an incredible organism."

"But it should hurt. And how could I survive falling out of an airplane into a tree?"

"Whacky physics."

"See, I don't believe you."

"You never really did."

"I'm sorry."

"I don't mind. I like you anyway."

"That's nice," Kate says. "Hey, can I ask you a question?"

"Of course."

"What happened? Engine failure? Pilot error?"

"Friendly fire."

"Huh?"

Hark hoists himself up into a more comfortable notch in the tree.

"Your plane got shot down by American missiles by mistake. The air war has begun."

"The air war?"

"Yeah. I don't think it will end well. I mean, in the long run it might. But the period of adjustment will be brutal. But that's all history ever is. Trauma and adjustment. I mean, it's also a fat boy with

a sparkling gem up his bum, but mostly it's trauma and adjustment.
You've just been that lucky minority in the right region at the right
time. You avoided the worst. Until now. But from here on out, boy,
howdy."

"How do you know all this?"

"I pay attention. I'm a major noticer."

"And you're the son of God."

"The son? Please. These days I'm more like a barely tolerated
nephew."

"But still. You are the light."

"It doesn't make me good, per se. It's just like anybody. You come
from somewhere. You have parents at some point."

"But you're up there."

"Sort of. It's not an up or down thing."

"Do you ever see Fraz?"

"Fraz?"

"He died. He drowned. A few months ago."

"Yeah, I heard."

"But you don't see him?"

"Well, where I am, I wouldn't."

"What, you mean he didn't make it to heaven?"

"He's a kike."

"Excuse me?"

"I mean, he's of the Jewish faith."

"What does that matter?"

"Personally? I don't care. But there are some sticklers."

"That's stupid and racist."

"I agree. But heaven is a Christian nation. Let's not forget that.
Still, you're right. We need to move past these obsolete modes of
thinking. Like, you know that idea that all religions are basically the
same, all different paths leading to the same conclusion?"

"Yes."

"Well, that's bullshit. But what does link them together is me. I
play big roles in all of them. Still, I agree about Fraz."

"Is this how God or whoever wants it?"

"No, not really. There's this . . . well, it's going to sound bizarre
out of context, but there's this very influential catfish."

"What?"

"It's hard to explain. Also, Fraz is probably not the best person to build a diversity crusade around. Anyway, do you want to come with me now? You can if you want. It's pretty awesome. The coffee's amazing. The beans are shit out of the souls of elephants. You just have to do whatever I say."

"Nobody's the boss of me."

"Here, sure. But where we're going, I'm pretty much one of the main bosses. You'd be, like, my bride. One of them. But it's not sexist or anything. Some of my brides are men, or somewhere in between, or even somewhere else. They're just all my brides."

"It's a Mormon thing?"

"No, in this case it's a celestial thing."

"Can I think about it, make a decision?"

"How do you know I'll be into you then?"

"That's an interesting thing for you to say. Kind of hostile, no?"

"What do you want, Kate?"

"I guess I just want to find out once and for all if I can be happy here."

"Nobody can be happy here. Here is over. Here never was."

Vein claret, plasma surprise, the incarnadine flip.

"Fix me," Kate whispers. "My body. Please. Do a miracle. Let me continue to live on Earth."

"I can't," Hark says. "Or maybe I won't. I never really did most of that stuff. Those were stories. I could have pulled off some of that loaves and wine crap, but it always seemed so tacky. You know: too on the nose. But I'm happy to forgive all your sins."

"Please don't," Kate says. "Just get me back to normal."

"This *is* normal, Kate."

"The new normal?"

"It was always the same old normal."

"Huh?"

"Think about it."

"I'm having trouble doing that."

"Well, if it's any consolation, it has always been very bewildering to me as well. I'm never really sure who I am until I die. Maybe I have an inkling, but I really just think I'm a weird kid from LA. Or, like, you know, a nerd from Nazareth. A freak from Mecca. Or Ur. A loser from Lumbini. Or wherever. Maybe I still am. Are you familiar with the concept of eternal return? Actually, I know that you are. What I can't figure out is the suffering. Mine and everybody else's. What's the point? Why do I have pretty much the same awful childhood every time? Is it because I don't change enough? Probably I've changed a lot. It's just that I'm not that self-aware. I'm a doer. A leader. The fact is I'm really just a ceaselessly mutating mass of energy. Which can be a very cool thing. But it's why I've always been so fidgety. I used to say my motto was 'Cut to the chase.' Never took time to reflect much. But I'm beginning to realize that the chase is a big fucking bore. It's always the same old chase. I thought mental archery might do the trick. But it was just another trap. The catfish was right about that, at least. Anyway, I guess I'm the eternal child. Never satisfied. Maybe if I'd been a little more mindful, more focused, things would be different."

"What things?"

"Everything. Or maybe not."

"Hark!" Kate shouts. "Please!"

"Hey," Hark says. "Yeah. The best thing for you to do right now is focus. Apple, yes. Boy, no. Or apple, yes, boy, howdy. Like that. Because the pain is about to kick in, Kate. It's really going to fucking hurt."

Tincture of Mars, river of roses.

"I thought you were love," Kate says.

"Pardon?"

Kate hears a screech, a high scrape in the sky. A squadron of fighter drones banks into view.

"Go get 'em, you fine metal fellows," Hark says.

The tip of a nearby mountain explodes.

The wizard serum. The ruby fondu.

"Yikes," Hark says, turns to Kate. "How's it going, darling?"

But Kate doesn't answer. She's already lost in her litany.

ACKNOWLEDGMENTS

The author wishes to thank Yaddo and the Civitella Ranieri Foundation, as well as Ira Silverberg, Eric Simonoff, Alex Abramovich, Lorin Stein, Ben Marcus, and Ceridwen Morris for assistance in the completion of this book.

Keep in touch with
Granta Books:

Visit granta.com to discover more.

GRANTA

THE FUN PARTS

Sam Lipsyte

'Hilarious'
Observer

'Sublime mayhem!'
New York Times

'Brilliant'
Financial Times

In these masterful, tragicomic stories from one of America's
greatest living satirists, a gang of lonely boys suffers under the
tyranny of a maniacal Dungeon Master; a recovering addict and
cardio ballet instructor struggles to stay clean; a misery memoirist
is out-miseried and outsold by his homeless gay punk protégé;
and a substitute gym teacher turned male birthing coach teaches a
couple that bringing home a newborn is not all cuddles and fluff.

'The riffs come thick and fast, and the gags are sprayed on with a
machine gun . . . a whole lot of fun' Kevin Barry, *Guardian*

'I'd wholeheartedly direct you towards this sour and scintillating
new collection of short stories . . . You won't read finer
sentences this year' *Scotland on Sunday*

'Dementedly imaginative . . . Sharp and deeply, blackly funny'
Metro

'*The Fun Parts* is funny because it is true to what is sometimes
missing in all the wisecracks, one-liners, grotesques and
gussied-up endings elsewhere – life' *Sunday Times*